PRAISE FOR SUSAN STOKER

"Susan Stoker knows what women want. A hot hero who needs to save a damsel in distress . . . even if she can save herself!"

—CD Reiss, *New York Times* bestselling author

"Irresistible characters and seat-of-the-pants action will keep you glued to the pages."

—Elle James, *New York Times* bestselling author

"Susan does romantic suspense right! Edge of my seat + smokin' hot = read ALL of her books! Now."

—Carly Phillips, *New York Times* bestselling author

"Susan Stoker writes the perfect book boyfriends!"

—Laurann Dohner, *New York Times* bestselling author

"These books should come with a warning label. Once you start, you can't stop until you've read them all."

—Sharon Hamilton, *New York Times* bestselling author

"Susan Stoker never disappoints. She delivers alpha males with heart and heroines with moxie."

—Jana Aston, *New York Times* bestselling author

"Susan Stoker gives me everything I need in romance: heat, humor, intensity, and the perfect HEA."

—Carrie Ann Ryan, *New York Times* bestselling author

"Susan Stoker packs one heck of a punch!"

—Lainey Reese, *USA Today* bestselling author

DEFENDING EVERLY

DISCOVER OTHER TITLES BY SUSAN STOKER

Mountain Mercenaries Series

Defending Allye
Defending Chloe
Defending Morgan
Defending Harlow
Defending Everly
Defending Zara (March 2020)
Defending Raven (TBA)

Ace Security Series

Claiming Grace
Claiming Alexis
Claiming Bailey
Claiming Felicity
Claiming Sarah

Delta Force Heroes

Rescuing Rayne
Rescuing Aimee (novella)
Rescuing Emily
Rescuing Harley
Marrying Emily
Rescuing Kassie
Rescuing Bryn
Rescuing Casey

Rescuing Sadie (novella)
Rescuing Wendy
Rescuing Mary
Rescuing Macie (novella)

Delta Team Two Series

Shielding Gillian (April 2020)
Shielding Kinley (TBA)
Shielding Aspen (TBA)
Shielding Riley (TBA)
Shielding Devyn (TBA)
Shielding Ember (TBA)
Shielding Sierra (TBA)

Badge of Honor: Texas Heroes Series

Justice for Mackenzie
Justice for Mickie
Justice for Corrie
Justice for Laine (novella)
Shelter for Elizabeth
Justice for Boone
Shelter for Adeline
Shelter for Sophie
Justice for Erin
Justice for Milena
Shelter for Blythe
Justice for Hope

Shelter for Quinn

Shelter for Koren

Shelter for Penelope

SEAL of Protection Series

Protecting Caroline

Protecting Alabama

Protecting Fiona

Marrying Caroline (novella)

Protecting Summer

Protecting Cheyenne

Protecting Jessyka

Protecting Julie (novella)

Protecting Melody

Protecting the Future

Protecting Kiera (novella)

Protecting Dakota

SEAL of Protection: Legacy Series

Securing Caite

Securing Sidney

Securing Piper

Securing Zoey (Jan. 2020)

Securing Avery (May 2020)

Securing Kalee (TBA)

Beyond Reality Series

Outback Hearts

Flaming Hearts

Frozen Hearts

Stand-Alone Novels

The Guardian Mist

A Princess for Cale

A Moment in Time (a short-story collection)

Lambert's Lady

Writing as Annie George

Stepbrother Virgin (erotic novella)

DEFENDING EVERLY

Mountain Mercenaries, Book 5

Susan Stoker

Published by Montlake, Seattle

www.apub.com

ISBN-13: 9781542015387
ISBN-10: 1542015383

Cover design by Eileen Carey

Cover photography by Wander Aguiar Photography

Printed in the United States of America

Ashley L. . . . this one's for you!

Chapter One

Kannon "Ball" Black knocked on the door of the apartment in front of him and waited impatiently for it to open.

He wasn't happy.

The only thing mollifying him at the moment was knowing the woman on the other side of the door wasn't happy either.

He'd been an ass when they'd first met, and Everly Adams had every right to be pissed at him. In his defense, while the night in question had been a great one for his friends, he'd been struggling, seeing everyone paired up with amazingly awesome women when he didn't have one of his own. And the way he was going, he probably wouldn't *ever* have one. It wasn't that he didn't like women; he did. He loved his buddies' women and would do anything for them.

But he'd been burned, badly. First by his ex-partner. Then after, during one of the worst times in his life, when his girlfriend should've been there for him, Holly had screwed him over instead—big-time. It was a blow he wasn't sure he'd ever recover from.

So the night his friends had celebrated Gray's and Arrow's engagements, he'd been out of sorts. It was just bad luck that they'd learned about their new mission that same night, and the fact that a civilian would be highly involved.

And that the civilian was a woman.

He'd run off at the mouth about how he was sure she would mess everything up and they'd have to babysit her. Turned out she'd been standing behind him the entire time and heard everything he'd said. Classic.

The couple of days since had been tough, as she'd spent quite a bit of time with the Mountain Mercenaries, going over the information they had—which wasn't much—trying to find out where Everly's missing sister had gone.

Last night, they'd determined that someone was going to have to travel to Los Angeles to get more information. Everly was going for sure. As a Colorado Springs police and SWAT officer, she actually had a few loose connections with officers in the LAPD. Since this was a fact-finding mission, the entire team wasn't needed, and somehow Ball found himself being volunteered to travel to LA with Everly.

He didn't want to go.

But it wasn't fair to separate Gray, Ro, Arrow, and Black from their women just because Ball had his doubts about working so closely with Everly. Meat could've gone, but he was helping Rex, their handler, with another case.

So that left him.

Ball had little doubt Everly was a good cop. But his ex-partner Riley'd had the potential to be a good Coastie, and look what had happened with *her* . . .

The door in front of Ball opened, but all he saw was Everly's backside as she immediately turned and walked away from him without any kind of greeting.

More bemused than annoyed, Ball pushed the door open and stepped inside her apartment. The complex itself was nice. The cars outside were all in the mid- to upper-price range, and the lights were all in working order in the parking lot and inside the complex itself. The hallways smelled of eucalyptus, and there were fresh flowers in the lobby area. He wasn't surprised that a cop lived in a safe and clean apartment complex—but her apartment *did* surprise him.

Ball knew he'd judged Everly harshly from the first moment he'd learned of her existence, but seeing her apartment made him reassess even the little he thought he knew. He wasn't sure what he'd been expecting when it came to her living space, but it wasn't the unfussy, comfortable home she'd made for herself.

He'd lived in enough apartments to know how hard it was to make them feel like your own. The walls were always white, and there always seemed to be a sterile feel to them. But not Everly's apartment. She'd managed to make her space feel inviting and lived in without stuffing it to the gills with extra crap.

The door opened into a large living space. She had a tan suede couch with pillows strewn haphazardly on it and a gray, fuzzy blanket shoved into one corner. Instead of a coffee table, she had a large, square ottoman with some remotes and a few other odds and ends on top. A bookshelf sat in the corner, overflowing with books. Her TV was huge and took up most of one wall. There were also pictures on the walls of Everly and a young girl, who he knew was her missing sister.

Her kitchen was small but functional. She had a coffee maker on one mostly uncluttered counter, and he could see a bowl and spoon in the sink from her breakfast. A small table with enough room for two sat between the kitchen and living areas. And for some reason, that table made Ball sad. He imagined Everly sitting there by herself, eating meals. Even though he lived alone, he still had a table that could seat at least six people. He'd sat there many a night with his friends, laughing and talking.

Overall, her space was tidy, but not obsessively neat. Exactly like his own.

"Are you gonna stand there all day judging me for how I live, or are we going to get moving?" Everly asked with a hand on her hip.

Ball didn't feel guilty for checking out her place. The more time he spent with her, the more curious he became. Not in an I-want-to-know-how-she-lives-because-I-want-to-date-her kind of way, though. No, Everly Adams was the last person he would go out with. She wasn't his type at all. He definitely didn't want to date a woman employed in a field similar to his.

He didn't even want to *work* with a woman. And if he ever got married or into a serious relationship, it would be with someone he liked and respected—but who he wasn't madly in love with. His heart would be safer that way.

Though, looking at Everly as she impatiently stared at him, he couldn't deny she was beautiful. Her red hair fell past her shoulders in disarray, which made him want to smooth it down. Her green eyes were currently shooting sparks at him in irritation. She was tall—he estimated about five-ten—but was still half a foot shorter than he was. Everly was also muscular but managed to rock her curves. He had a feeling in her CSPD uniform, she'd make quite a stunning figure.

"Ball?" she asked. "Are you listening to me?"

That got him moving. His former partner in the Coast Guard, Riley Foster, used to ask him that same thing all the time. He'd found it amusing before the accident. Now, it annoyed him.

"Do I have a choice?" he asked a bit harsher than he'd intended.

He pretended he didn't see her scowl before she turned away. He wasn't here to make friends. He had to work with Everly on this case, but once they'd found her sister, he hoped their paths wouldn't cross again.

"Right," Everly said as she picked up a duffel bag sitting on the floor of the kitchen. Without another word, she headed for the front door, not looking back to see if Ball was following.

Knowing he was fucking things up with her already, Ball sighed. It wasn't that he didn't respect her for being a cop and for wanting to find her sister. He just wished *he* wasn't the one who had to go to Los Angeles to help her.

She waited until he'd exited her apartment, then locked the door behind him. They walked without a word toward his black Ford Mustang. Ball loved his car. It drove like a dream, and it looked cool as hell to boot. Everly didn't seem fazed or overly impressed. Ball pushed the button on his key fob to open the trunk and debated reaching for her bag, but decided she probably wouldn't appreciate him trying to help.

She slammed the trunk after putting her bag inside and headed for the passenger side. Both seated, Ball pulled out of the parking lot and headed for the small Colorado Springs airport. They were flying from there to Denver, and then on to Los Angeles.

"Have you heard from your grandparents today?" he asked once they were on their way.

"Yeah, but they still haven't heard from Elise."

Elise was Everly's missing fifteen-year-old half sister. The whole reason they were in his car heading to the airport. "Do your contacts at LAPD have any new information?"

Everly sighed and rubbed her forehead. "No. They're doing their best, but I think some suspect she's merely another runaway and will show up at some point. They're overworked, of course, and while they're doing their best to help, nothing is really happening. We're all stressed, but Me-Maw and Pop are taking this especially hard, since Elise was living with them."

Ball thought it was cute that she called her grandparents by the silly names, but he'd never tell her that. "Have they taken her computer in for analysis yet?"

"Not that I know of. The detective who was assigned the case has ordered her phone records, but they're taking a while to come back from the phone company. Me-Maw said the detective came out to their house yesterday, but all he did was look around a bit. He'd tried to trace her phone already, but didn't have any luck, probably because if it's off, it won't be pinging on the towers."

"What do *you* think happened?" Ball asked. They'd been over and over the facts of the case in their meetings with the other Mountain Mercenaries, but there wasn't any one scenario that had stuck out as being what likely had happened to the teenager.

She'd left for school as normal, but never returned home. After asking her friends and talking to her teachers, they found out that she'd been at school and everything seemed okay with her that day. But once she'd left the building to walk home, like she did every day, no one saw her again.

"I think she met up with the wrong person and was snatched. Elise isn't like me," Everly said. "Because she's deaf, she's always taken everything much more to heart than I ever did. She's sensitive, and it's hard for her to make friends, which is one of the reasons she's still living in LA. I didn't want to take her away from the few she has, and frankly, Elise didn't want to leave either. The littlest things stress her out, and she can be in a funk for weeks as a result."

"And you're not like that?" Ball asked.

"Not really. I've seen too much at work to get stressed out about little things, and I definitely don't get in bad moods that can last weeks. Part of that is because of her age. She's a teenager, I get it. But sometimes it drives me crazy. I also can't stand drama, and if someone can't take me as I am—super blunt and to the point—then I'm done with them."

Ball sensed there was a story there, but didn't press. "So did something happen recently that would stress out Elise?"

"I'm honestly just not sure. Elise used to tell me everything, but in the last year or so, she hasn't kept in touch as much, and when she does, she just claims everything's fine."

"What about your mom?"

"What *about* my mom?" Everly asked.

"Could she be a part of this?"

"I don't think so. My mom's a bitch, and after I moved in with Me-Maw and Pop, I didn't have a lot to do with her. I don't think Elise has either. But her scenario is different. She's always taken everything Mom does personally."

"She does?"

"Yeah. She blames herself for Mom's relationship with her dad breaking up . . . which is bullshit. Maybe if Mom got off the drugs, she'd be able to have a normal relationship for once in her life. With her daughters, her parents . . . *someone*."

"And that's why Elise went to live with her grandparents, right?"

"Right. My mom disappeared for a week, and eventually Elise took the bus to Me-Maw's. Pop was pissed, and immediately drove over to Mom's house to bitch her out, but since she wasn't there, he had to settle for grabbing all of Elise's stuff and moving her into their place."

"When was that?"

"About four years ago."

"And she hasn't seen your mom since?" Ball asked. It was hard for him to fathom simply leaving a kid alone in a house for days like Ella Adams had done.

"Not that I know of, but I'm not there. Knowing my mom, she's probably been texting or emailing Elise. Giving her a guilt trip or something."

"Maybe Elise went to move back in with your mom," Ball suggested.

Everly shook her head, but she looked worried. "No."

"You don't know that for sure."

Everly shifted in her seat so she was facing Ball. "Ella Adams doesn't care about anyone but herself. Elise knows that. We've had long conversations about it. She knows she's better off at Me-Maw and Pop's place."

"But it's possible," Ball pushed, frustrated that Everly wasn't even considering the possibility.

She huffed. "Fine. You're right. It was a possibility."

"Was?" Ball asked with an eyebrow raised.

"Yes, *was*. I talked to Detective Ramirez about it. He went and talked to Mom. Found her in a pay-by-the-hour shitty motel room with some guy. He questioned her, and he said she seemed very surprised to hear that Elise was missing. Even squeezed out some tears or something. She was high, and as I said earlier, she really only gives a rat's ass about herself. He said he'd keep an eye on her to see if she led him back to an apartment or something where Elise could be hanging out, but after a day and a half of surveillance, she hadn't left the motel where he'd originally found her. I know you think I'm white trash and a gutter rat, Ball, but just because my mom's a drug addict doesn't mean she passed her stupid gene to me and my sister."

"I don't think you're white trash," Ball said, genuinely shocked that she'd think so.

Everly sighed heavily and refused to look him in the eye.

"I don't," Ball insisted. "I know we didn't exactly start out on the right foot . . ."

She snorted.

". . . but that doesn't mean I don't respect what you do."

Everly eyed him. "But you don't want to work with me."

Ball shrugged. "It's not personal. I don't like working with women."

"Why?"

"It doesn't matter."

She let out a harsh chuckle. "I think it does, since we're going to be working closely together for the next week or so."

"So if Elise didn't go back to live with your mom, would she want to stay with anyone else?" Ball asked.

For a second, he didn't think she was going to let go of her question about why he didn't like to work with women, but eventually she sighed.

"I don't know. I wanted Elise to come stay with me, but the school she's at right now is awesome, and all her friends are there. So I send money every month to help my grandparents, and Elise knows when she graduates from high school that she's more than welcome to come out here to Colorado Springs to live with me."

"Do you have any objections to Meat remotely logging on to her computer when we get to Los Angeles?" Ball asked. They'd already discussed it, but he wanted to be sure.

"None."

Ball nodded. He tried to think about what else they should discuss, but nothing came to mind.

He'd never been this . . . weird . . . with a woman before. He knew it was because he couldn't figure out exactly how he felt about Everly. He admired her for excelling in a job that was typically male dominated, even as he resented having to work so closely with her. He felt sorry for her because her sister was missing and she was so worried . . . but he also had a feeling that maybe the LA cops were right, and the girl was just sowing some wild oats.

His feelings about both his ex-partner and his ex-girlfriend had been brought to the forefront thanks to this case, and he'd been dealing with those for the last few days, even while trying half-heartedly to make up for the shit he'd said about Everly when he'd first learned she'd be tagging along on the mission.

Luckily, they arrived at the airport quickly, so he didn't have to attempt any small talk. They parked and headed for the ticket counter. Within an hour, they were seated on the plane and taking off for Denver. Of course Rex had put them in adjoining seats on the plane. Ball would've preferred to have a break from her, but instead they were sharing an armrest.

Wanting to ease the awkward silence between them as they taxied to the runway, Ball looked over at Everly in the window seat. Her eyes were closed, and her head was resting against the seat back. Her hands were clutched together in her lap, and it was more than obvious she wasn't a good flier.

She also wore a ring on her right pointer finger that he hadn't noticed before. It was a thin, gold band that could've possibly passed for a wedding ring if it had been on her other hand.

Thoughts of her jewelry were quickly replaced yet again by memories of his ex.

Holly hadn't been a good flier either. She hated the feel of the plane lifting off and always thought they were going to crash. They hadn't flown together very often, but Ball would always put his arm around her shoulders, telling her to hang on to him, that he'd keep her safe.

Forcing away thoughts of his ex, Ball looked out the opposite window across the aisle so he didn't have to see Everly struggling with her fears. His fingers twitched with the urge to cover her hands with his own, to reassure her. It was a stupid notion. Being in each other's company was just as distasteful to her as it was to him.

Thankfully, takeoff was smooth, and soon they were at cruising level and headed for Denver. Everly pulled out a set of earbuds, plugged them into her phone, put them in her ears, then turned slightly to face the window, effectively blocking him out.

Ball sighed. It was going to be a long trip.

Chapter Two

Everly put the earbuds in her ears, but didn't bother to turn on any music. She needed to be able to hear in case of an emergency. She hated flying. *Hated* it. She usually drove to Los Angeles when she wanted to visit her sister or grandparents, but time was of the essence right now. She had to get to LA and find Elise.

Whenever she thought about where her sister might be, terror threatened to overwhelm her, but she forced the feeling back. She would find her. She had to. The alternative was unthinkable.

She and her sister had gotten the short end of the stick early in life. They'd had to scrape and fight from the time they were toddlers. Their mom was in the running for worst mother ever, but at least they'd had Me-Maw and Pop.

Everly hadn't been surprised when her mom had gotten pregnant with Elise. Honestly, she'd been shocked it hadn't happened sooner. Ella Adams was a drug addict who'd been in rehab several times since her teens, but the bottom line was that she just didn't want to quit. She liked the high the drugs gave her, and she liked to party. She was also pretty, even after all the years of self-abuse. Everly and her sister had inherited her auburn hair, but Ella seemed to have that little something extra that men were always drawn to.

The crux of the problem was that Ella didn't care about anyone but herself. Neither the fathers of her children nor her kids themselves.

She didn't care that she'd caused her parents untold hours of worry, or that she'd sometimes forgotten to feed her kids. Ella just wanted the next high . . . wanted to be the center of attention. She was selfish and self-absorbed.

Ball had asked how Everly knew her sister hadn't gone to their mother. Because Elise hated the woman as much as Everly did. She would never in a million years go back to live with her. But that didn't mean Elise wasn't going through teenager growing pains. She thought her grandparents were too strict and was yearning for more independence.

And Everly understood why Elise wouldn't come to Colorado Springs to live with her, though it didn't mean Everly was completely happy with that decision.

She knew Elise wasn't willing to give up her school and friends, even if it meant getting out of Los Angeles, and Everly just wanted the best for her little sister. She was one of the smartest people she knew. That was the only thing keeping Everly calm right now. Knowing that if something *had* happened to her, Elise would be able to keep calm until Everly found her.

Then there was the man next to her . . .

Ball had hated her before he'd even met her—and that stung. She wasn't exactly Miss Congeniality, but she'd never had someone take an immediate dislike to her simply because she was a woman. Everly was well aware that she worked in a male-dominated field, but most men she met at least hid the fact they didn't think she could do the job, and talked about her behind her back.

On one hand, she grudgingly respected Ball for speaking his mind, but on the other, it pissed her off. How dare he judge her without even knowing her? How dare he decide that just because she had boobs, she couldn't get the job done?

Having spent a few days near him, she now understood that his problems stemmed from his own history and didn't really have anything to do with her specifically. But she still couldn't shake the hurt his words had caused that first day they'd met.

She was stressed out and worried, and had to deal with two flights before she'd get to hug her me-maw and pop. Flying wasn't helping her stress level. Takeoffs and landings were the worst parts, in her opinion. Statistics were clear that most plane crashes happened during the few minutes after the plane took off or right before it landed. So every time she flew, she did her best to endure those ten or so minutes at the beginning and end of each flight.

On top of everything else, over the last few days, she'd slept a total of about six hours. Every time she closed her eyes, images of Elise's dead body being found haunted her. She was a cop. She knew the first forty-eight hours were the most crucial to finding a missing person. And those two days had long since passed. The local cops thought she was a runaway, but Everly knew they were wrong.

Yes, Elise had been feeling down lately, but she'd never just disappear without a word to anyone. Someone had her. Everly felt that down to her very bones. They just needed to find out who, and where she'd been taken.

Everly prayed the kidnapping wasn't what one of the LA detectives suspected—human trafficking. Most of his coworkers were still operating under the assumption that Elise was a runaway, but he'd been concerned enough about the possibility of trafficking that he'd mentioned it to Everly, and now she couldn't get it out of her mind.

Human trafficking happened way more than the world thought it did. Apparently kidnappings and disappearances were on the rise in Los Angeles. And because of Elise's age, and the number of other girls and women like her who had disappeared without a trace recently, the detective in LA suspected this was another trafficking case.

Everly didn't want to believe it, but she'd had her own share of investigations in which someone had disappeared, and the suspicion had centered on the victims being taken into an underground network of sex workers. But like every single person she'd interviewed over the years, she'd never thought it would happen to someone she knew and loved. No way.

But maybe it had.

In any case, Elise was simply gone.

Everly had heard previously about the Mountain Mercenaries, and she'd been able to get in touch with their elusive leader, Rex. After she'd presented her case, and he'd done some research, he'd agreed to take it on. Rex hated sex trafficking. He'd seemingly made it his life's work to end it, one victim at a time. When he'd heard from the detective in LA that this was a suspected case of abduction for the purposes of sex trafficking, Rex had been much more willing to assist. Even allowing Everly to be involved . . . but she suspected that had more to do with the fact that Rex worked closely with the Colorado Springs Police Department, and he wanted to keep that relationship flourishing.

Elise wasn't exactly helpless—Everly had taken the time to teach her basic self-defense, but she was also only fifteen. And deaf. And she'd taken after her father in the size department. At only five-three, she wasn't really strong enough to take on a grown man.

Like many girls her age, Elise loved social media. She was constantly talking to her friends and sending silly pictures and posting selfies. If Everly had to guess, she'd suspect her sister had caught the attention of someone who liked her looks—her red hair and green eyes. Maybe talked to the wrong person online and had gone to meet up with him.

If that was the case, Everly didn't think Elise had done so with the intention of being gone that long. She didn't take any of her overnight things, and she didn't tell Me-Maw or Pop where she was going. Her sister was responsible . . . but she was still a teenager. Didn't really think about the consequences of her actions.

Everly had done her best to be a good influence, but it was hard when she'd been gone so much. First it was college, then she'd gotten a job at the Phoenix Police Department. She'd worked her ass off and hadn't been able to travel home as often as she would have liked. Then she'd gotten the job offer from the Colorado Springs Police Department and settled there.

She went to LA for visits as much as possible, but ultimately the job of raising Elise had fallen on Me-Maw and Pop.

Just then, the sound of the flight attendant saying something came over the speakers. Everly reached up and took out an earbud, but had already missed the announcement. "What'd she say?" she asked with a hint of trepidation in her tone.

"Just that we'll be starting our descent soon," Ball said.

Shit. She hated landing as much as she hated taking off.

Without pause, Ball reached over and grabbed her hand. He laced his fingers with hers and rested their clasped hands on the armrest between them.

He didn't look at her, and he still had the crinkles in his brow that she'd come to understand meant he was feeling stressed or annoyed, but she couldn't care about that at the moment. The simple act of being connected to someone helped make her fear more manageable.

Telling herself she was only holding his hand because she was so freaked and hadn't gotten enough sleep in the last few days, Everly closed her eyes and leaned her head back on the seat once more. She was sure once they landed, Ball would go back to being his usual annoying self, but for right now, this moment, she was going to take the comfort he offered.

Hours later, when they finally landed at LAX, Everly was more than grateful.

Ball hadn't held her hand on the flight to Los Angeles because Everly had volunteered to switch seats with a woman who'd been separated from her husband when the seat assignments were handed out. So Everly sat six rows behind Ball, trying to forget how reassuring the feel of his hand around hers had been, and how he'd kept the worst of her panic at bay with that simple gesture.

Now the only thing she wanted was to see Me-Maw and Pop. It had been too long since her last visit. They were in their midseventies now, but looked more like they were in their fifties. Allison Adams had the same red hair as her daughter and granddaughters. Even though age had dulled the auburn, it was still obvious she was a natural redhead, and she was petite like Elise. Landen Adams was tall, around six feet, and Everly had always loved how he smiled indulgently at his wife when she was acting crazy . . . which happened a lot. He never seemed to get embarrassed by her antics, and he always had a hand on her. Touching her back. Holding her hand. Resting his own on her leg when they were sitting. Running his fingers through her hair.

Their relationship was one of the reasons why Everly was still single. She'd never met a man who looked at her the way Pop looked at Me-Maw.

It was heartbreaking that two such amazing people had a daughter who'd turned out as Ella had.

The second she and Ball exited the secure section of the airport, Everly saw Me-Maw and Pop. Without worrying if Ball was following, she headed straight for them. They'd said they would meet her at the airport, but Everly had told them not to worry about it, that she and Ball were going to rent a car and she'd meet them back at their house.

Of course they ignored her and came anyway.

Not caring about anything other than feeling her grandma's arms around her, Everly dropped her duffel bag and practically dove into the hug waiting for her.

For the first time since she'd heard about Elise's disappearance, she broke down.

Smelling the familiar scent of Me-Maw and seeing how fragile she looked, Everly just lost it. It took several minutes, but eventually she got herself under control and looked up at Pop. He was standing behind his wife, as usual, and had a hand on her back as she held Everly.

She went to hug him and felt someone touching her. For a moment, she'd forgotten all about Ball. Turning her head, she saw him take a step back, and realized only then that he'd had his hand on her lower back the entire time she'd been hugging Me-Maw, lending silent support.

Before she could process that, Pop enveloped her in a hug. He smelled the same too . . . like the cigars he liked to smoke even though his wife scolded him for it.

"Hey, Pop," Everly said.

"Hey, kiddo. You okay?" he asked.

Everly took a deep breath and nodded. She wasn't, but she had to be strong. Her grandparents should be enjoying their retirement. Instead, they'd been busy raising their second granddaughter, and now were full of guilt and self-recrimination over her disappearance.

"We're going to find her," she told her pop with more confidence than she felt. She had no idea if they would find Elise, but with the Mountain Mercenaries at her back, hopefully there was a chance. Even a slim chance was better than no chance at all.

"Did you guys drive here?" Everly asked as she bent to pick up her duffel bag. It wasn't at her feet, and she looked up to see it slung over Ball's shoulder. She wanted to insist that she could carry her own bag, but she knew Me-Maw would scold her and tell her to let the "nice young man" carry her stuff.

"We Ubered," Pop said proudly.

Everly chuckled. "Seriously?"

"Yup. Didn't want to drive all the way down here, and we knew you were renting a car, so we figured we'd just ride back with you," Me-Maw said. "Now . . . introduce us to your friend."

"Right. Me-Maw, Pop, this is Kannon Black. He's a part of a special group that will be helping me find Elise. This is my grandmother, Allison Adams."

Allison held out her hand in greeting. "It's very nice to meet you, Kannon."

"Same here. I only wish it was under better circumstances. And please, call me Ball," he said, shaking her hand in return.

"Ball . . . how unusual," her grandmother murmured. "Let me guess . . . cannonball?"

"Pardon?" Ball asked.

Allison chuckled. "Is that how you got that nickname? Because of your first name? Kannon. Ball?"

Ball smiled. "Actually, no. But that's very appropriate."

Everly couldn't suppress the grin at her grandmother's words. "And this is my grandfather, Landen," she said, gesturing to her pop. Ball shook her grandfather's hand.

"Thank you for your service," Pop said.

Everly blinked in surprise. "How did you know he was in the military?"

"I can just tell," Pop said, then turned to Ball. "What branch?"

"Coast Guard, sir."

"It's Pop. Or Landen, if you want. None of that sir crap."

"Sorry," Ball said. "It's ingrained in me. I grew up in the south. My mom would smack the back of my head if I didn't show my respect by calling you sir."

Pop chuckled. "Fine. You've shown me respect. Now enough. It's Pop or Landen to you."

"Come on," she said. "Let's get the car. I'm eager to get home and get to Elise's computer."

Her words were a reminder about why she was there, and Everly could've kicked herself when she saw Pop frown and the worry lines appear on Me-Maw's forehead. She linked her arm with her grandmother's and pulled her toward the rental car area of the airport. "We're gonna find her, Me-Maw," she said softly. "I swear I won't give up until she's home."

"I'm not an idiot," Allison said. "I know the statistics just as well as you do. And I know all about sex trafficking. Elise is beautiful, like you, and I'm terrified that we'll never see her again."

Ball responded before Everly could. "From what Everly tells me, Elise is smart. She knows her sister will do whatever it takes to find her. Have faith, Allison. We're going to look under every rock and in every crevice and find your granddaughter."

"Thank you," Me-Maw said with a sniff. Then she took a deep breath and seemed to straighten. "I've got a roast in the Crock-Pot," she told Everly. "You're too skinny. You need to keep your strength up. Have you been sleeping?"

Everly smiled. Some things never changed. Her grandmother was always trying to feed her, always concerned that she wasn't getting enough rest. "I'm sorry it took me so long to come visit," she told her. "I'm going to try to do better in the future."

Pop wrapped his arm around his wife's waist, and the three of them walked side by side. "You don't have to visit for us to know you love us."

"True, but I miss you," Everly said.

Me-Maw elbowed her husband in the ribs. "Quit telling her it's okay if she doesn't come home."

"I didn't say that!" Pop defended himself.

"You did so!"

As her grandparents continued to mock-argue back and forth, Everly turned to make sure they hadn't lost Ball. She met his gaze for a split second—and what she saw there surprised her. Instead of the cynical or distrustful expressions she'd gotten used to, he looked more relaxed than she'd ever seen him.

~

Luckily, there wasn't a long line at the car rental place, and Ball was able to check in fairly quickly. He upgraded to an SUV since Everly's grandparents would be traveling with them.

He liked Everly's grandparents. They seemed subdued, and were upset about their missing granddaughter, but the tight connection between the two of them was hard to miss. Landen kept his hand on his wife's back or on her arm while they were talking, and the way he looked at her made it clear he was still very much in love with his wife.

Not only that, but Everly's me-maw was amusing in her attempts to push him and her granddaughter together. He'd also actually caught Allison checking out his ass at one point, and it made him laugh.

And for the first time since he'd learned he'd have to work with Everly, he'd seen her let down her guard. Her response at first seeing her grandparents had tugged at him.

He hated when women pulled out the crocodile tears. Holly, his ex, had done that all the time. Squeezed out tears when she didn't get her way. And his partner Riley had cried buckets during the investigation into what had happened to Ball. Though he couldn't prove it, he had a pretty good idea her tears had swayed a few of the officers in charge of her fate.

But Everly's tears had been genuine, unavoidable . . . coming from the soul. He suspected a mixture of relief at being in the arms of her grandmother and despair that her sister was missing. Throughout their talks the last few days, she hadn't shown even half the emotion she had upon seeing her me-maw. It hammered home the fact that this wasn't just another job for her. Not at all.

She might not be close to her mother, or even like her much, but she was extremely close with her grandparents and her half sister. Seeing their reunion created a sense of urgency in Ball that he hadn't felt before today.

Previously, Elise had been just another missing girl. But now, she was far more real.

Ball still wasn't too happy about having to work with Everly, but seeing her with her grandparents had already changed something in him. He just had to figure out *what*.

Everly insisted Me-Maw sit in the front seat, and she spent most of the drive to the house talking with her pop in the back. Meanwhile,

Allison Adams spent the ride grilling him. Asking him personal questions about how old he was, where he lived, whether he wanted children—until Everly told her to cut it out.

When they got close to the house, Ball started paying closer attention to his surroundings. The neighborhood the Adams lived in was nice. It wasn't super expensive, but it wasn't in the middle of a bad part of the city either. The lawns were all manicured, and there were flowers along many of the walkways.

"Two decades ago, this place was filled with children," Allison said. "But now everyone's grown up and moved away. It's just us old folks left."

"You're not old," Everly said from the back seat.

"I'm just seasoned," Allison replied easily, as if it was a running joke between her and her granddaughter.

"It's nice," Ball said.

"It is. But unfortunately, with every year that passes, it gets less and less nice," Pop said. "There's more crime, and the gangs are pushing their way in, slowly and steadily."

"Do you think Elise somehow got involved with a gang?" Everly asked.

"No. But then again, as of several days ago, I would've said there was no way she'd ever disappear without a trace either," Pop said.

He had a point.

After pulling into the driveway, Ball stopped and turned off the engine. "I'll come around," he told Allison.

"No need," she said with a small smile. Her husband had already climbed out of the back seat and had her door open. He held out a hand and helped her out of the SUV as if he did it every day of their lives . . .. which he probably did. He started walking her to the front door, leaving Ball and Everly behind.

Ball turned to open Everly's door, but found her already out as well, and at the back of the SUV, opening the hatch to get her bag. Hurrying back there, he tried to take her bag along with his.

"I've got it," she said, snatching the handle out of his hand.

"I'm just trying to be polite," he told her.

"Well, stop it. This isn't a date. I'm well aware of what you think of me."

"Everly—"

"Save it," she told him. "I heard you loud and clear the day we met—when you were talking behind my back. You don't want to work with me, and I'm sure you're pissed you were the one who got stuck coming to LA. I get it. You think I don't? I work with men like you all the time."

"Men like me?" Ball asked.

"Yeah. Men who don't think a woman can do the job as well as they can."

"That's not—"

"It is," she said, interrupting him once more. "But news flash—we can do the job just as well as you, if not better. I don't care that I'm shorter, or outweighed by most men. I've learned how to fight most effectively for my body size. I can fight dirty when I need to. I can run just as fast as any man, even faster than a lot of the cops on the Colorado Springs force. I can shoot a gun and search a building just as well too. When I'm wearing my SWAT gear, you can't even tell that I *am* a woman.

"I don't know what your beef is with women, Ball, and I don't really care. You can treat *me* like shit, and I won't even blink. But don't for one second think you can treat Me-Maw and Pop with disrespect. I won't stand for it. Hear me?"

"Have I done anything but show them respect so far?" Ball asked. He didn't wait for her to answer. "No, I haven't. They seem awesome, and you're lucky as fuck to have them. I wish I knew *my* grandparents, but they died when I was little, and I don't remember them. And I might not like working with women, but it has nothing to do with you. I had a bad experience. That's on me, and I'm doing my best to not let it affect this case. And I know I was a dick when I first heard that you'd be involved, and I'm sorry. But your sister needs us to work together, so that's what I'm trying to do. Okay?"

She stared at him for a beat, then nodded and headed for the door without another word.

Ball followed along—and the moment he stepped inside the small house, he felt himself relax. The smell of the pot roast permeated the air, making Ball's stomach rumble. The living room was a bit cluttered, but in the way that proved Allison and Landen had been living there for a long time.

There were pictures on every available surface and most of the walls, and Ball studied them briefly before making a mental note to check them all out later. From the glances he'd gotten already, Everly seemed happy as a young child, but as time went on, the photos captured someone more serious. He was curious about the pain he saw in her eyes in the more recent photos. Pain she did a good job of hiding in person, but which still leaked out every now and then.

He knew he hadn't been hiding his attitude about working with her, but he also hadn't suspected she'd cared much about what he thought. He'd obviously been wrong. Despite her words outside, she cared very much. And that surprised him.

He made a mental vow to try harder to put his prejudices aside. Elise deserved every ounce of his professionalism and expertise. If he and Everly were constantly at each other's throats, it would take their attention away from why they were there.

The plan had been for him to stay at a hotel nearby and for Everly to stay with her grandparents, but when Me-Maw was informed, she put her foot down.

"I've already prepared the room," she told them.

"What room?" Everly asked.

"*Your* room. Yours and your man's."

Ball pressed his lips together to keep from laughing at the look of horror that appeared on Everly's face.

"We're not together, Me-Maw. I *told* you that."

The older woman crossed her arms, and she got a stubborn look on her face. Pop rolled his eyes at his wife.

"You're really not? I thought you were just trying to be polite," Me-Maw said a little sadly. "I mean, you're thirty-four, you're old enough to bring a boy home. Besides, how else am I going to get great-grandbabies?"

Ball choked on the sip of water he'd just taken.

"Me-Maw!" Everly complained.

"What?"

"We're not dating. He doesn't even like me!"

"I like you," Ball countered immediately. Surprised to realize in that moment that, not only did he genuinely like her, he *respected* her. He might not be happy she was working with his team, but that didn't diminish the fact that the more time he spent with her, the more he got to know her, the more he begrudgingly liked her.

"No, you don't," she said.

"I do."

"No. You *don't*," she insisted.

Ball grinned.

"And stop smiling!"

That made his smile grow even wider. He glanced at Me-Maw and saw her standing in the kitchen, grinning at the two of them. He turned to her. "I appreciate the offer of lodging. I do. But I think Everly needs some quality time alone with her grandparents. I also have a lot of research I need to do, and I'll be talking to the other men on my team back in Colorado Springs a lot."

"Don't think you're going to keep anything from me," Everly said, putting her hands on her hips.

She did that a lot, and Ball couldn't help but notice how it stretched her shirt over her chest. Damn, she had a fine rack . . . and he was a dick for noticing. "I wasn't planning on it," he said.

"Fine. He can stay," Everly said, turning to Me-Maw.

"Seriously, I'm perfectly all right with—"

"I'll sleep out here, and he can have the guest room," Everly said, interrupting him again.

"We had a king-size bed put in there a few months ago," Pop said, getting into the conversation for the first time. "The couch out here stinks. Trust me, I know. I've fallen asleep on it more times than I can count."

Everly stared at her grandfather in disbelief. "Not you too."

"I'm sure I don't know what you're talking about," the older man said with a smirk. "All I'm saying is, if Ball's going to be doing research into the night, I'm guessing you'll need to be discussing that with him, and it'll be easier if you're in the same room. Your me-maw and I don't sleep that well, and if you were out here in the living room, we'd be able to hear you."

Ball couldn't help but be impressed by the way the couple so easily manipulated their granddaughter. It wasn't that he wanted to sleep in the same room she was in, but it sure was fun watching her squirm. He kinda thought it was weird that her grandparents were so willing to throw her into an intimate situation with a man she wasn't dating . . . but then Ball studied the couple more closely.

Allison's brow was furrowed, her hands wringing together slightly but steadily. And even though Landen was currently teasing Everly, Ball heard the note of concern in his tone.

They were probably using their granddaughter's lack of love life as a means of distraction from the situation with Elise. He already knew they felt tremendous guilt. They had no control over where Elise was now, or what might be happening to her . . . but they could control where Everly slept, maybe even have a hand in helping her find someone to spend her life with.

Teasing him and Everly was something they could focus on instead of the worry that had been heavy on their shoulders for the last week.

"It's fine," he said, letting Everly off the hook. "I can stay at the hotel like we planned. I promise to tell you what I find out."

"No," she said. "I don't trust you. We'll both stay here."

Her response surprised and bothered him. He needed time away from her. He couldn't be with her twenty-four seven. No way. "I've already got the hotel room reserved. I'll stay there."

"What if Elise calls? Won't you need to be here? What if whoever *has* her calls? We can't be taking eight or ten hours off each night just because you're too weirded out to work with a girl."

Ball clenched his teeth together. She was right. Damn it. "Fine."

"Fine," she repeated. "But"—she turned to her grandmother—"I can sleep in Elise's room. There's a perfectly good bed in there. That way, Ball can still do his research in the relative quiet of the guest room, and if he needs to ask me anything or consult, I'll still be around to assist."

At the mention of her missing granddaughter, Allison sighed heavily, and her shoulders drooped as if the weight of the world was once more pressing down on her, the momentary playfulness with Everly already forgotten. "Okay, honey."

Figuring he'd get out of the stressed couple's way and get to work, Ball said quietly, "If someone will point me to Elise's room, I'll just take a look around, if that's all right."

"I'll show you," Landen said. He headed down a short hallway, and Ball followed. Before he left the living room, he saw Everly heading for the kitchen to comfort her grandmother.

"Here it is," Landen said as he pushed open one of the doors. "If you have any questions, don't hesitate to ask." And with that, he headed back to his wife and granddaughter.

Ball stepped into Elise's room and simply stood there a moment, taking it in, trying to get into the head of the missing fifteen-year-old.

It didn't look like the Adamses had touched it since she'd left for school almost a week ago.

The comforter on the bed was thrown back, as if she'd just climbed out of bed and hadn't looked back. There were pink sheets on the bed, and the comforter was also pink with big white flowers. The walls had posters of Beyoncé and Drake, as well as Thor and Wonder Woman. There was also a poster of a young actor he didn't recognize. Making a mental note to ask Everly about it later, he continued looking around.

She had a desk that was an absolute mess. There were papers and books all over the surface. A bulletin board hung on the wall behind it. Ball stepped closer so he could get a better look. Ticket stubs, a few pictures of who he knew was Elise with other girls, a poem, and other silly mementos were tacked up so she could see them every day.

Dirty clothes were lumped in a corner near an already full hamper, and clothes spilled out of the small closet on the other side of the room.

Ball walked over to the window and tried opening it. Locked. He peered out, and saw it would be easy to open the window and sneak out of the house, as the room was on the first floor, but there weren't any footprints that he could see outside, under the window itself. Besides, she'd gone to school the day she'd disappeared. She hadn't snuck out of the house to meet up with someone.

"It looks like a normal teenage girl's room, doesn't it?"

Ball wasn't surprised by Everly's sudden appearance. He'd heard her enter a few seconds earlier.

"Yeah. But there's something missing," he said.

"What?"

"A computer." He turned to look at Everly.

"She's not allowed to use it in her room, much to her annoyance. Me-Maw and Pop let her have one, but she had to use it in the living room, with them there. They didn't want her up all night talking to her friends or whatnot."

"Hmmm."

"What are you thinking?" Everly asked.

"Nothing yet," Ball said. "I just have a feeling that while your grandparents' hearts were in the right place, and that was a smart idea, maybe they weren't as careful as they'd thought when it came to the computer. Who's that?" he asked, using his chin to indicate the poster.

Everly looked at the poster of the young man and said, "Sean Berdy. Why do you think they weren't careful?"

Walking over to the poster, Ball slowly lifted the bottom edge that wasn't tacked to the wall and looked behind it.

"Ball? Are you going to answer me?"

"Who's Sean Berdy?" he asked, ignoring her question for now.

Everly sighed. "He's a deaf actor. He was in the movie *The Sandlot 2* forever ago, and lately he was in the TV show *Switched at Birth* . . . which has been credited with increasing awareness of deaf culture. Elise loves that show, and is pretty much in love with Sean too."

Ball lifted the poster higher until Everly could see the back.

Gasping softly, Everly went to his side. She took the poster from his hand and tilted her head to better read what Elise had written on the back.

Elise Berdy had been written over and over, and there were hearts doodled everywhere. "Wow," Everly breathed.

"I'd have to agree with your assessment that she was in love with Sean," Ball said with a chuckle.

Everly didn't respond, but lifted the poster even higher. Above the hearts and the name Elise had doodled were lines and lines of extremely tiny writing. She squinted as she read them.

Ball frowned as he leaned closer and read over her shoulder.

Me-Maw is so mean! She won't take me to Hollywood to meet Sean. I know if he saw me, he'd totally fall in love with me. I'm not too young. We'd be perfect together. I hate it here. I hate Me-Maw, I hate my sister, I hate my mom. I hate everyone!

I woke up today and the flowers outside on the porch had bloomed overnight. They're so pretty.

I got to talk to Ev today, and as happy as I am for her, I'm sad for me. I hate LA and can't wait to get the hell out.

I got an A on my creative writing paper. I rock!

I wish I was dead.

Carrie's a bitch! She told Rick that I was a virgin and they all laughed at me. Some friend she is.

The notes were clearly some sort of diary. The words were obviously written at different times, as they were in different colors and scrawled haphazardly on the back of the poster. Sometimes horizontally, sometimes diagonally, other times upside down.

"Don't freak," Ball said softly, wanting to put his hand on Everly's suddenly stiff shoulders to comfort her—but also wanting to put distance between them for his own self-preservation.

"Don't freak?" she echoed. "How can I not? She said she wished she was *dead*! Said she hated me."

"She's a teenager," Ball said. "Her hormones are all out of whack, and she literally feels every emotion ten times as strongly as we do. This looks like her way of venting."

He watched as Everly took a deep breath. "You're right." Then she dropped the poster and turned to him. "How'd you know to look behind it?"

Ball shrugged. "Every other poster in the room has thumbtacks neatly in each corner. This one only has them in the top corners to hold it to the wall. It's also a lot more ragged than the others . . . as if it's been handled repeatedly."

Everly turned her eyes back to the poster and examined it for a moment. Then she nodded.

"I'm going to need to take pictures of what she wrote and send them to the others, so they can help figure out who the people are she's mentioned, look into their backgrounds," Ball said gently.

Everly sighed. "I know. I don't like it, but I know."

"And it's good that she didn't have a computer in her room, probably did keep her from staying up half the night, talking to her friends . . . but what about her phone? I know you said the detective has tried to track it with no luck, and that they're waiting for the records to come back. She probably used it to message people. Did your grandparents inspect her phone, or the computer each time after she used it? Check to see who she was talking to and on what sites?"

Everly shook her head. "I doubt it. They're awesome and pretty hip, but I don't think they'd know how to do that."

"That's where we'll start. We'll go over this"—he motioned to the poster—"to see who her friends were that she talked to the most, and look into that computer. Tomorrow, I'll go to her school and interview her teachers and friends, as well as check out the surveillance cameras. You can check in with the detective and see if he's gotten anything back, and maybe even have him pressure them to hurry it up."

"That's not going to work," Everly said.

Slightly annoyed that she was already questioning him, Ball asked, "Why?"

"Because you don't know sign language. You can't talk to the people at Elise's school."

Duh. Ball had forgotten all about the fact that Elise was deaf. Rather, he hadn't actually forgotten; being around Everly had made him temporarily lose track of that small detail. "Right. Of course. So we'll both go to her school, then head to the police department."

She was staring at him with a weird look on her face.

"What?"

"Just like that?"

"Just like that what?" he asked, confused.

"Change of plans, just like that?" she asked.

"Yes, Everly. What the hell?"

"I figured you'd say you'll find a way to talk to them, or that you'd be able to handle it, or that you'd stay up all night and learn sign language or something. I'm sure it bothers you to rely on me for anything, since you don't want to work with me."

Her constant reminders about his previous attitude were starting to piss him off a little, but Ball tried to hold his temper. "It's not you, specifically, I don't want to work with."

"Right."

"The last woman I partnered with almost got me killed," Ball blurted.

Everly didn't back down. "I'm not her."

Sighing, Ball ran a hand through his hair. "I know."

"Do you? Because from where I'm standing, since we met, it's seemed an awful lot like I'm being punished for someone else's crime. I don't know what happened, and it sucks that it happened to you at all, but did it actually happen *because* she was female? Or is gender, in your mind, just the easiest thing to blame for what happened?"

Standing in the middle of a teenager's bedroom, Ball felt his world shift on its axis at her words.

Had he been unfair to Riley? He hadn't thought so before now, but Everly's words made him wonder. She was definitely right about one thing—he was letting his personal prejudice get in the way of his mission. He wasn't going to immediately start jumping up and down with joy that he had to work with Everly, but at the moment, he *did* need her.

"I'm sorry my past experiences have made me difficult to work with. I'll do my best to put them behind me so we can find your sister."

"Thank you."

"I'm assuming you don't want to get a good night's sleep before we tackle this?" he asked, gesturing to the poster once more.

"Absolutely not. I haven't been sleeping well anyway. If I'm up, I might as well be doing something to find Elise."

Ball didn't like hearing that she wasn't sleeping, but it wasn't exactly a surprise. The dark circles under her eyes were more than enough evidence that she wasn't taking care of herself. He wanted to tell her that if she got sick, she wouldn't be helping her sister, but figured that might be taking things a bit too far. He let it go. "You grab the poster, and I'll go ask your grandparents for the computer she used."

Everly nodded.

Taking a deep breath, Ball headed out of the room.

Working with Everly was turning out to be harder than he'd already thought it would be . . . but not for the reasons he'd thought even just a day ago.

He *did* like her.

Admired her strength.

Admired the way she stuck up for herself and didn't put up with his shit.

She wasn't anything like his old partner in the Coast Guard. Riley Foster had been eager to do a good job, but she hadn't been terribly confident. She'd only been driving on that fateful day because it had been less intimidating than manning the gun at the bow of the small boat.

Ball suspected Everly would've relished the chance to be the gunner on that boat. She wouldn't have hesitated to volunteer for the position—and would've had the time of her life while doing it.

Not wanting to think about Riley any longer, Ball headed for the kitchen. He needed that computer so he could contact Meat and get him working on trying to figure out where the hell Elise Adams had disappeared to.

~

Elise Adams sat on the cold floor in the basement where she'd been stashed. Her lips were dry, and she hadn't eaten more than a few bites of the food her captor had brought her in the last couple of days. She didn't trust him not to drug and attack her when she was vulnerable. The room was dark, and no matter how many times she blinked or squinted, the darkness didn't dissipate, not that she really expected it to.

The man who'd brought her to the house had talked to her, but she'd only been able to catch snippets of his words by reading his lips because he was always looking around, as if he was worried someone would see them.

She had no idea where she was, but she was scared and miserable and wished she could go back and change the decision she'd made at the end of that fateful school day. She'd never imagined that agreeing to meet the boy she'd been talking to for months could result in being chained to a pole in the basement of some run-down house.

A light flicked on at the top of the stairs, and Elise blinked. Her eyes refused to adjust to the light after being in the dark for so long, and she had to look away. By the time she looked back, there was a man standing in front of her.

He was a lot taller than her own five-three, and his brown hair wasn't short, but it wasn't long. If she passed him on the street, she wouldn't have looked twice at him, because he looked so ordinary. So normal. He was old, way older than she was . . . at least forty . . . and had on a pair of jeans and a black T-shirt.

It was the same man who'd picked her up after school. He'd held out his phone, where he'd written something in the notes app about being Rob's dad, and she'd stupidly believed him. She'd been a little nervous, but she trusted Rob, and therefore trusted his "dad" by extension.

God, could she have *been* any more stupid?

Her eyes went to his face, but he was just standing there staring at her. Finally, he gestured downward.

Elise looked down to see that he was holding a fast-food bag. Her mouth immediately started to water. She was *so* hungry. She didn't know if he'd drugged the food he was holding, but she'd gotten to the point where she didn't care anymore. She was starving. She would have to risk being drugged.

Without thinking, she stood and reached for it, but the man backed up, holding it out of her reach. He placed it on a table on the other side of the room. Then he came back toward her.

Her eyes focused on his lips as he began talking. She only caught some of his words, because of the low light in the room and because she was still working on learning the art of lip reading. She could tell he was speaking slowly, as if to help her understand him easier. Why he didn't have a note prepared to show her, like he had when he'd picked her up, she didn't know.

"Food . . . quiet . . . go home . . . nice to me . . ."

Then he stared at her as if waiting for an answer.

Not knowing what else to do, and not wanting to provoke the man, Elise nodded.

He smiled then, and Elise immediately panicked. What had she agreed to?

She shook her head, but the man didn't see it—he was already taking off his shirt.

Elise tried to back up, but forgot about the chains around her ankles. She fell to her ass on the hard concrete floor and looked up into the eyes of pure evil. He smirked at her as he bent and reached for the buttons on the cute shirt she'd picked out to wear all those days ago.

Gasping in horror, she smacked his hand away and scrambled as far away from him as she could get.

When he stepped toward her again, Elise screamed in terror.

The man stopped and tilted his head, frowning as he studied her.

Elise had no idea what he was thinking at that moment. She wasn't naive; she knew what he *wanted*, but there was no way she was going to lie there docilely and let him assault her. She knew he could overpower her, but Everly had taught her how to fight. She'd stab her fingers into his eyes, kick him in the balls, and basically do anything and everything to keep him from touching her.

She flexed her fingers, ready to do what harm she could—when the man suddenly smiled.

But it wasn't a happy smile. It was malicious. That, combined with the look in his eyes, made Elise shiver in dread.

He walked back over to where he'd dropped his shirt and slowly pulled it back over his head. Elise wanted to be relieved, but she couldn't forget the look in his eye. He had something planned, but the question was, what?

The smell of the fast food, which had previously made her mouth water with anticipation, now made it water from nausea. She wanted to cry. Instead, she prayed with all her heart that Everly would find her. She had to. She was a police officer, and Elise knew she was awesome at her job. She'd track her down. It was what she did.

She stared at the man as he once again spoke slowly and haltingly, as if wanting to make sure Elise could read his lips.

"You . . . good girl. Pure. Waiting . . . Better. If you . . . eat, you behave."

Then the man walked over to the table where he'd placed the bag of food and picked it up. He brought it over to her and dropped it in her lap.

"Good . . . home . . . soon."

Then he turned and walked back up the stairs. Before Elise could even look into the bag to see what her apparent purity had bought her, the light went out, and she was plunged into the pitch black once more.

She thought about refusing to eat the food again, but that would be stupid. She needed her strength. If it was laced, so be it. If he came back to finish what he'd obviously wanted to do, and she was knocked out from some drug, that would be good, right?

Elise shivered at the thought of the man touching her.

At one point, she'd actually hoped Rob might be the man she gave her virginity to, but it looked like that would never happen. There *was* no Rob.

Now she had to do whatever it took to stay alive, including keeping her body strong by eating, until Everly could find her. Elise had no doubt she would.

Fingering the ring on her right pointer finger, she prayed harder than she'd ever prayed in her life.

She couldn't taste the food, but she ate it anyway.

Then she cried.

Chapter Three

Everly's stomach clenched in frustration. They'd called Meat, and he'd walked them through setting up the computer so he could remotely log on to it. He'd instructed them to leave it exactly as it was and to let him do his thing. They'd done as he requested, had a quick meal with her grandparents, and then begun examining the impromptu journal on the back of the poster, line by line.

Me-Maw and Pop had stuck their heads in hours ago to tell them good night, then headed off to bed.

It was now two in the morning, and Ball had just called it quits.

"I'll stay up just a bit longer," Everly said.

"No. We're both whipped. I think we should get some sleep, then start tomorrow when we're fresh," Ball suggested.

"I'm fine. If you want to go to sleep, you can," Everly said absently, not taking her eyes off her computer screen.

Without a word, Ball grabbed her hand and physically pulled her out of the chair she was in, out of the dining room, and down the hall. Everly didn't protest too loudly, ever aware of her grandparents sleeping in their room nearby.

Figuring she'd humor Ball and, when he fell asleep, go back out to continue examining her sister's poster for any kind of clue, she went into the bathroom across the hall from her sister's room and changed into a T-shirt and leggings to sleep in. She didn't even look at Ball when he went into the bathroom after she was done.

She crawled into her sister's bed and turned on her side.

It felt weird to be in Elise's room. Sad. Heartbreaking. Everly shouldn't be there. It should be her sister under that soft comforter. Where was she now? Did she have a warm place to sleep? A bed?

Doing her best to turn her morose thoughts away from what her sister might be going through right that second, Everly briefly wondered what would've happened if she'd gone along with Me-Maw's suggestion and slept in the guest room with Ball.

It had been a long time since she'd shared a bed with someone, even just for sleeping. She'd had a few affairs, but they were mostly about relieving tension and not about connecting deeply with a man. She'd have sex, cuddle for about two-point-three seconds, then either she or the guy would inevitably get up and go home.

But being here in her grandparents' house, in her sister's bed, and thinking about Ball . . . it was all too weird.

Even more so because Everly had such mixed feelings about the man in the other room. She was well aware of the fact that he didn't want to be here, and when she'd called him on it, instead of bullshitting her, he'd owned up to the fact that he didn't want to work with a woman. He'd even apologized for how he'd treated her, which had shocked her.

Ball didn't strike her as the kind of man who said he was sorry a lot, simply because she didn't think he made a habit out of doing things he had to apologize *for*. Sure, he was a jerk, but even *she* had to admit he'd been conscientious around her since his major foot-in-mouth moment the day they'd met. And he was respectful and kind to her grandparents.

She hadn't known him long, but the more she learned, the more she almost liked the guy. *Almost.* He obviously respected his teammates as well, and she'd seen him interacting briefly with the other men's fiancées. He'd seemed downright gentle with them.

His animosity hadn't made sense to her then, but hearing that he'd almost died at the hands of a woman he'd worked with . . . it made everything much clearer.

Twisting the ring on her finger, Everly closed her eyes and turned her attention back to Elise. The ring was as familiar as breathing. It was one of the most precious things Everly owned. She'd never taken it off before, and *would* never take it off.

As she turned over Elise's disappearance in her mind, she couldn't stop some of her darker thoughts from creeping in. Was her sister hungry? Hurting? Was she even alive?

She had so many questions and not a single answer. And Everly *hated* not having answers.

Everly was so lost in thought about her sister that she hadn't heard Ball open the door to Elise's room. She jumped when she felt him sit on the bed behind her—and was full-on shocked when he lifted the covers and crowded into the bed behind her. He wrapped an arm around her stomach and shoved his other arm under her neck.

She could smell the mint of his toothpaste, he was so close, and Everly swallowed hard. "What the hell are you doing?" she asked, struggling slightly to get out of his embrace.

"Sleeping," he said calmly. "Or I would be if you'd stop wiggling."

"Wiggling?" she seethed. "Let go of me!"

"No. Now hush and go to sleep."

"Seriously, Ball. This isn't funny. You're supposed to be sleeping in the other room. Let me go."

His arm only tightened around her belly, and she felt him move even closer. His lips brushed against her ear as he spoke. "You've been sleeping like shit. There's nothing more we can do for your sister right now. Meat will probably stay up all night, working on her computer, and he'll call the second he finds anything. We're going to have a long day tomorrow, and we both need to get a few hours of shut-eye."

"I can sleep just fine with you in the other room," Everly informed him.

"The second I fall asleep, you're going to be up and out of this bed, rereading that damn poster for the hundredth time. There's nothing there that will help us. It's just her way of blowing off steam. Now again . . . *hush*."

How did he know what she'd planned? She'd definitely been hoping after enough time had passed for him to fall asleep, she could sneak out to the dining room to see if she could find something on Elise's computer.

"I will not," she lied. "And I can't sleep with you touching me like this."

"Try," was his unsympathetic response.

"Ball—"

"Shhhh. I'm exhausted," he said.

"Then get out of this bed, and go into the guest room to sleep," she said snarkily.

He inhaled deeply. "You smell good," he whispered, so softly that Everly wasn't sure she'd heard him right.

"What?"

"Go to sleep," Ball said a little louder. "Just try. If you still can't sleep after a while, I'll leave."

"Fine," Everly huffed. Anything to get him to let go of her. Having him this close, holding her as securely as he was, made her suddenly want things she couldn't have. At least not from him. She and Ball were like oil and water. They'd never work out.

But she couldn't deny that being plastered together on the full-size mattress like they were . . . felt good. Really good.

She wasn't sure sleeping with Ball in her sister's bed was appropriate, but she couldn't muster up the energy to kick him out.

"I'm scared for her," she said quietly after a tense silence.

Ball tightened his arms around her and nuzzled her neck gently. It tickled a little bit, but took her mind off her sister for a brief second.

Several minutes went by, then he whispered, "We're going to find her. I fucking promise."

It took a lot, but Everly beat back the tears that threatened to fall.

She liked this gentler, more supportive Ball. Too much.

Her entire life, she'd felt as if it was her against the world. But for a moment, just this moment, she felt as if she truly had someone on her side.

~

Ball knew he was pushing his luck, but he'd watched Everly getting more and more stressed as the evening went on. When she didn't even get upset after Me-Maw made a slightly suggestive comment about the two of them, he knew she was officially done.

After her grandparents had gone to bed and she'd worried herself sick overanalyzing every word her sister had written on the back of the poster, he'd physically dragged her away and told her in no uncertain terms they were done for the night.

As she went into the bathroom to get ready for bed, he knew she was only humoring him, that the second he fell asleep, she'd sneak out and go right back to obsessing over the poster. So when *he'd* finished getting ready for bed, he decided to do something he'd never done before.

Oh, he'd slept with women, of course. But generally for sex, and afterward, he'd roll over to sleep on one side of the bed while they stayed on the other. Ball was *not* a cuddler.

However, the second he'd entered Elise's room and climbed under the girly comforter on the bed, he'd wrapped his arms around Everly, effectively trapping her. At first he'd done it mostly because the bed was so small—and because annoying her in the process was just a bonus—but the second her warmth seeped into him, he knew he'd made an error in judgment. He liked this a little *too* much.

He was surprised by how good it felt. How good *she* felt. He tried not to dwell on that fact, but he could feel every inch of her body against his. He wasn't aroused, but he felt . . . content. He was also exhausted. He'd used up a lot of energy being stressed over working with a woman, and then trying to figure out where Elise might have gone. He was in a strange city, in a strange house, and he'd had more than his share of being polite and courteous. He just wanted to relax and sleep for a bit.

Somehow, holding Everly in his arms seemed to make all the stress he'd been feeling fade away. She was tense and stiff at first, but the longer they lay there, the more he could feel her relax.

He drew in a deep breath, and the scent of whatever shampoo she used further eased his tension.

After she admitted her fear, Ball whispered, "We're going to find her. I fucking promise."

He felt her body tense again, heard a small hitch of breath, but she controlled herself and relaxed once more. In ten minutes, her even inhalations and exhalations told him she'd fallen asleep.

It made him feel good that she'd been able to shut down enough to finally get some rest. Ball had no doubt that she'd be up and raring to go in a few hours. He would be, too, if it was his sister who was missing.

But for now, he relished the quiet of the house with only a muted ticking of a clock somewhere breaking the silence—the feel of Everly against his large frame, as if she were made to be there.

Closing his eyes, Ball ran his thumb over the ring on her right hand. He had no idea what the significance of it was, but he'd seen her turning it around and around and around all night. As if the simple act of touching it calmed her.

He fell asleep with the scent of her in his nostrils and the feel of her in his arms . . . and never slept better.

~

"I've got bad news," Meat said the next morning when Ball and Everly were sitting at the table after eating breakfast. Everly had tried to tell Me-Maw they would grab something on their way to the school, but she wasn't having any of it, and had insisted on making them eggs, bacon, and pancakes.

"You need a good meal to start your day. I know you, Ev, you'll grab crap, and then you'll be sagging by the end of the day. If you and your man start off with a full belly, you'll be able to think better."

She couldn't argue the "full belly" thing. She let the "your man" thing go.

Everly had woken up feeling more refreshed than she had in a very long time. She'd immediately known where she was—and whose arms she was in. Sometime during the night, Ball had turned onto his back, and she'd woken up using his chest as her pillow. His arm was around her shoulders, and she'd been in a tight little ball, curled up next to his side. It was disconcerting how comfortable she'd been.

She'd slipped out of bed, grabbed her stuff, and headed to the bathroom, glad he hadn't been awake. She quickly showered, only thinking a little bit about whether Elise had been able to do the same since she'd disappeared, and by the time she'd arrived in the kitchen, Ball was already there. Dressed and looking as awake as ever . . . damn him.

She just hoped that Me-Maw hadn't seen him coming out of Elise's room. Hopefully he'd been smart enough to muss up the guest bed so as not to let on where he'd actually slept. Her grandmother would never let her hear the end of it if she knew Everly and Ball had shared a bed last night, after all.

They'd made small talk, avoiding the heavy topic that was on all their minds as they ate. As soon as Me-Maw disappeared back into the kitchen with the dishes, Ball had called his teammate.

"Don't make us wait," he scolded Meat. "Spit it out."

They had Meat on speakerphone. Even though Everly had wanted to spare Me-Maw the details, she wanted even more to hear firsthand what Meat had discovered.

"I was able to get into her Facebook account, but she doesn't use it very much. There were a few messages, but nothing exciting."

"And?" Everly asked impatiently.

"Hang on, I'm getting there. There *were* a ton of other apps on the computer, though. Instagram, Snapchat, Sarahah, Yubo, Musical.ly, Kik, WhatsApp . . . those are the main ones it looks like she's used in the past."

"I haven't even heard of some of those," Everly said, stunned.

"Kids are resourceful, and they'll use whatever their friends are using. Anyway, the thing is, a lot of these apps are so attractive because they don't keep a record of conversations between two people, or they're even totally anonymous."

"Even if they're anonymous, there's still some IP addresses and things to follow up on, right?" Ball asked.

"Well, yeah, but it doesn't look like Elise really used the computer for talking to her friends," Meat said.

"She used her phone," Allison guessed.

Everly turned to look at her grandmother. She was standing at the end of the kitchen nearest them, listening.

"That's my assumption, yes," Meat said.

"She did. She was always tapping away at it," Allison said sadly. "Said she was talking to her friends, and we didn't really think much about it. Didn't think that she might be lying or anything. We told her she wasn't allowed to use it at the dinner table and insisted she finish her homework first, but the second she was done, her face was buried in that thing."

Everly didn't even think about it; she began signing to her me-maw: *It's not your fault.*

Isn't it? Me-Maw signed back.

No. Believe me, every teen is obsessed with their phone. It doesn't mean you're a bad guardian, Everly signed.

I bet it wouldn't have happened if she was with you. You would've been on her. Asked more questions.

Stop, Everly signed.

"What's going on?" Meat asked from the speaker of Ball's phone.

"Everly and her me-maw are having a discussion," Ball told his teammate.

"But . . . I don't hear them talking," Meat replied.

"Oh, they are," Ball said.

Everly couldn't read his tone. "I'm sorry. That was rude. I didn't even realize I was doing it. Meat, I was talking to Me-Maw in sign language. She thinks this is her fault."

"It's not," Ball said immediately.

"And I was telling my granddaughter that *she* would've been more strict with Elise. Everly wouldn't have let her talk to strangers on the internet."

"Me-Maw, you know that's not true, and you don't even know that she *was* talking to strangers. Why do you think these apps exist? Because teens want a way to get around their parents. If Elise wanted to chat online, she would've found a way. Stop beating yourself up about it. Meat?"

"Yeah?"

"So there's no information on the computer?"

"I didn't say that exactly. I've got a few conversations that she had with people on WhatsApp on the computer, and the pictures she posted on her story on Snapchat. For some reason, probably by design, no conversations from her phone have carried over to the apps on her laptop. So I'll need her phone to track down any conversations she had on it. And if she used Kik, it'll be really hard to find out who she was talking to. The biggest lure of that site is how private and anonymous things are."

"But you can figure it out?" Everly asked.

"Given enough time, yes."

She understood what he was saying. They might not have the time they needed for him to track down her sister's conversation partners . . . but worse, if they didn't have the phone, they might not even get to try. "Can we subpoena her phone records and get the data that way?"

"Yes and no," Meat said. "We can get phone numbers she texted and called, but the apps are different. We could probably subpoena each of the apps we know she used, but it will take forever to get the information."

Sighing when she really wanted to scream, Everly nodded. She got it. They needed the phone. But that was probably impossible. The police had already tried to track it, and it was either turned off or smashed to pieces by now.

"We're headed over to Elise's school this morning," Ball told Meat. "Then we're going to go talk to Everly's contacts at the PD. We'll know more after we talk to them and find out what, if anything, they've done to look into things further."

Meat said, "I'll be in touch if I find out anything more from the computer. Mrs. Adams?"

Everly turned to her grandmother. She was still standing nearby, listening.

"Yes?"

"I don't know your granddaughter all that well—Everly, that is—but between her and Ball, and the rest of us back here in Colorado, we're doing everything we can to find Elise."

"Thank you."

"If it's okay, please don't use the computer today. I haven't finished cloning the hard drive yet."

"I won't," Me-Maw said.

"Thanks," Meat told her.

"I'll call later," Ball told his friend.

"Sounds good. Bye."

"Bye."

Ball clicked off the phone.

"So the rest of your friends are in Colorado?" Allison asked, though Everly guessed it wasn't really a legit question, as Ball had already told her that. "Please tell me you're not with the Mob or anything."

Ball chuckled. "No, ma'am. We're just an organization that helps find missing people."

"Okay." Then she signed to Everly. *You okay?*

I'm fine.

You look better. Like you got some sleep.

I did.

You two would probably sleep even better in the king-size bed in the guest room, rather than the full-size one you slept in last night.

Everly shook her head and knew she was blushing. Of course her grandmother knew Ball hadn't slept in the guest room. Sighing, she couldn't deny that she'd slept well the night before. She'd been exhausted, yes, but she had a feeling that a lot of the reason was because of the man who'd held her in his arms all night.

Maybe she'd simply give in and go for comfort tonight and stay in the guest room, after all. Me-Maw didn't mind. And obviously, neither did Ball.

Wondering what in the world she was thinking, she looked away from her grandmother and caught Ball's eye.

"I really need to learn sign language," he drawled. "I'd pay good money to know what put that blush on your face."

"Nothing." Everly looked at her watch. "School is about to start. Our appointment with the principal is in forty minutes. We should get going."

Ball nodded and stood. Everly hugged Me-Maw and told her to tell Pop that she loved him, and they headed out.

On the way to Elise's school, Everly told Ball everything she knew about the place. When it was founded, how many students there were, which grades, the fact that everyone was deaf or very hard of hearing, and how the test scores of the students were some of the highest in the state.

They pulled into a parking space when they arrived, and Everly hopped out, not waiting for Ball to come around and open her door. She'd grown up watching Pop do that for Me-Maw, and once upon a time she'd wished for a man who would do the same thing for her. Maybe she still did. Though she also wanted a man who'd be proud of her and the job she did, who wouldn't insist on treating her as if she wasn't capable of taking care of herself.

"Don't be offended if people stare at you," she told Ball as they headed for the front door of the school.

"Why would they stare?"

Deciding to be blunt, she explained, "One, because you're hot. I'm sure you know that, so don't think it's me coming on to you. Second, because in their world, you're the outcast. They're going to talk about you, knowing you can't understand them. Don't take it personally."

"I won't." He paused a moment, then said, "I'm hot?"

Everly rolled her eyes. "I knew you couldn't *not* comment on that. Surely you know that about yourself."

He shrugged. "I guess I don't think about it much. I am who I am."

Everly paused at the front door and stared at him. "Ball, you're tall and muscular. Your blond hair and blue eyes are heart stopping. You have that square jaw, and enough swagger in your step that it just screams confidence. You might be 'old' to these teenagers, but you also have an aura about you that says 'Don't fuck with me.' If you married any of their mothers, you'd be a total DILF. So yeah, you're hot."

"What the hell is a DILF?"

She chuckled. "You don't know?"

"No."

"Then that's for me to know and you to find out," she told him with a smile, then opened the door. She heard Ball hurrying in behind her, and she had to smile wider at getting the upper hand with him—for once.

They got there in the middle of a class change, and her smile died as she caught snatches of conversations going on between groups of students. She'd been wrong. They weren't talking about Ball at all.

They were talking about her sister. About Elise being missing.

Most thought she'd run away.

Ashamed that she'd let herself enjoy even one minute of her day when Elise was out there somewhere, probably terrified, Everly pressed her lips together and refused to look around at the kids as they made their way to the front office.

"What's wrong? What are they saying?" Ball asked, pulling her to a stop with a hand on her upper arm.

"Nothing."

"Everly, tell me. I don't give a shit if they're talking about me, but considering how you just shut down, I'm thinking it's something else, right?"

Feeling as if she was on the verge of losing it, Everly shut her eyes and took a deep breath. Ball pulled her off to the side, but she didn't open her eyes. When she felt a wall at her back, she did finally open them, and looked up to see Ball standing between her and the hallway. His hand rested on the wall next to her head, and he was leaning close.

"Talk to me. Whose butt do I need to kick?" he asked.

She couldn't help it—she chuckled. "You can't get into a fight with a kid, Ball."

"Why not?"

"Because!" She stared up at him in exasperation.

"That's not an answer. Tell me what they were saying."

Everly shook her head. She couldn't discuss it now. "We have to go meet with the principal," she stalled.

"Everly," he said, putting one hand under her chin, "tell me."

"It's nothing. They're just talking about Elise. Wondering who you are, and why I'm here. They know I'm her sister, and apparently some think I abandoned her. They were just gossiping, Ball . . . saying she probably ran away because no one cared about her."

Ball turned and glared at the few students still milling around in the hallway. "Who? I'll kick their ass."

Everly grabbed his arm. "Ball! Stop it."

He turned back to her. "You didn't abandon your sister. Don't for one second let that shit sink into your head. You dropped everything to be here for her now. And don't think I don't know that you're taking unpaid leave from your job to be here."

"How'd you know about that?"

"I know everything," he said, and Everly had a funny feeling that he really did. "Ev, don't let these little shits get to you. We're going to find Elise."

"What if we don't?"

"We are."

"Ball, you can't know that."

"I do. I don't know how, but I do. Someone as beautiful as your sister—and I mean who she is as a person as much as her physical looks—can't have her life ended this soon."

"You don't know what she's like inside."

"I've listened to you talk about her. I read her thoughts written on the back of that poster. She feels hard. About everyone. If she only cared about herself, she wouldn't be nearly as emotional. I've met Me-Maw and Pop, I've seen her room, I see how much you love her. How could she be anything else?"

Everly just stared up at him. She wasn't sure she'd even liked Ball all that much until now, but given what he'd just said, she felt herself softening. "I'm scared," she whispered.

"Me too," he admitted. "But that's not going to stop us, is it? Elise needs us. She's counting on you to find her. And dammit, that's what we're going to do, no matter what these gossipy teenagers say about the situation. All right?"

"All right."

"Good." Then he grabbed her hand—not romantically, almost impatiently—and towed her down the hallway. Apparently the look on his face was somewhat scary, because the few kids who were still lurking about rushed to get out of his way.

~

Ball sat next to Everly in the principal's office and watched them talking.

Everly was translating as they signed so he could understand what was being said. It was odd being on the outside like he was, and now he fully understood why Rex had insisted on Everly being involved with the investigation. He wouldn't have been able to talk like this with the principal. He would've had to resort to writing things down on paper and having the principal do the same.

It would've been awkward, and there was no way the man would've opened up like he was with Everly. It was obvious the two knew each other, that they'd had many chats in the past about her sister.

The man was worried about Elise, and he told Everly that no one had reported anything being off with her the last day she'd been at school. He'd talked to all her teachers, and everyone said the same thing, that it had been a normal day. She'd gotten a history test back and had earned a B. She was seen chatting happily at lunch with a group of girls she hung out with, and she hadn't said anything to anyone about where she was going or who she might be meeting after school.

The only useful thing that came out of the conversation was when the principal said that one of the bus monitors had seen Elise walking the opposite way from the direction her grandparents lived.

That was new. And Everly picked up on it immediately.

"Why didn't someone tell the cops?" she asked.

I think they did. They were here yesterday and talked to a handful of Elise's friends, the principal signed as Everly translated.

After talking for another twenty minutes, and not getting any other useful information out of the man, Everly thanked him. He told them they were welcome to talk to any of the students if they wanted to.

"Should we track down her friends and see if they'll talk to us?" Everly asked, back out in the hall.

He shook his head. "I don't know that it'll do any good. I believed the principal when he said that no one had seen anything unusual. Your sister is kind of a private person, right?"

"Yeah. I didn't even know she had a crush on that Sean Berdy guy. She made me watch that *Sandlot* movie one time when I was visiting, but I didn't think anything of it."

"Right. And does she have one friend that she hangs with all the time? A best friend?"

"Not really."

"I'm thinking if she was talking to someone on one of those apps, that maybe she was keeping it to herself. You said it yesterday, she's sensitive. If she shared that she had a cyber-boyfriend, she might've been afraid someone would talk her out of it, or tease her, or tell her that he might not be who she thought he was. Maybe he was older, and she was worried someone would tell her grandparents."

Everly thought about everything he'd said. "You're probably right. But what now?"

"Let's take a walk."

"A walk? Are you crazy?"

"Nope. Come on. Trust me."

And oddly enough, she did. They exited the school the way they'd come in and turned left . . . away from the direction Elise would've gone if she was walking home.

~

Ball was unsettled. And not just about the case.

The more time he spent around Everly, the more he liked her.

She wasn't prone to hysterics, and in fact had been way more stoic than he could've imagined, under the circumstances.

She didn't expect him to do things for her simply because he was a man and she was a woman. He clearly remembered Riley standing back and letting him coil rope on the boat they'd operated together. She'd also let him pump the gas, troubleshoot the engine, and clean out the boat at the end of the day.

Then again, he'd done all those things without thought or hesitation.

Maybe he'd perpetuated some of the stereotypical gender roles she'd fallen into. He'd been all too eager to be the first one to make entry on any boat they stopped, and to stand in front of her when shit went sideways.

Had it always been that way? He honestly couldn't remember.

But Ball had a feeling if he tried to do any of that stuff with Everly, she'd push him aside and do whatever needed to be done herself.

It wasn't a comfortable thought that maybe, just maybe, he'd done Riley a disservice over the years.

He hadn't let her do a lot of things because he'd thought she didn't *want* to. But what if she did? What if she could've been a better Coastie if he'd let go of his habit of coddling her, or his need to keep her safe?

What if it had been *his* actions that ultimately caused the accident that cost him his career?

Shit.

But it was more than that. Yes, being around Everly was slowly changing his mind on working with women—which was crazy, as he'd only known her, *really* known her, for a day or so—but it was also slowly chipping away at the shield he'd built around his heart. Holly had ripped it out of his chest when she'd left him while he was recuperating, but witnessing Everly's devotion to her sister and grandparents, even when she didn't live in the same city, he knew without a doubt that she'd never turn her back on a man she supposedly loved.

"What are we looking for?" Everly asked, bringing him out of his musing.

"I'm not sure. But someone saw your sister walking this way. It's as much of a clue as we've had since we started looking into things."

Everly nodded, her head constantly swiveling as she kept her eyes peeled for anything that might be related to Elise.

"When you were getting ready to go this morning, Gray sent me an email," Ball told her.

"Yeah?"

It was progress. She didn't immediately lambaste him for not telling her earlier. "Yeah. He contacted the FBI office out here in LA and got information about sex trafficking."

His words seemed to hover between them like the proverbial huge fucking elephant in the room. It was a risk bringing it up out of the blue, and he might not have mentioned it at all a few days ago, but after spending the last twenty-four hours with Everly, Ball figured she could take it. And that she'd prefer he be blunt. He was right.

"And?"

Her question didn't sound antagonistic. He heard the sorrow, but her training kicked in, and she was obviously curious too.

"They've been investigating a very aggressive group that seems to be based here in LA that uses social media and various apps to lure vulnerable teenagers into their web. Gray informed them about Elise's disappearance, and she's on their radar. They have her picture and description, and they'll be on the lookout for her in any future raids."

"Do they have any leads on who might be involved? When is the next raid planned?" Everly asked.

"Unfortunately, as you know, sex trafficking isn't just a one-man or woman job. There are layers upon layers of players, making it almost impossible to find the head of the snake. They've been able to rescue some women and make some busts on brothels that were forcing women and girls to work without consent, but finding the person or persons behind the operation can take years."

Everly's shoulders slumped. "God. I can't even imagine what those poor girls and women go through."

"I know." Ball wasn't sure what else he could say. Everly knew as well as he did that the chances of finding Elise got slimmer and slimmer with every hour that passed. If she'd been conned by someone in the human trafficking world, she could be in the back of a semi or in the bowels of a ship, leaving the United States right now. Because they were so close to Mexico, it wouldn't be out of the realm of possibility that she was already long gone across the border.

Just then, Everly inhaled sharply—and took off running.

Ball immediately gave chase, concerned because he had no idea what she was running toward or away from. She didn't go far, though, stopping about twenty yards from where she'd started.

She stood on the edge of the sidewalk, staring into the grass alongside the road.

Lying in the tall grass and trash was a small black purse.

Thankfully, Everly hadn't touched it . . . although of course she wouldn't. She was a police officer. She understood the importance of evidence and how crucial it was not to contaminate it.

"Elise's?" Ball asked.

Everly nodded. She kneeled down to get a better look, even as Ball pulled out his phone to take a picture.

"The strap's broken," Everly said.

"There could've been a struggle," Ball guessed.

Everly nodded and stood up. She turned in a complete circle, trying to get the lay of the land.

Across the street from where they stood was a gas station. They weren't in the best area of town, but it wasn't the worst either. Ball knew there was a chance there might be cameras at the gas station. And if there were, they might've caught a glimpse of what had happened. If Elise had been grabbed and put into a car, maybe the vehicle would be on film.

There weren't any stoplights around, so unfortunately there weren't any traffic cameras Meat could get footage from, but if they knew what kind of car they were looking for, he could absolutely work with the FBI and see if they could track it from the nearest traffic camera to the next.

"Come on," Ball said. "Let's go talk to the employees at the gas station. See if they saw anything suspicious in the last week. We can check for cameras too."

Everly nodded, then hesitated. "Her purse . . ."

"We'll call the cops after we check in with the store. Her purse has been here since she went missing. I think it'll be okay for another fifteen minutes or so. We'll be right across the street. If we see anyone over here, one of us can run back, okay?"

She nodded. "You're right. Okay."

It was easy to see that Everly was shaken by the discovery, but it was also the first really big clue they'd had. They hurriedly crossed the street and headed toward the convenience store.

"Do you want to look around or talk to the cashier?" Ball asked, doing his best to work with her and not order her around.

She looked up at him, one brow arched.

He shrugged. "I'm trying."

She obviously knew what he meant, because she simply said, "I'll talk to the cashier. If it's a female, she might be less intimidated talking to another woman. And if it's a guy, I might be able to flirt information out of him."

"Flirt information out of him?" Ball asked. "Is that a thing?"

"I know I'm not exactly model material, but I've done my share of flirting to get information, and I'm not ashamed of it either."

"I definitely wasn't questioning your looks," Ball told her honestly. "You're beautiful. I was just questioning the phrase."

She looked startled, as if she wasn't used to getting compliments. It was a shame, really, because the longer he was around Everly, the more attracted he became. She turned heads wherever they went, and Ball had definitely noticed.

"Whatever. Come on, let's get this done so we can call the cops and have them pick up the purse and look inside to see if there are any other clues." With that, she turned her back on him and opened the door to the convenience store.

Ball watched through the glass as her gait changed from the no-nonsense "cop walk" to a more seductive swagger. Her hips were lush, and the way the jeans hugged her ass should be illegal.

Shaking his head and smiling to himself, Ball turned to have a look around the outside of the building—and ran right into someone standing way too close to him.

The man immediately kneed him in the groin, and Ball folded in half, excruciating pain pulsing through his body.

Taking advantage of his momentary incapacitation, the man grabbed an arm and forced him around to the side of the building.

Ball struggled to get his wits about him. The asshole who'd kneed him pushed hard, and Ball fell to his knees in the gravel parking area. He was immediately on his feet again, but not before two other men grabbed him by the arms and held him between them.

Ball was taller than the three men, but waves of pain were still shooting from between his legs, and the man who'd attacked him first was able to get in two punches before Ball came to his senses. In a way, the hits to his face helped redirect the pain he was feeling away from his balls to his head.

Using some of the moves he'd learned in the Coast Guard, as well as those his fellow Mountain Mercenaries had taught him, Ball fought back.

But after a minute, he was dismayed to realize he was still losing the fight. Three against one wasn't exactly fair, but the men didn't care. They hadn't demanded anything of him, and Ball had no idea why they'd targeted him.

Until one of the men who'd been waiting around the corner of the store said, "Knock him out already so we can get the girl!"

Fuck that. They weren't getting their hands on Everly.

"Fuck that!" a feminine voice said from nearby, and before Ball could warn her away, Everly was in the thick of things.

Now that he wasn't fighting three men at one time, it wasn't long before Ball had knocked one of the assholes unconscious.

He turned to assist Everly—and instead could only stare. The man who'd kicked him in the groin was moaning in pain on the ground, and she had the other guy in a headlock. She was shorter than he was by two or three inches, and yet he was still bent backward, totally under her control.

A man wearing khakis, a polo with the name of the gas station on it, and a ball cap ran around the corner. "The cops are on their way . . . Holy shit!"

Ball had to give it to the young man. He collected himself and said, "I've got some rope in the back!" He then turned and ran around the corner, presumably to get the rope so they could secure the punks who'd attacked them.

Ball couldn't help himself. He walked up to the first man—who was now on his hands and knees, looking like he was thinking about getting up—and kicked him in the balls, just as the man had done to him.

The man fell to his side, crying out with pain.

Satisfied, Ball turned to Everly. She'd effectively cut off the guy's oxygen enough to knock him out and was lowering him to the gravel.

So many feelings and thoughts were running through his mind in that moment.

"Are you all right?" she asked.

Ball nodded but didn't say anything.

Her eyes narrowed. "Are you sure?"

"I'm sure," he said, after a beat. "Thank you."

Everly nodded, and then turned to make sure the men she'd incapacitated weren't going anywhere anytime soon.

Ball couldn't believe how fast she'd taken the two men down. And she hadn't even hesitated. Had just waded into the fight and done what needed to be done. She'd had his back. And his front. It hadn't mattered that she was female. She'd just done it. And quite effectively, at that.

As if struck by lightning, or smacked on the back of his head à la Gibbs on the TV show *NCIS*, Ball knew that it wasn't women in general he had a hard time working with . . . it was only Riley. She'd been almost a decade younger than he'd been, and she'd admitted once that she'd joined the military for the benefits. Her heart wasn't in the job, ever . . . and he'd missed it. Well, he hadn't exactly missed it, but maybe he'd been conceited enough to think that he could change her mind.

But as he stood there, blood trickling from his split lip while he continued to stare at Everly, who didn't even seem to have a mark on her, he realized he'd always known it wasn't gender that made someone a good partner. It was passion. Passion for the job. And Everly had it in spades.

He owed her an apology. A *big* fucking apology. But now wasn't the time, as their hands were full with these assholes, dealing with Elise's purse, and seeing if there was any other information they could glean at the gas station about Elise's disappearance.

But one thing he already knew for sure . . . Ball had been wrong about working with Everly. She was one hell of a partner, and he wouldn't hesitate to let her know that she could have his back, and he'd have hers, any day of the week.

Chapter Four

Everly was exhausted. After the run-in with the petty thieves—who had nothing to do with her missing sister and had only wanted to make a quick buck—and giving statements to the cops, they'd stood by impatiently as an officer accompanied them across the street to pick up Elise's purse on the side of the road. They'd both been shocked to see her cell phone inside as well. It had been turned off, but it was there.

Ball wanted to take it and give it to Meat, but the cop insisted that it go to the LAPD's own forensic technicians. Everly knew Ball was upset, and frankly, so was she. She had a feeling Meat would be able to get results a hell of a lot faster than the LAPD.

They rode to the station with the officer at the scene, and talked to Detective Diego Ramirez, who'd been assigned to Elise's case. He'd discussed with them the hundreds of teenagers who were reported missing every week . . . and how most weren't actually missing.

Ball had almost lost his cool.

"I don't care what the statistics say, Elise Adams is missing. Pure and simple. I get it, you don't want to waste resources looking for someone who isn't actually in trouble, but Elise is not on drugs. She's not acting out. She's fucking *gone.* A runaway wouldn't have dropped her purse with money *and* her phone in it. No way in hell. Now, you can either help us look for her, or you can give us back her purse, with her phone, and let us find her on our own."

Detective Ramirez had stared at Ball for a beat, then nodded. "I believe you, and I've been doing my best to follow leads, but there just *aren't* any leads to follow right now. The purse is the first."

Ball didn't back down, and he didn't look away. "So what's the plan, then? How are we going to find Elise?"

They'd ended up talking for another hour and a half. They'd gotten a much more complete rundown of the trafficking situation in the area, and it scared the shit out of Everly. If her beloved sister had been taken by one of the recruiters, they'd probably never find her. She'd live the rest of her life as a plaything for whoever wanted to pay for the privilege—and she most likely would have already been shot up with drugs to keep her more compliant and docile.

It was terrifying, and as if he could sense all the horrible scenarios that were going through her mind, Ball put his hand on her knee and squeezed.

Just that small touch grounded her and let her know she wasn't alone. That Ball had promised to do whatever it took to find her sister.

Ever since the earlier fight at the convenience store, he'd been . . . different. It was subtle, but there. Everly felt him staring at her frequently, but when she turned to see what he wanted, he'd look away. At first she thought he was pissed that she'd come to his assistance, but it wasn't that. She couldn't figure it out, but as they'd had no time to talk about the attack yet, she'd just have to wait to see where his head was at.

They'd promised to come back to the police station in another day or so to touch base with the detective about the case. Everly didn't want to go back to her grandparents' house yet. It felt like she should be *doing* something. Not just sitting around and shooting the shit.

"Come on," Ball said once they'd left Ramirez's office.

"Where?"

"I'm hungry, and I know you have to be as well."

"Me-Maw's probably been cooking all day," Everly warned.

Ball smiled. "Awesome. I have a feeling I'm gonna have to work out extra hard to keep the grandma weight off me."

"Grandma weight?" Everly asked with a small smile.

"Yeah. Your me-maw is an excellent cook, if that meal from last night was any indication."

"Yeah, and?"

"I do okay in the kitchen, but my weakness is home-cooked meals—that *I* didn't have to make. I'm gonna make a pig out of myself, and you'll be embarrassed when I have to undo the button on my jeans in order to be able to breathe. A few meals like that equals grandma weight."

Everly chuckled. He wasn't wrong. But she didn't think he had anything to worry about when it came to gaining weight. The man was built like a brick house. There was no way he would let himself get out of shape. He was too committed to the Mountain Mercenaries. "When you were saying goodbye to Ramirez, one of the other officers told me about some food trucks parked a few blocks away. We could get something to tide us over until dinner tonight."

"Sounds good," Ball said. He held open the door to the station for her, and they walked out into the humid and hot afternoon air.

Neither said anything for a while as they walked, and finally Everly couldn't stand it anymore. "You haven't said anything about what happened."

She didn't need to elaborate; he knew what she was talking about.

"I know."

She waited, but he didn't say anything else. Deciding to let it go, but feeling disappointed at the same time, Everly walked alongside Ball toward the food trucks. He settled on a Greek-style kabob, and she got a sushi bowl. There were a few benches under some trees nearby, and they made their way over to them and got settled.

They ate in silence for a while, then Ball said, "I've been a dick."

The statement came out of the blue, and Everly frowned at him. "What? When?"

He wasn't eating, instead just staring down at his kabob like if he took his eyes off it, it would lunge and attack him. "In general. I judged you before I even met you, and worse yet, I let my previous experiences overshadow what all my friends, and Rex, were telling me about you." He looked up then, and the emotion in his eyes made Everly freeze. "Thank you for what you did today. Intellectually, I knew you were a cop, and SWAT, but emotionally, I still saw you as merely a woman."

Everly refused to drop her gaze. Merely a woman? What the hell did he mean by that? "Go on," she said quietly, her own lunch forgotten in the seriousness of their conversation.

"When I was in the Coast Guard, I was partnered with Riley. She was fresh out of the academy and so excited to be assigned to patrol. I was older than her by about a decade, and I was happy to show her the ropes. After a while, we got into a comfortable routine, but we weren't equals. I was her mentor and reveled in the role. Looking back, I know I treated her differently because she was a woman. I wasn't as hard on her as I would've been with a male partner. Did far too much for her. But she didn't complain. She did her job, but when shit got tough, and it did, she'd step back and let me take the lead."

He stopped, and everything in Everly wanted to tell him to keep going, to tell her what happened to make him so bitter and dead set against working with a woman again. But she kept quiet. Taking a chance, she reached over and put her hand on his.

Her encouragement seemed to help as he took a big breath and continued. But this time he wasn't looking at her, he was staring off into space as if he were reliving the events he was describing.

"We were down in the Gulf of Mexico in our twenty-five-foot Defender-class boat. We were on our normal patrol duty when we got a call about a suspicious boat in our area. Riley was in the cabin, as usual, and I was standing at the front manning the M240."

Everly could picture it in her head and knew without a doubt that Ball probably made a very imposing picture. His feet braced, biceps bulging, as he held on to the machine gun, ready and willing to do whatever it took to defend his country. She made a mental note to ask to see a picture of him in his uniform. "What happened?" she asked.

"I don't know what you know about boating, but apparently Riley thought she saw something in front of us, and she executed a high-speed maneuver known as a power turn, without warning me first. I wasn't prepared and was thrown into the water . . . but my arm got caught in one of the lines on the side of the boat when I tried to keep myself from falling."

Everly gasped.

"Yeah," Ball chuckled, but it wasn't a humorous sound. "I was dragged alongside the boat for at least two hundred yards before Riley got the boat slowed down. My shoulder had been jerked out of its socket, and I tore just about every muscle and ligament as well. The irony is that I was actually lucky. There was a case a while back where someone was killed when the same thing happened. The propellers struck him in the head when he was thrown overboard.

"Riley wasn't showing off or trying to be overly aggressive in her maneuvers to try to intimidate someone. She was simply reacting to something she thought she saw. And the kicker was that she *had* seen something. A boat without any lights was lurking in the area. I managed to get myself back on the boat, and no matter how badly my arm hurt, we had a job to do.

"Turns out the boat was hauling drugs. Riley was in charge of searching the men, as my shoulder was out of commission. I had them at gunpoint, but when she went to handcuff them, one of the men pulled a pistol from wherever he'd managed to hide it and shot me."

Everly inhaled sharply again.

Ball nodded. "I shot and killed both of the men in the drug boat, and Riley freaked the fuck out. She'd messed up so many times that night it wasn't even funny. She was hysterical and couldn't drive the boat, so I had to hook up the drug boat myself and drive us all in. Riley was reprimanded, and reduced in rank, but was allowed to keep her job. Her lawyer claimed she hadn't been trained properly and that the stress of the situation made her act out of character. What really got to me was how, during her hearing, her lawyer twisted things so much, claiming me getting shot was somehow *my* fault."

"Seriously?"

"Seriously," Ball said. "Here I thought we were partners, but when shit got real, she showed absolutely no loyalty to me whatsoever. She never even apologized. My shoulder took forever to heal, with the gunshot on top of the torn ligaments. Eventually the Coast Guard medically discharged me. I was bitter about that for a long time."

"I can't say that I blame you. But, Ball, I would never do that to you, or *anyone* I worked with."

"I know," he said quietly.

"Do you?" Everly asked.

He turned to look at her then. "Yes. That's what I'm trying to explain, badly. When those guys were beating on me, not once did I imagine you'd come to help. It didn't even cross my mind. If I had been with one of my teammates, that's the *first* thing that I would've expected. But then there you were. Kicking ass and taking names. I swear to God, you didn't even break a sweat. I'm ashamed of myself, Everly. And I'm so sorry."

Any animosity she might've been harboring after overhearing him bitch about how he didn't want a woman on any mission dissipated. "It's okay, Ball."

"Thank you for letting me off the hook so easily. But I'm afraid it's going to take me longer to forgive myself. Women are just as capable as men. I know that, I've seen it firsthand, but somehow it all got mixed up in my head after Riley. I still thought they were capable—as long as I didn't have to work with them. It was stupid."

"How old are you?" Everly asked.

"Old enough to know better."

She raised her eyebrows at him.

"Forty."

"Right. So you've got another twenty years before retirement to make up for your caveman attitude."

He smiled, and Everly relaxed. She was glad she could tease him out of his bad mood.

"Seriously, you kicked ass today."

"I did, didn't I?" Everly said. "Although I have to admit, it's a lot easier to fight hand to hand without all my gear on. I didn't have to worry about either of them grabbing my weapon or cuffs. And it didn't hurt that you'd already damaged them."

He shook his head. "Nope. Don't downplay what you did. You're like my own personal Wonder Woman."

"Now *that* comparison I'll take," Everly told him with a smile.

They both turned to their lunches and ate for a bit without speaking. Then Ball said, "Meat has to get access to that phone."

The comment was an abrupt change of topic, but Everly went with it. "How?"

"I'm not sure. But I bet Rex'll have an idea."

"Call him."

"Now? Are you sure? We were taking a break."

Everly gave him an incredulous look.

"Right," Ball said, and pulled out his phone. He clicked on a button, and they waited. Within seconds, they heard the electronically distorted voice of Ball's handler on the phone.

"What ya got?"

Ball spent a few minutes updating him on the events from earlier that day, then got to the reason for his call. "Meat's still working on Elise's computer, but we have the feeling, if she was targeted by a trafficker, most of her communication with him will be on her phone. But the cops have it now, and they said they didn't know how long it would take their computer forensics division to look into it."

"What's the name of the detective again?"

"Ramirez. Diego Ramirez."

"Give me some time to talk to him. I don't know him personally, but I do know some of the other people over there. Is Everly there?"

"I'm here," she said.

"Don't give up hope," he ordered. "Until you know for sure what happened, don't assume anything. Okay?"

"Okay," she said quietly.

"I'll be in touch," Rex said, and disconnected.

"What was that about?" Everly asked as Ball put away the phone. "I mean, that was nice of him and all, but something in his tone seemed . . . off. Almost desperate."

Ball paused, as if considering what to tell her. Then he said, "This isn't something Rex talks about. I only know because Arrow told the rest of the team. I'm telling *you* because, after what you did for me today, I feel like maybe we've gone beyond being just two strangers trying to solve a case. Rex's wife disappeared one day, just like Elise did. She was there when he went to work one morning and gone when he got home. There weren't many clues, and it's been a decade now, and there haven't been any confirmed sightings of her."

"Confirmed?"

Ball nodded. "The reason Rex started the Mountain Mercenaries is to help find other missing women and children. Over the years, he's gotten some clues and tips about his wife, and none have panned out, though he's been able to help so many others. But he'll never stop looking, either until he finds her, or her remains are found and identified."

Everly looked at Ball in disbelief, shaking her head. "Ten years?"

"Yeah."

The sushi she'd eaten threatened to come back up. "I can't go ten years without knowing what happened to Elise. She'd be twenty-five . . . No. I can't do—"

Ball put his half-eaten kabob to the side and took her hand. "Shhh. I didn't mean to upset you. I'm an idiot."

"Seriously, I can't do it," Everly responded.

"Listen to me," Ball ordered, putting his hands on her shoulders and half turning her on the bench. "We're close. I can feel it. I'd tell you straight up if I thought she was gone. I *would*. But something's telling me she's still here . . . somewhere. Hear me?"

Everly nodded. She wanted to believe him. So badly.

"Right." He stood and held out his hand. "Come on. Ramirez said when we needed a ride back to the school, that he'd take us. We'll get the rental and head back to Me-Maw's. We'll call Meat and see what he's been able to get from the computer. And if I know Rex, he'll be getting access to that phone sooner rather than later."

"Okay." She let Ball pull her upright, and was only a little surprised when he pulled her into his embrace. The jolt of electricity she felt between them was intense. He held her close for several moments, then pulled back. He gathered up what was left of their lunch and threw it away in a trash can nearby, then he gestured for her to precede him. She did, and felt his fingertips against the small of her back.

A sudden image of Pop doing the same thing with Me-Maw sprang to her mind, and she stopped abruptly.

"What? What's wrong?" Ball asked.

"Nothing. I'm good," Everly tried to reassure him. She had no idea if he felt the chemistry arcing between them like she did, but the last thing she was going to do was ask. He'd only just come to the conclusion that she could actually be a good partner. No way was she going to throw sex into the mix.

~

Ball sat in the comfortable armchair with a smile on his face. If someone had told him he'd have anything to smile about before he'd left for Los Angeles, he would've told them they were crazy. He was working with a woman, there was a missing teenager, and he wouldn't have his team at his back. It was a potential disaster in the making.

But even though the day had been long, he'd had some pretty serious epiphanies about himself. And now he was currently stuffed with Me-Maw's homemade meat loaf and listening to her banter back and forth with Everly.

And speaking of Everly, she'd been extremely magnanimous, forgiving him for being an ass. She hadn't exactly saved his life today—or maybe she had. At the least, she'd certainly prevented him from receiving a worse beating than he'd gotten.

"I tidied up after you left this morning and noticed that you didn't bring much," her grandmother said. "Do you need me to do your laundry? Did you bring enough panties?"

"Me-Maw!" Everly exclaimed, turning beet red.

"What? Oh, you don't want me saying *panties* in front of Kannon? You don't mind, do you?" she asked, turning toward him.

"No, ma'am."

"And you probably have some underwear that needs to be washed too. I can just throw your stuff in with Everly's."

"Kill me now," Everly mumbled.

Ball did his best not to laugh. "I'm okay for now," he told Me-Maw. "But thank you."

"How long do you think you're going to be here?" she asked.

That was a harder question to answer. "I'm hoping when my friends get their hands on the data from Elise's phone, it'll speed things up," Ball said, being diplomatic.

"Oh, that would be such a relief," the older lady said.

Ball could tell how stressful the situation was for them. Despite their teasing, both Allison and Landen were struggling hard with their granddaughter's disappearance. He wanted to tell them that it wasn't their fault, that Elise was vulnerable not only because of her mother being the way she was, but because of her disability as well. But he didn't want to bring down Me-Maw's current lighthearted mood.

"Oh! Everly, I know. Go and get your scrapbooks so I can show Kannon."

"Oh, hell no!"

"Everly Adams! Language!" Me-Maw scolded.

Ball couldn't keep the smile off his face that time.

"This is not funny," Everly hissed.

"It's a little funny," he countered.

"Ball isn't interested in seeing newspaper articles about me from high school. That was forever ago."

"Yes, he is," Ball countered.

"See?" Me-Maw crowed. "Now go on, go get them. If you don't, I'll find the old picture albums from when you were in high school."

At that, Everly stood up and stomped out of the room without another word.

Me-Maw smiled, but the second Everly was out of earshot, she turned to Ball with a severe look on her face. She leaned forward and said, "Be straight with us, Kannon. Do you think our Elise is still alive?"

Taken aback by the question—and the swift change in demeanor—Ball immediately nodded. "I do. I know I'm not supposed to really say that, though, especially not to family. But finding her phone was huge. It won't help track where she is right now, but it'll give us insight into what happened. Who she was talking to."

Allison Adams nodded.

Then Landen spoke up. He'd been letting his wife do most of the talking that evening, content to sit next to her. "Lord knows we've made some mistakes, both with our daughter and now with our granddaughter, but we love Elise so much, and we'll do just about anything to bring her home safe and sound. If money is needed, we have retirement accounts we can take from, and we can refinance the house if necessary. All we want is Elise home."

Ball couldn't help but be impressed by the sentiment, but money wasn't going to help Elise right now, unfortunately. "I don't think that'll be necessary, but if we can't find anything and the case goes cold, it might be worth looking into hiring a private detective."

Landen nodded. He looked beaten down, but not out.

Then he changed the subject . . . and started talking about his *other* granddaughter.

"You should know, Everly has a very tender heart under her brash exterior. She hasn't had an easy life, has had too much responsibility on her shoulders for way too long. Our daughter was a terrible mother. Didn't care about anyone other than herself. Still doesn't. Everly was making her own dinner, if there was even food in the house, by the time she was six. Even when she moved in with us, she was trying to take care of Allison and me and downplaying the shit that went on in her mother's house. We've despaired of her ever finding a man who can understand that, while she's perfectly capable of taking care of herself, sometimes she needs someone to lean on."

Ball felt uncomfortable talking about Everly behind her back, but he also didn't want to mislead her grandparents. "I like your granddaughter, sir, but we're not dating," he explained gently.

"Why not?" Allison asked with more curiosity than animosity.

"We just met less than a week ago," Ball told her. "And until today, I really wasn't all that keen on working with a woman."

"But Everly's a police officer," Pop said indignantly.

"She's more than that," Me-Maw said, nudging her husband. "Everly is beautiful. And smart. And kind. And brave. You'd be crazy not to want to date her. What's wrong with you?"

Ball's lips quirked at that.

"Besides, a week is plenty of time. Landen kissed me the day after we met. He asked me to marry him a month later, and we've been together ever since. When you know, you just know."

"That's awesome for you guys, but—"

"Are you not attracted to her? Are you gay? It's okay if you are, but that would make sense as to why you don't want to date her," Me-Maw said.

Ball about choked. "I'm not gay, and I think your granddaughter is beautiful."

"Then why don't you want to date her? Get to know her better?" the older woman demanded.

"I didn't say that." Ball tried to backpedal, beginning to sweat. Shit, Everly's grandmother was a better interrogator than Black, and that was saying something.

"So you *do* want to date her! That's what I thought. Good. I'm glad I put you in the same room, then. You can get to know her better, maybe share a few kisses. Back in our day, we had to sneak around when we stayed at my parents' house. I didn't want either of you having to roam around in the middle of the night. Sometimes we get up to get a glass of water or something, and it would be awkward if you ran into us."

He opened his mouth to respond—not even sure where to begin—but luckily Everly returned, saving him. She had a large notebook in her hands, and she handed it to him with a huff, then plopped down on the floor in front of the sofa where her grandparents were sitting.

"No, dear, you have to sit next to Kannon and explain what he's looking at," Me-Maw said not so innocently.

Everly looked at her as if she'd lost her mind. "Sit next to him? Me-Maw, he's in the armchair."

"So?"

"So, there's no room for me!"

"Sure, there is. Look, he'll scoot over a bit . . ."

Ball did as directed, leaving a minuscule amount of space between his leg and the side of the chair.

"There. See?"

As if she was used to her grandmother being bossy and knew the woman wasn't going to shut up until she did as ordered, Everly slowly stood and came over to where he was sitting. She had a resigned look on her face and mouthed, "Sorry."

Ball gestured to his side. With a sigh, she gingerly sat on the arm of the chair next to him.

Wrapping his hand around her waist, Ball tugged until she slid off the arm and was squished between him and the side of the chair. One of her hands landed on his thigh for balance, and the other hovered in the air in front of her. He could feel the warmth of her body along the length of his own.

He raised his arm, wrapping it comfortably around her shoulders, and she fell deeper into him. Her hair brushed against his jaw, and that familiar scent wafted up until it was all he could smell. Ball felt surrounded by her—and surprisingly, he wasn't in the least bit bothered by it.

He saw the smirk on Me-Maw's face before she turned away to hide it.

Hating that Everly was embarrassed—and she was clearly uncomfortable, judging by the pink color in her cheeks—Ball opened the scrapbook.

The first picture was a newspaper cutout of a much younger Everly wearing a store-bought skeleton costume and a huge smile with two teeth missing. "Cute," he said with a grin.

Everly rolled her eyes. "There was a neighborhood Halloween party. My mom forgot to get me a costume, but Me-Maw found this at the drugstore down the street. Of course there was a newspaper photographer there to capture my dorkiness."

"Not dorky—cute," Ball told her. He felt her relax against him a bit as he turned the page.

He spent the next hour viewing glimpses into Everly's past. There were a few more pictures, but most were articles about various competitions Everly had excelled in. There were a few poems she'd written and some papers from grade school. It was more than obvious how proud her grandparents were of her.

By the time he got to the end of the scrapbook, Everly had relaxed completely and was resting most of her weight against him. She was wedged into a tiny corner of the chair, and had to be uncomfortable, but she didn't make a move to get up when he was done.

"We're going to head to bed," Pop said quietly. "Allison's done in."

Ball looked over and saw that Everly's grandma had fallen asleep against her husband's side.

"Need any help?" he asked.

"Nope. I've got her. She does this just about every night. I used to be able to pick her up and carry her to bed, but now we just hobble there together. We'll see you both in the morning." And with that, Landen gently shook his wife awake, and, just as he'd said, they walked with their arms around each other's waists down the hall to their bedroom.

"They've been through so much in their lives, and I hate that they're dealing with this now too. It's not fair."

"How'd your mom become the person she is?" Ball asked. "I mean, your grandparents are awesome. I don't get it."

"Don't think they haven't asked themselves the same thing," Everly said. "And the short answer is, I don't know. I guess it's that old nature-versus-nurture question. Was my mom born to become a drug addict, or was it a factor of her surroundings? I'd have to guess the latter. Me-Maw says she saw no indication of her having any kind of addictive personality before high school. Then she got in with the wrong crowd, and the rest is history. It's my understanding that she didn't start out slow, as far as the drugs go. She went straight from sneaking a drink now and then to doing cocaine. And that was that. She was hooked after the first hit, and from then on out, her life continued on a downward spiral. She didn't finish high school. Got pregnant with me, and even though she went through the motions of trying to quit, she never really wanted to."

"That sucks."

"It does. But don't feel sorry for me. I had Me-Maw and Pop. They were awesome. They stepped in when it was obvious my mom didn't care about even trying with me anymore. I graduated high school, won a ton of scholarships, and got my two-year degree at a community college, then went on to get my bachelor's. I've worked my ass off, and I have them to thank for supporting me."

"I wasn't criticizing you or your grandparents," Ball said gently. "I wish I knew mine, but they died when I was young."

"What are your parents like?" Everly asked.

Ball shrugged. "They're good. I don't talk to them nearly as much as I should, but they're living out in North Carolina. They have an RV and are gone a lot, just driving around the country, seeing the sights. I designed a website for them so they can keep all their friends informed about where they are and what they're doing. It's super simple, but that's what they wanted."

Everly sat up a bit. "You designed a website for them?"

"Yeah, why?"

"You say that like it's no big deal."

"It's not. Well, *technically* it's not. There are templates for blogs and websites out there that almost anyone can set up. But I didn't want one of those, I wanted to make something custom just for them, that would be easy to keep up and Mom could use from her phone. Besides, it's what I do for a living."

She blinked. "No, you work for the Mountain Mercenaries."

"Yeah, but most of the time it's not a full-time gig. I design websites as my day job. I even did some work on the CSPD site last year. They wanted to update it, make it easier to navigate."

"Wow. I had no idea."

"You thought I was just a dumb former Coastie, didn't you?"

She chuckled. "No."

"Liar, you so did." Ball loved seeing Everly smile. He dug his fingers into her side, and she shrieked softly and squirmed.

"Stop it!"

"Admit it and I will."

"Never!" she exclaimed, and began to fight back. Her fingers went for his sides as she tried to tickle him.

Thankful that he'd never been ticklish, Ball grabbed her around the waist and pulled her up so she was straddling his thighs, giving him better access to her very ticklish sides. She laughed and undulated on his lap as she tried to pry his fingers off.

"Stop—oh my God, I'm so ticklish! Uncle, uncle!" she cried.

"Admit that you thought I was stupid," he urged.

"Fine! I admit it. But for the record, I'd admit just about anything right now to get you to stop."

Ball stilled his fingers and simply held on to her. "Yeah?" he asked.

"Don't get that gleam in your eye," Everly warned as she smiled down at him.

They stared at each other for a beat—and then they both seemed to realize at the same time how intimate their position was. Her legs were spread open as she straddled his thighs. Her hands were resting on his chest. And his thumbs had somehow gotten under her T-shirt, where they were rubbing absently against her warm skin at her sides.

Neither said anything . . . but they didn't move either.

Ball's phone ringing interrupted the electric moment.

Everly slid off his lap and stood awkwardly in front of his chair for a second before turning to the small table next to the couch and grabbing the glass her grandmother had been using earlier, taking it to the kitchen.

"Hello?" Ball said as he answered his phone, noting the call was from Rex.

"I'll have the data from Elise's phone in the next twenty-four hours or so."

"Really?"

"Really."

"Do I want to know how you accomplished that?" Ball asked his handler.

"I know some people who know some people," Rex said. "How are things going with you?"

"Good."

"I want the truth, Ball. I know you weren't happy about having her join you."

"I wasn't. But it's fine," Ball told Rex.

"Look, I know I've been absent lately, and I'm sorry. But I'm back now, and if you're having issues, I need to know. I can probably send Ro or Black in to relieve you if you want. We need Everly. She can talk to Elise's friends, and Elise herself when we find her. But if you—"

"I said it's fine," Ball interrupted. "I mean it." He caught Everly's gaze. She was standing in the doorway of the kitchen, giving him space but still listening in. He couldn't blame her. If it was *his* sister who was missing, he'd be listening too. "You were right, we *do* need Everly. She's been very useful so far, and honestly, it's possible she may have saved my life today."

There was silence on the other end of the phone, as if Rex was too shocked to speak. So Ball continued. "I was jumped by some run-of-the-mill punks who were trying to get me out of the picture so they could grab Everly. I was losing the hand-to-hand fight, as I was outnumbered, but then Everly was there, and she kicked two of their asses while I was busy with the third. She also got the principal of Elise's school to open up to her, and that conversation ultimately led to us finding her sister's purse and phone. I wouldn't have been able to communicate with the principal or the students. I was wrong—and I can admit it."

He was talking to Rex, but speaking directly to Everly. He needed her to know that he hadn't been blowing smoke up her ass earlier. He really was trying to change his mind-set when it came to working with women . . . at least working with *her*.

"I need to go check my weather app," Rex said under his breath.

"What? Why?" Ball asked.

"To see if hell has frozen over," Rex quipped.

"Fuck off," Ball told him.

"Seriously, though, I'm glad, because I've heard nothing but really good things about Sergeant Adams. She'd be a good resource to have back here in the Springs."

Ball hadn't taken his eyes from Everly's. She hadn't moved from where she was standing either. "You'll call as soon as you've got anything from the phone?" Ball asked.

"Of course. If you need anything in the meantime, anything at all, call," Rex ordered.

"I will."

"Later."

"Bye." Ball clicked off the phone, and still Everly didn't say anything. Finally, he said, "That was Rex. He's using his connections and should be able to access Elise's phone in the next day or so."

Everly nodded.

"Ev? You okay?" he asked, getting concerned.

"Did you mean it?" she asked quietly.

Ball didn't ask what she was talking about. "Every word."

"I didn't save your life today."

Ball shrugged. "You could've. One of the cops found a knife on one of those guys."

"I think I'm going to head to bed myself . . . unless you have anything you need me to do?"

Recognizing it for the retreat it was, Ball shook his head. "No, I'm good. I'm just going to go over the notes from the principal again and see if I can find anything on Elise's computer. Everly?"

"Yeah?"

"There's more space in the guest bed than the one in Elise's room, and I could tell you weren't all that thrilled to be in your sister's bed in the first place. Also . . . I slept better with you next to me last night than I have in a long time."

"Are you asking me to sleep with you in the guest room?" Everly asked point-blank.

"Yes," Ball said.

He could see her thinking about it, then she nodded slowly. "I slept better than I have since Elise disappeared too, and you're right about me feeling weird, staying in Elise's room. I'll stay in the guest room with you as long as you don't get any ideas."

"I promise," Ball said immediately, feeling relieved she'd acquiesced.

"Okay. If you need me, wake me up."

"I will."

Everly nodded and headed for the hallway. Ball watched her go. Once he was alone in the living room, he put his head on the cushions behind him and rubbed a hand over his face.

What in the world was wrong with him?

He was attracted to Everly.

He shouldn't be, and not only because they were working together. He didn't want to lose his heart to a woman again. Not after Holly had ripped it out of his chest.

But somehow, he had a feeling it was already too late. Everly Adams had snuck under his shields and was slowly but surely chipping them away completely. And the thing of it was, she wasn't even trying. He knew without a doubt that she was as weirded out by their attraction as he was . . . her retreat tonight made that clear.

Now wasn't the time or the place to explore this. They had to find her sister. But maybe, just maybe, once she was home safe and sound and things were somewhat back to normal, Ball could call Everly and see if she wanted to have lunch or something.

Yeah, that was a good plan. Find Elise. Go home. Get back into his normal routine. Then see about going out with Everly a time or two . . . and getting this attraction out of their systems.

Feeling better now that he had a strategy in place, he relaxed.

Slow and steady. That would work perfectly.

Chapter Five

Everly woke abruptly, confused. She wasn't sure what had roused her.

She looked at the clock. Three fourteen in the morning. It was dark and quiet, but she immediately knew she was alone in the king-size bed in the guest room.

Hours earlier, she'd withdrawn because she wasn't sure what to do with this new Ball.

She was used to him being standoffish and grumpy. The man who'd flat-out told his handler that he needed her, and that she'd saved his life, was someone she wasn't sure how to deal with.

Of course, she was glad they were getting along, but it was getting harder and harder to fight her attraction to him. She suspected it had started when he'd snuggled up behind her the night before. It had felt good. Too good.

But now he wasn't in bed with her.

Before she'd headed up to the guest room, he'd said he was going to work for a while longer, but she'd assumed he meant an hour or two. It had been way longer than that.

She hoped he was still up because he'd found something important that might lead to Elise, but if he had, wouldn't he have woken her up to share it?

What if he'd found something bad . . . and didn't want to tell her because he was afraid of what she'd do or say? What if Rex had found evidence that Elise had been killed?

Worried now, Everly threw back the covers and headed for the door.

She crept down the stairs and saw Ball at the dining table. He sat in front of a computer screen, the slight glow lighting up his face as he frowned in concentration. Everly opened her mouth to ask him if he'd found anything—but paused when he made a subtle hand gesture, still studying the screen intently.

She couldn't see the screen of the computer because he was sitting in profile, but it looked like he was . . .

Yes . . . he was signing the word for *safe.*

As she watched, confused, he then signed, *You're safe.* Then he clicked on something on the laptop in front of him and did it again. And again.

Then he signed, *My name is Ball. You're safe.*

His signs were slow and hesitant, but when she realized what he was doing, Everly's knees threatened to buckle.

She must've made some sort of noise, or maybe Ball just sensed he wasn't alone anymore, because he turned his head and saw her standing there.

"Hey," he said softly.

"What are you doing?" she asked, even though it was obvious.

Ball shrugged and gestured to his computer. "There are a ton of videos on the internet on how to do sign language, but it's not as easy as it looks."

He sounded discouraged, and Everly hated that for him. "You were doing a good job."

"I suck. It's okay, you can say it."

"You don't. Like you said, it's not as easy as it looks. And I knew what you were saying—and so will Elise."

"I couldn't sleep," he admitted. "I searched Elise's computer for a while. Then I started working on a website I'm designing, just to keep busy, hoping Rex would call and have more information about her phone. But I kept thinking about your sister. I couldn't stop. I thought about what would happen if we had to bust a house that she's being kept in or something. How I might scare her because she wouldn't be able to hear me. So I thought if I learned a few things, it might keep her calm until you could get to her."

Everly wanted to cry. In her entire life, that was probably the most amazing thing a man had ever done for her. "If you really want to learn, I'll help you."

"Yeah?" Ball asked, looking at her once more.

"Yeah."

"Thanks. What are you doing up? You were sleeping soundly when I checked."

It was such a strange conversation. One that two lovers might have. Or a husband and wife. Everly forced the thought from her head. She did like that he'd checked on her, though. It was . . . nice. She shrugged. "I just woke up."

Ball closed the laptop and stood. He came toward her. She looked up at him when he stopped right in front her. Neither moved. Everly couldn't even breathe.

"Come on, there's still time to get a few more hours of sleep before we'll need to be up and at 'em again."

Ball reached out, and for a second Everly thought he was going to hug her, but his hand rested lightly on her lower back, and he turned her. She walked ahead of him, back toward the room they were using.

He kept his hand on her until she reached the side of the bed. "Climb in," he said softly.

She did, scooting across the mattress until she was on her side again. Not surprised when he followed a minute later and wrapped an arm around her waist, Everly relaxed into him.

After a couple of minutes, she said, "When I woke up, I was worried because you hadn't come to bed. For a second I thought maybe you found out something bad about Elise and didn't want to tell me."

"I told you I wouldn't do that."

"I know. But I've been lied to before, Ball. Lots of times."

"You're a cop. I get it."

She shook her head. "Yeah, but that's not what I mean." She felt him stiffen slightly behind her. Everly hadn't told anyone this story before, but after what she'd just seen—Ball trying to learn sign language to soothe a scared teenager—she felt like he deserved her honesty.

"My mom lied to me all the time. *All* the time. From as far back as I can remember, she'd lie straight to my face and not even care."

"I'm so sorry," Ball said. Everly's arms had been tucked up against her chest, and Ball moved the hand around her waist to cover her clenched fists. "What'd she lie about?"

"Everything. That we didn't have any money for food. What time she'd be home. That she'd be there to pick me up after school. That her current boyfriend wouldn't hurt me . . ."

She felt Ball's hand tighten over her fists at that one, but he didn't interrupt.

"She told me Me-Maw and Pop didn't want me living with them when I asked about it once. I believed her for over a year before I outright asked Me-Maw if it was true. She cried and told me that of course it wasn't true. If I wanted to live with them, they were one hundred percent all right with that. They knew how their daughter was. They knew she wasn't taking care of me. But they also knew if they tried to take me from her, she'd dig in her heels and probably treat me even worse."

"Damn," Ball said.

"Yeah. She continued to lie even after I moved out. She'd tell me how much she missed me and how hard she was trying to clean herself up so I could come back. By then, I'd pretty much stopped believing anything she said. I got so cynical, it took me a long time before I trusted anyone ever again. But you know what the worst thing was?"

"What?"

"She swore that she was being careful. That she wasn't going to accidentally get pregnant again. Stupid me, I believed her. But one night, when I was about nineteen, I went to visit her and found her on the floor of her shithole house, bleeding between the legs. My mom had used drugs in the past to purposely miscarry, and I thought she'd done it again. She'd get pregnant, then take some stupid cocktail of pills that someone had told her would abort the fetus. I decided then and there I was never talking to her again."

"But you did," Ball surmised.

"Yeah. When I'd walked in on her bleeding, I'd been so disgusted with her—and myself, for believing her lies. But I still got her to the hospital. That's where I found out she was bleeding because of complications with the pregnancy, not another self-inflicted abortion. By some miracle, she'd done her best to avoid getting high while she was pregnant, and despite Mom being too stubborn to call for an ambulance when she'd first realized something was wrong, Elise was born relatively healthy . . . except for her being deaf, of course.

"Because she'd managed to clean herself up during pregnancy, the hospital didn't see any reason to sic child services on her." Everly snorted, a weird half-desperate, half-derisive sound.

"But within a year, she was up to her old tricks. Me-Maw and Pop did what they could to take care of Elise anytime Mom was on one of her benders, but they didn't want to involve the courts. So for the first ten or so years, Elise lived half of her life at the stable and loving home of her grandparents, and the other half in hell at our mom's house. Luckily, Elise was a lot smarter than me. She decided she was done and was going to live with Me-Maw and Pop full-time before she entered middle school.

"Anyway . . . yeah . . . my mom is a pathological liar. I'm surprised Elise and I are as normal as we are, all things considered. But back to my point. For a second, I thought you were keeping things from me about Elise's case . . . something bad. I'm sorry. You said you wouldn't do that, and the first chance I got, I doubted you."

"Ev, cut yourself some slack. You've had a tough week. Your sister's missing, and you're a cop who's used to doing everything possible to solve cases. Face it, sitting around isn't either of our strong points. I hate that we're here, comfortable, with our bellies full, and we have no idea where Elise is or what she's going through. But I swear to you that I will never keep you out of the loop. When I find out information, *you'll* find out information."

"Okay." She was quiet for a long moment. "Ball?"

"Yeah, Ev?"

"Even though Elise has been deaf her entire life . . . my mom hasn't bothered to learn how to talk to her in sign language. Even if you can only say a few things, it'll mean the world to Elise."

Ball squeezed her tight in a backward hug, but didn't speak.

Feeling as if they'd crossed some sort of line, but not knowing how it would change the nature of their relationship—just knowing it had definitely changed—Everly fell asleep with Ball's thumb brushing back and forth over the ring on her finger.

~

Elise had no idea what time it was, or even what day it was, but hours had passed since she'd last seen the man who'd kidnapped her and chained her up in the basement of the decrepit old house.

Earlier, she'd gotten up the courage to explore her small prison, to the limits of her shackles, and had discovered a bucket nearby that was obviously for her to use to relieve herself. Elise was glad she hadn't had much to eat or drink, because using that bucket was extremely humiliating and gross.

She would also gladly go hungry if it meant she didn't *ever* have to see the man again. He hadn't taken off his shirt a second time, but she didn't like the way he looked at her. She wasn't an idiot; she knew she'd been extremely lucky so far that he hadn't sexually assaulted her. She didn't know *why* he hadn't. And not knowing if her luck would run out at each visit freaked her out.

She no longer worried he'd drug her food, but every time he brought any—which wasn't often—she had to do exactly what he said to get it. Stand up. Look to the right. Smile. Turn around. Lift her shirt to show him her stomach . . . her breasts.

He never made her disrobe completely, but she felt as if she were a puppet, and he the puppet master. It was degrading and demoralizing, but if she didn't do what he wanted, she wouldn't get fed. It was as simple as that. She'd tried defying him once, and he'd left her alone in the dark for what seemed like forever. By the time he came back and began playing his mind games again, she was starved enough to do whatever he wanted.

Elise knew she smelled horrible, and she was weak from lack of sustenance. She'd played his games and done what he'd wanted in order to get food and water. But it was never enough. Just sufficient to keep her alive and desperate for him to show up once more.

Psychologically, she understood he was grooming her to associate his appearance with the basic needs of food and water, but she was determined to fight him in any way she could. She'd act like a trained pony when he demanded it, but he couldn't control her thoughts or emotions.

Unfortunately, she couldn't hear if someone else was in the house with her or not. She had no idea what was going on above her. There weren't many times in her life when she'd regretted not being able to hear, but this was definitely one of them.

Elise wanted out.

She wanted to go home.

To see Me-Maw and Pop again.

To talk to her sister over the internet.

All the things she'd thought were so terrible about her life didn't seem so bad anymore. She'd spent so much time online, trying to feel normal. Online, she wasn't deaf. She wasn't the short redhead with a million freckles. She was whoever she wanted to be.

And Elise had loved the freedom all the chat rooms she'd participated in had given her. But she'd been stupid. Everly had warned her about some of the dangers on the internet, but she'd just thought her older sister was being overly protective.

Of *course* the people she was talking to were teenagers, like her.

Of *course* they were boys, not men.

Of *course* they were harmless.

Until they weren't.

She'd been talking to Rob for months. She'd opened up to him regarding how she felt about her mother. About how lonely she felt most of the time. They'd talked for hours. It had been exciting . . . and Elise had fallen in love with seventeen-year-old Rob.

But it was all a lie.

Every single word.

And she'd been stupid to agree to meet him.

She'd gotten into the innocuous white van with the man she'd never seen before simply because he'd said he was Rob's dad and was going to take her to him.

So stupid.

There was no Rob.

Never had been. She was almost sure of it.

Just an old guy with scary black eyes, a guy who hurt her.

She didn't think she had any more tears left, but they rolled down her face as if she hadn't already cried herself sick again just hours ago.

She twisted the ring on her finger, the same one her sister had, and hoped like hell that Everly was as good at her job as Elise always thought she was. She knew things in real life didn't work like they did on television, but she couldn't help but pray that someone had found her purse. The man had turned off her phone and thrown the purse out the window almost as soon as he'd picked her up. Hopefully, Everly would be able to hack into it and figure out what was going on.

But just as soon as she had the thought, her shoulders slumped.

She'd thought she'd been talking to a seventeen-year-old boy named Rob. Not this old guy. She wasn't sure anything they'd talked about would help Everly find her now.

As the tears continued to roll down her face, Elise signed, *I'm here. Please, someone find me.*

~

Thirty-six hours later, Ball was beyond frustrated. Rex had been given permission to have Meat access Elise's phone, but so far he wasn't having much luck. He'd been able to get into the texts and phone-call log easily, but there wasn't much there.

Elise did have the apps on her phone that Meat had found on her computer, but as he'd warned, many were geared toward anonymity, and in most cases, any communications were deleted as soon as the apps were closed.

An alarming thing that *had* been found was a tracking app. It looked like it had installed automatically when Elise opened a picture that had been sent through one of the apps. The picture was just a meme of a dog doing something silly, but as long as the picture was on her phone, she could be tracked.

Everly was nearly at the end of her rope, and Ball wasn't sure what else he could do to distract her. They'd walked the entire journey from Me-Maw's house to the gas station and back, several times, finding no new clues. It was looking more and more like Elise had gotten into a car with someone and disappeared into thin air.

Me-Maw had done their combined laundry last night, and when Everly wasn't even fazed by it, Ball had realized she wasn't doing well. Then she'd broken down and cried in his arms in bed later that evening—and Ball was done. Too much time had gone by with no leads. If Elise had gotten involved with a trafficking ring, soon she'd be buried so deep, they'd never find her.

"Come on," he told Everly. She was sitting at the dining room table, staring blankly at her laptop, trying to think of something else to research. Someone else to contact. Some other reporter to beg to put her sister's case on the six o'clock news. Unfortunately, teenagers disappearing in LA wasn't exactly newsworthy.

"Where?" she asked.

"We're going to the station to meet with Detective Ramirez again. We'll go over his notes and see if we can glean anything new. Maybe by then, Rex will have something new for us. An address. A phone number. *Something.*"

The spark of hope in her eyes killed him. Everly had been holding up extremely well, under the circumstances, as had her grandparents. But the strain was starting to get to them all. Ball hated that.

Everly gathered up her things without a word. She grabbed her purse and went into the living room to tell Me-Maw and Pop where they were going. Ball heard her telling them to call if they heard anything, and then she was next to him.

Without a word, they made their way to his rental car and headed for the police station. Every now and then, he looked over at Everly and saw that her head was turned and she was hyperaware of everything and everyone they passed.

After a while, she asked, "Should we go downtown and talk to some of the prostitutes? Bring Elise's picture and see if they've seen her?"

Ball's stomach clenched at the thought. "As a last resort, maybe. But you know as well as I do if she's been taken for trafficking, they wouldn't put her on the streets. Not at first. They'll keep her under wraps until she's beaten down psychologically, and they aren't afraid she'll run or alert anyone to her situation."

"I know," Everly said softly. "I'm just at a loss as to what else to do. I know what the statistics say. I know it's very likely we're looking for her dead body, but a part of me refuses to believe that."

Ball saw her worrying the ring on her finger, and it reminded him of a picture Me-Maw had shown him last night. A picture of Elise and Everly, standing next to each other. Everly had her arm over Elise's shoulder, and her sister was holding on to her wrist. He'd seen the ring on her finger that looked exactly like Everly's.

"Tell me about your rings?" he asked, to try to get Everly's mind off the worst-case scenarios that were most likely going through her head.

"The day Elise was born, Me-Maw told me that Elise would be the one person I'd know longer than anyone else in the entire world. Longer than any friends I might have, longer than my mother, longer than her, and even longer than the man I'd hopefully someday meet and marry. She asked me if I accepted the responsibility that came with being a sister. The responsibility to look after her. To play with her, to laugh with her, to cry with her when necessary. To always be there for her, no matter what. Of course I agreed. Me-Maw gave me the ring as a physical reminder of my commitment to my sister.

"And when Elise was ten, Me-Maw got her a ring as well. I remember how happy she was, how grown-up she felt to be wearing that ring. Me-Maw made the gift of the ring a huge ceremony and party.

"I know people don't understand our bond. I mean, I'm way older than Elise. But the second I saw her, something clicked. I helped teach her sign language when she was little, and I did whatever I could to be there for her. The rings bind us together, even when we're physically separated." Everly held up her hand, looked at her ring.

It was gold, with little squiggles around it that were fading with time. It didn't look particularly expensive, but there was no doubt that it was absolutely priceless to her.

Her next words proved Ball's thoughts correct.

"I never take it off. Never. It's as though, as long as I'm wearing it, my sister is there with me." She shrugged. "That probably sounds stupid."

"Not at all," Ball said. "I would assume it's much how a wedding ring works. Yes, it tells others that you're in a relationship, but more than that, it's a commitment. If I had a wife, I'd want her to feel the same way about the ring on her finger as you do about yours. I'd want her to look at it and think of me. To know that I've got the same ring on my finger and I'm thinking about *her*. To know you're that close to someone in this world is a beautiful thing, and I think your grandparents are pretty awesome to have given that to you and your sister."

"I think so too," Everly agreed.

They were both lost in thought for the rest of the trip to the station, and when they pulled into the parking lot, Ball finally said, "I'm going to find your sister, Everly. Maybe not today. Maybe not tomorrow. Even if it takes the rest of my life, I'm going to find out what happened to her so you can be at peace."

"Thanks," she said softly. "That means a lot."

"Come on," Ball said. "Let's go see what Ramirez knows."

Nodding, Everly climbed out of her side of the rental, and they walked into the station.

Thirty minutes later, they were sitting alone in an interrogation room with the file about Elise's disappearance sitting between them. There wasn't much in it, and even though Ramirez was doing what he could, he hadn't found any information that they hadn't already discovered for themselves.

"Shit, this was a waste of time," Everly said in disgust.

Just then, they heard a commotion outside the room.

Everly stood up and went to the door. She opened it—and stepped back in surprise when Detective Ramirez almost bowled her over.

Ball was up and at Everly's back in a second. "What's happened?" he asked.

"A 911 call just came in. A man said he was walking his girlfriend's dog and heard someone calling for help from a house he'd thought was vacant. The girl had broken out a window in the attic and was frantically waving her arm, screaming. A unit is on the way, but I thought you might like to know."

"Did she sound funny?" Everly demanded.

"Sound funny?"

"Elise is deaf. If she was screaming, it would've sounded off to a hearing person."

"I don't know. But I'm on my way to the scene. I'll be in touch and let you know."

"We're going," Everly said.

"No, you're not," the detective told her.

"Look, it's my sister who's missing, and if this *is* her, and you guys go in there and start screaming directions at her, she's not going to understand you. And if whoever kidnapped her is still around, she won't be able to tell you what he looks like or anything. You *need* me."

The detective looked undecided.

"She's a cop," Ball added. "She knows how to stay out of the way and what the protocol is. She's not a regular civilian."

That did it. Ramirez nodded. "Okay, but I'm leaving right now."

Without a word, Everly sprang back to the table, gathered up the few papers they'd been looking at, and was back at Ball's side. "We're ready."

Within a minute, they were in the back of Ramirez's SUV. The siren was on, and they were driving hell-bent for leather toward the run-down neighborhood where the man had said the house was located.

Ball reached over, grabbed Everly's hand, and clasped it tight in his own. Neither said anything, they just held on to each other and prayed the girl yelling for help was Elise.

Chapter Six

The neighborhood was in complete chaos when Ramirez pulled into the area. Cop cars were already lined up and down the narrow street, and there were ambulances staged, waiting for the all clear to get closer.

Ball climbed out, pulling Everly after him. She could hear police dogs barking excitedly, as well as neighborhood dogs joining in the fray. But her eyes were glued to the house currently surrounded by police.

The SWAT officer inside her wanted to join in, but the sister in her couldn't make her legs work to take a step closer to the house. It was three stories, including an attic. The white paint on the outside was peeling, and the yard was full of waist-high weeds. Wooden slats hung tenuously off the side of the house in random places, and the leaning porch looked like it would blow away in a small breeze.

"Stay here," Ramirez ordered. "I'll go see what's going on." He didn't wait for their agreement, but turned and headed for what looked like the officers in charge.

Everly couldn't move a muscle. She could only hold on to Ball's hand as if it was the only thing keeping her from falling into a million pieces. When he'd become her lifeline, she wasn't sure. But sometime over the last several days, he'd become her support system. It was crazy. She'd never relied on anyone in her entire life, save her grandparents. She'd learned from a young age that she could only count on herself. But, despite their rocky start, Ball had begun to mean something to her.

It should've freaked her out. At the moment, she could only feel gratitude that he was there with her.

The possibility of her sister already being dead had definitely been at the forefront of her mind, especially as more and more time passed since she'd been seen, but the reality of one of the cops coming out of the house and telling her that they'd been too late, that Elise truly was gone, wasn't something Everly was sure she could handle.

There were shouts from inside the house, and Everly squeezed her eyes shut.

"Easy, Ev."

She nodded, but didn't open her eyes.

Then there were more shouts and a call for an ambulance.

Everly's eyes opened just in time to see a teenager being led out of the house with a police officer at her side. Her heart rate jumped, but a second later, her shoulders slumped.

The girl wasn't Elise.

She was older than Elise. And taller. And had the wrong color hair. She had on a pair of jeans and a black T-shirt. Her brown hair was in disarray, and she wasn't wearing any shoes. The teenager was holding her bleeding arm as the officer steered her toward an ambulance, which had pulled up in front of the house.

"It's not her," Everly whispered desolately.

"Maybe she'll know something," Ball told her gently.

But their attention was diverted from the girl being helped into the ambulance by more shouting from the house. Everly hoped they'd caught the person responsible for kidnapping the poor young woman.

Then she watched in confusion as another teen was helped out of the house. This one had blonde hair and was short like Elise. She was probably younger than Everly's sister, though, maybe twelve or thirteen.

"There were two of them?" Everly asked, shocked.

"Come on," Ball said, pulling her closer to the door.

Everly went willingly. The police officers around them weren't paying attention to them. They were more concerned about what was being relayed via their radios.

"This looks like a trafficking situation," Ball muttered. "More than one victim usually means they were collecting them before sending them off. Don't lose hope, Everly."

His words sent adrenaline shooting through her. She reacted without thinking, heading for the nearest officer.

"My name is Sergeant Adams, out of Colorado Springs. I'm here because my teenage sister is missing. She's about five-three, has red hair, but she's deaf. If she's in there, she's going to be scared because she can't hear anything."

The officer looked distracted at first, but as Everly continued to talk, he nodded. "I'll relay the information."

"Do you know how many are inside?" Ball asked.

"Unknown at this point. They're doing a sweep of the house from top to bottom. So far, they've found four."

Four. Everly inhaled sharply. Four kids. Scared out of their minds and taken from their families. Sex traffickers were the lowest of the low. The scum of the earth.

"Sergeant Adams knows sign language," Ball told the officer. "If her sister is inside, she can talk to her. Keep her calm. Please relay that."

Surprisingly, the officer did.

"We'll be right here," Ball told the man, and he nodded.

Ball led Everly back a few steps and pulled her into his side. They watched as another girl was led from the house, sobbing. Then another. It was obvious the girls were traumatized. They were all dirty, and one of the girls was only half-dressed. The implications were horrifying, but Everly kept her gaze on the front door. Praying harder than ever before that the next person to be led out would be her sister.

Five agonizingly long minutes went by, and then another girl appeared. Then another.

"Six," Ball whispered. "Has to be trafficking."

Everly held her breath—then heard a sound she somehow recognized, even though she'd never heard it before in her life.

Elise. Screaming in terror.

She tore herself out of Ball's loose embrace and sprinted toward the house. She heard shouts behind her, and Ball yelling something, but she had eyes only for the front door. She ran inside, knowing Ball was at her back, then she stopped and had to force herself to breathe for a second.

The house smelled awful. Like human waste, body odor, and mildew. She'd been in some pretty terrible environments as a cop, but knowing her sister was inside, had *been* inside this place for who knew how long, made it that much worse.

Elise screamed again, and Everly turned toward a set of stairs that were just off the front foyer. She ran down them and pushed through the four officers who were blocking her way to her sister.

There, on the far side of the basement, was Elise.

She was wearing the same blouse and shorts Me-Maw had said she'd worn to school the day she'd disappeared. Her feet were bare, and she sat huddled against the wall, staring at the police officers as if they were devils incarnate. Everly saw a bucket that her sister had obviously been using as a toilet out of the corner of her eye, but she ignored it, wanting to reassure Elise more than anything else.

Stepping closer, she began trying to calm her.

You're okay. It's me. Are you hurt?

Elise raised her eyes to her sister's, and Everly almost staggered under the weight of the confusion, pain, and fright she saw there.

It's me. I'm here. She took a step toward Elise, relieved when she didn't flinch. *I'm coming closer.*

When Elise nodded slightly, Everly took another step forward. She heard Ball telling the officers to give her some space, that she was the victim's sister, and she'd never been so thankful for his presence. She couldn't concentrate on them and make sure they gave her the room to do what she needed to do to reach her sister.

She glanced behind her briefly and saw that Ball had stepped forward, closer to both her and Elise. The support she felt with that small act was immense. He was close by just in case she or Elise needed him, but he didn't insert himself into what was going on.

Everly got close, then eased down onto her knees. She crawled the remaining three feet or so until she was right in front of Elise. *Are you hurt?* she signed again.

Not really. But I can't move far because of the chains. Elise pointed to her ankles.

Okay. We'll get those off. I've been looking for you since you disappeared.

I'm sorry, Elise signed frantically. *I'm so sorry. I was so stupid. I did exactly what you told me never to do.*

Shhhh. We'll figure it all out later. You're okay now. Can I hug you? Everly asked.

Elise shook her head. *No. I'm disgusting.*

I wouldn't care if you were covered head to toe in dog shit, Everly told her sister honestly. *I just need to hold you.*

The small nod was all she needed. Right before she gathered her sister in her arms, Everly gave another quick glance over her shoulder. Ball was right there with a pair of bolt cutters in his hand. She didn't know where he'd gotten them, but it was obvious he was hesitating, giving her time for a moment with her sister.

"We need to get her out of here," he told her softly, minutes later.

"I know," Everly said as she wrapped her arms even tighter around Elise. "Just give us a second." She felt her sister trembling, not moving otherwise, but after another long moment, she put her arms around Everly and clung tightly.

Everly felt like sobbing, but knew she had to be strong. There would be time later to break down.

"I need to touch her to get the chains off," Ball said. "Can you please warn her?"

Everly nodded and pulled back, moving to Elise's side. Her knees were still touching her sister, both needing the connection at the moment. *This is my friend. He's going to get those chains off. Okay?*

Everly looked at Ball, and she had to swallow hard to keep the tears from escaping as he painstakingly signed what he'd tried so hard to learn the other morning.

My name is Ball. You're safe.

Elise nodded at him, then turned to Everly. *Wow, his signs suck.*

Everly burst out laughing, feeling relief for the first time since she'd heard her sister scream. She was going to be all right. Something awful had happened to her in this room, that was pretty obvious, but she was alive, and her sense of humor was still intact.

She quickly signed back, *Yeah, but as of a day and a half ago, he didn't know any signs, so cut him some slack.*

Ball? Elise asked. *What kind of name is that?*

A nickname.

What's it mean?

Everly turned to Ball, who was waiting patiently for permission to touch Elise's leg. "She wants to know how you got your nickname."

Ball smiled, and even though it was a bit strained, she was so thankful he was doing his best to put Elise at ease. "Will you translate for me?" he asked.

"Of course," Everly told him, doing just that as he spoke.

When I was in the Coast Guard, I was a bit anal. Everything had its place, and I hated to be disorganized. I also had a knack for being able to tell when things were about to go sideways. When someone was about to lie to me. When they were going to try to flee. My fellow Coasties always said that I was really "on the ball." That got shortened to Ball. My last name is Black, but it's a good thing they didn't call me that, since I have a friend back in Colorado Springs whose nickname is Black. Can you imagine having two people in the same group of friends with the same nickname? But what's funny is, they should've called me "Ball" because my first name is Kannon. You know—like cannonball.

Everly hadn't known the origin of his nickname, and after the last few days, she was interested in learning just about everything about him. They'd been thrust into a very intense situation and had gotten close in a short period of time. But they didn't know some of the smallest things about each other.

Elise smiled a little at the cannonball joke, but turned to Everly. *So you know him from Colorado?*

Yes. Now, can he please get those chains off you so we can get out of here?

Elise turned to Ball and nodded. Then she gestured toward the chains and straightened her legs, giving him access.

Within seconds, Elise was free, and Everly was helping her stand.

"Are you good?" Ball asked.

Everly nodded.

Then he did something that shocked the hell out of her. He turned to Elise and signed very slowly, and not exactly correctly, but enough that they understood him, *Your sister was never going to stop looking for you. She loves you very much.*

Everly had no idea he'd looked *that* up online.

Elise looked from Ball to her sister, then back to Ball. Then she signed with one hand. *I love her too.*

Stay strong, Ball signed next, then he turned to Everly. "Go with your sister. I'll stay here and try to find out as much information as I can. I'll come to the hospital when I'm done. If they're going to keep her overnight, I'll make sure you have what you need to stay with her. I'll also call your grandparents and let them know Elise was found and she's okay, and bring them to the hospital as well."

He was matter-of-fact as he spoke, as if it was no big deal how he was taking over care of her, Elise, and her grandparents. She didn't have anyone else in her life to lean on like this, someone who would take on all the things that needed to be done so she could concentrate solely on her sister. Everly knew she should probably be the one to call her grandmother, but right now, her focus was Elise, and Ball seemed to understand that.

"Thank you," she said, not able to find the words to express her feelings more properly.

Then he shocked her once more by leaning down and kissing her on the forehead. His lips pressed against her for a long moment, firmly and intensely, before he pulled back. He nodded at both her and Elise before turning to lead them out of the basement.

Got something you need to tell me, sis? Elise signed.

And once again, Everly was overcome with gratitude that Elise still seemed to be mostly herself. Whatever had happened hadn't killed the spark in her sister. She wasn't sure what to say about Ball, but she'd tell Elise everything if that would help her get through her ordeal.

The cops escorted them out of the house and ushered them into an ambulance. Everly didn't like the bruises on her sister, or how dirty she was, but she was alive. That was all that mattered. They could deal with everything else . . . together.

Chapter Seven

Ball paced Detective Ramirez's office. Back and forth. Back and forth. It was either that or hurt someone.

It had been two days since Elise and the other girls had been rescued from the vacant house, and the cops were no closer to finding the identity of the man who'd kidnapped them.

Everly sat on a chair in front of the detective's desk, watching him. She'd been amazing the last two days. Staying with her sister at the hospital before she'd been discharged, making sure she felt safe while Elise told the authorities what had happened.

Elise had sworn that she hadn't been raped, and at first Ball wasn't sure if he should believe her. He thought she might be trying to downplay what had happened, especially in front of him and the male detective. But after being reassured by Everly that the doctor had examined her and corroborated what Elise had said, he'd been immensely relieved.

But that didn't mean Elise hadn't been affected by what had happened to her. She'd been traumatized just the same. The mental abuse her abductor had heaped on her was hard to stomach, and Ball knew if it had taken too much longer to find her, the man would've moved on to sexual assault sooner or later. As it was, it almost seemed as if he'd been grooming her for some unknown role.

And that didn't sit well with Ball at all, particularly based on what he knew about traffickers.

He also wasn't sure about *Everly's* mental health. She'd been too busy taking care of her sister and her grandparents to care for herself. Ball had been the one to make sure she had something to eat that first night in the hospital. He'd brought over some things so she had clothes to sleep in, and he'd arranged for a cot to be brought into her sister's hospital room, so she didn't try to sleep in the uncomfortable chair.

Watching how attentive Everly was with her sister reminded him of how *inattentive* Holly had been when he was hurt. He'd expected her to do what Everly was doing now. To be by his side and at least *act* like she was worried about him.

Instead, she'd told him she didn't like hospitals and to just call her when he was discharged. When he had, she said she was busy and couldn't come get him. He'd ended up calling a fucking taxi to get to his house. And the few weeks after were progressively worse.

He'd honestly thought they were going to get married, he'd loved her that much. But in the end, Ball had realized she was a selfish bitch who'd just been looking for an easy ride, and figured since he was in the military, he was it.

Forcing back his bitter thoughts, Ball began another trek across the small office. He and Everly had come to the police station to talk to Detective Ramirez about the case. To learn any new details about the kidnappings. Everly had heard her sister's side of things, but now they wanted to know what was happening, to find the man responsible.

There had been seven girls in all. Three were being kept in bedrooms on the second floor, one in the attic, one in the living room on the main floor, and even one in the fucking kitchen. They were all chained like Elise had been. But unlike Elise, all the others had been assaulted.

And most of them told versions of the same story—they'd been talking to a guy online who they'd assumed was their age. After several months, they'd agreed to meet him, and when the guy's "dad" had shown up, they'd gotten into his car.

The oldest girl, though, had simply been in the wrong place at the wrong time. She'd been beaten unconscious and had woken up in the house.

The girl in the attic had been the one responsible for their rescue. That day, in a startling bit of sheer luck, her captor failed to completely engage the lock around the chain on her ankle. When he left, she'd waited a long while before going to the window and breaking it. When the unsuspecting man passed by, walking the dog, she'd screamed her head off and begged him to call the cops.

The girl had heard others in the house, but didn't know how many were trapped with her. Besides Elise, there was a twelve-year-old, two fourteen-year-olds, two sixteen-year-olds, and an eighteen-year-old. They all looked very different from one another. Some were tall, others were short. There was a blonde, two brunettes, Elise with her red hair, two with black hair, and the eighteen-year-old had dyed her hair pink.

"We think whoever orchestrated this was collecting different types of girls to sell on the black market," the detective continued.

"And what's being done about that?" Ball asked.

"Everything possible," Ramirez said calmly. "The FBI is involved, and we've got a description of the man's car, his physical description, and we're analyzing all of their interviews to see what other information we can pick up."

"You do realize that if that girl hadn't broken that window, we probably wouldn't have found them, right?" Everly asked.

It was what Ball had been thinking, but wasn't going to say . . . not in front of Everly. But he should've known she wouldn't back away from the truth.

"You don't know that," Ramirez said.

"Had you even connected the other missing girls to Elise?" Everly asked with crazy-good insight. "Did you dismiss them as runaways as well? None of their parents had the connections I did, so they weren't able to hire someone like my friend Ball here to help investigate and keep the pressure on. There's something really wrong with our society when a kid goes missing, and the first thing the cops think is that he or she is simply a runaway and they'll show up eventually."

"Statistics bear that out, Sergeant Adams," Ramirez said.

"I know, but I don't care. I also know that when I get back home, I'm going to sit down and have a talk with my chief of police. Even if three out of four disappearances are a simple case of a disgruntled kid, it's not fair to that fourth family to dismiss their worry so easily."

No one said a word for the longest time. Then Ramirez cleared his throat and said, "We might need to talk to Elise again. Sometimes victims can remember more details after some time has passed."

"If you need to talk to her, she'll be with me in Colorado Springs," Everly said.

Ball stopped pacing and turned to stare at Everly. They hadn't spent a lot of time together over the last two days; she'd mostly been with her sister. They hadn't discussed what was going to happen next. He figured Everly would spend a bit more time in LA with her family, then go back to Colorado Springs and try to get back to her life, just as Elise would do here. He should've known better.

"That might be best," the detective said.

"Actually, it's not. It's gonna suck," Everly said bluntly. "Her friends are here. Her grandparents. Her school. But I don't feel she's safe here, and neither does she. Until you find the man who kidnapped and assaulted her, along with whoever is behind the entire operation, she'll be as far away from here as I can get her. And that's Colorado Springs. With me."

"We'll need her to be available if we have questions," Ramirez said.

"Not a problem. We've got child advocates at the CSPD, as well as sketch artists."

"What about school?" Ball asked.

Everly turned to him, and he saw the emotion in her eyes. She was worked up, and he couldn't blame her. If the situation was different, if

Everly was the one who'd been kidnapped, and the man was still on the loose, he wouldn't be comfortable leaving her here.

The thought should've concerned him . . . but instead, rightness settled in his gut.

He also hadn't known Elise very long, but the little he'd learned had made him extremely protective of the girl. She was hurting and scared, but doing her best to act like she wasn't. She'd taught him a few signs, and teased him when he'd gotten them completely wrong. She was extremely strong and brave . . . just like her sister.

"Colorado Springs has a deaf school. It's not as prestigious as the one here, but all things considered, it'll be fine," Everly said.

"And Elise is okay with going?" Ball asked.

"She was the one who asked if she could come home with me."

Ball nodded. His mind whirled with plans.

"I'm sorry we couldn't find her sooner," Ramirez said.

"Me too. But we did find her, and at the moment that seems like a miracle. I appreciate how everyone has treated my sister since she was rescued. The professionalism and care has been impeccable."

The detective nodded.

Ball took Everly's elbow when she stood, then stepped back, giving her space. It was interesting watching her interact with her fellow police officers. It was as if a shroud fell over her. She became stiff, less emotional. He understood it, but hated it all the same.

The second they stepped outside, she sagged.

Ball's fingers itched to touch her, but he shoved them in his pockets instead. "I can get in touch with the rental car company and arrange to keep the car longer," he said as they walked through the parking lot.

"Why?"

"I just thought since you don't like flying, maybe you'd be more comfortable if we drove back. Your chief gave you another week off, right?"

"Yeah, but that's not necessary. We can fly."

He couldn't help it. Ball reached out and stopped her with a hand on her biceps. "Everly, you hate flying. We can drive."

"I hate a lot of things. Eating brussels sprouts. Working the overnight shift. Taking my sister away from Me-Maw and Pop. But that doesn't mean that I won't do them. I need to get back to the Springs, set Elise up in the school, make sure she's comfortable in my apartment, that she feels safe, *and* make sure my boss is okay with me working the day shift, at least for a while. I don't have time to drive back."

Ball stared at her. She was right, but he'd actually been looking forward to getting to know Elise better and spending more time with Everly. He'd missed sleeping with her when she'd been in the hospital with Elise, and the night before, she'd slept in her sister's room with her. Somehow, in the few days they'd been in Los Angeles, he'd gotten used to having her in his arms. What had started out as something he'd done mostly because he'd known it would annoy her had become much more. "Okay. Let me call Rex, and he'll get our tickets organized."

"That's not necessary," she protested.

"It is."

"No, it's not. I can take care of my sister on my own."

"No one said you couldn't," Ball replied, trying to figure out where her sudden attitude was coming from. "Rex is thrilled that Elise was found. Trust me, that's his goal with every case, but it doesn't always turn out as good as this one did. He's going to be happy to get both you and your sister out of LA so she can start to heal."

Everly's shoulders dropped, and she sighed. "I know. It's just hard to accept help."

"If it makes you feel better, think of it this way . . . it's for Elise, not you."

She chuckled. "Right."

"And something else."

"What?"

"I work from home. When I'm not on a mission, I'm happy to have Elise come to my place after school if you aren't home yet. She can help me with my sign language and hopefully feel safe in the process."

"You'd do that? Why?"

"Why?"

"Yeah. A week ago, you hated my guts."

"A week ago, I was an ass," Ball confirmed. "But you've made me see the error of my ways. I *like* Elise. She's a hell of a lot like her older sister. Besides . . . if she's at my house, that means I'll get to see you too."

"You want to? I thought for sure between Me-Maw, the newspaper clippings, the discussion about our underwear copulating in the washer, and great-grandbabies, that you'd run as fast as you could from me and never look back."

Ball shrugged. "Yeah, well . . . you thought wrong."

They stared at each other for a long moment before Everly sighed. "Thank you. That would be a big help. And this probably goes without saying, but don't let her use the internet unsupervised. I know she's fifteen, but that's what got her into this mess in the first place."

"Of course," Ball said.

"Thanks."

"How are *you* doing?" Ball asked.

"Me?"

"Yeah. You. You've been going nonstop for a while now. I know you were sleeping okay before we found Elise, but I haven't really seen you much in the last two days. You look tired."

"I *am* tired," Everly told him. "But I'm so very grateful that we found her. It's hard for me to put into words. I know better than most what the odds were of that happening. Even though I was trying to be optimistic, I had a small feeling she could've been gone. Finding her was a miracle, and I just want to get her out of here as soon as I can."

"I don't blame you."

"And Elise asked about our mom last night. Asked if Mom had known she was missing, and if I thought she'd come see her."

Ball didn't care that they were in the middle of the parking lot outside the police department, he pulled Everly into his arms. She didn't fight. Instead, she practically melted into him. Her hair brushed against his jaw, and he inhaled deeply, needing the physical intimacy as much as she did.

"I'm sorry," he said.

"Me too. I don't get it. Elise is her flesh and blood. Why wouldn't she care?"

Ball knew Everly already had the answer, but he had to say something. "Drug addicts literally can't care about anything but their next high. They crave it with every fiber of their being. They'd lie, cheat, and steal to get it. Things like jobs, family, and friends fall to the wayside in their quest to find and do drugs."

"I know," Everly mumbled.

They stood like that for a long moment, soaking in the comfort of human contact.

"Thank you for being here," Everly said. "I know you didn't want to come and that you could've left by now. Instead, you've been amazing. Driving Me-Maw and Pop back and forth to the hospital. Bringing Elise some clothes to change into. Making sure I ate something. I . . . It hasn't gone unnoticed."

That was just one more thing Ball liked about Everly. She didn't shy away from saying what she was thinking . . . good or bad. "There was no way I was going to leave you guys the second she was found."

Everly shrugged and straightened. Ball kept his hands on her waist, just as her hands stayed on his upper arms. She looked him in the eye. "A week ago, you would've."

She was right.

"What's happening with us?" she asked.

"I don't know," Ball said softly. "But I haven't felt like this in a very long time. If ever."

"Me either. I was perfectly happy being an independent, kick-ass SWAT officer and cop. I didn't need anyone, and I liked it that way. Now my little sister will be living with me, and I have no idea if the man who kidnapped her will try again. In the last two days, I've turned to tell you something at least a dozen times, only to realize you're not right there."

He chuckled. "We did spend practically every minute of every day together there for a while, didn't we?"

Everly nodded.

"If it makes you feel any better, I've been sleeping like crap. I fully admit that I was fucking with you a little that first night, when I spooned behind you. That bed was plenty big enough for us to sleep in and never touch . . . but the joke was on me, because now I can't sleep worth a damn when you're not there with me."

"We're a mess," Everly said with a small shake of her head.

"It's been an intense week," Ball agreed. "I'd like to see you when we get home."

"You just volunteered to help me with Elise. We're definitely going to see each other," Everly told him.

"No. Like, *see* you. Take you out like a normal person. Dinner. Bowling. Maybe a movie. See if there's anything to our attraction once we're back to our normal lives."

She stared up at him as if he'd just asked her to take off her clothes and streak through the police station behind them.

Feeling awkward, Ball hurried on to say, "If you want to. I know I was a dick, and I wouldn't blame you if you didn't want anything to do with me. I was totally chauvinistic, and I should've given you the benefit of the doubt, but you know my story, know why I didn't, and—"

Everly cut him off. "I'd like that."

"Yeah?"

"Yeah. Although I can't promise I'll have a ton of time. I don't know what I'll do with Elise if we go out. I don't feel comfortable leaving her alone, and I won't have Me-Maw and Pop to help me out."

"She can either come with us, or I'm sure one of my buddies will look after her. We won't call it babysitting because Elise is way too old for that, but my guess is that she won't really *want* to be alone for a while either."

"They'd do that?"

"Are you kidding? The second they hear I have an actual date, the others will fall all over themselves volunteering to have her over."

"You guys all seem pretty close."

"We are. I'd do anything for those guys. I thought I knew what brotherhood was from my time in the service, but it doesn't compare to what I've found with them."

"How did the Mountain Mercenaries come to be?" Everly asked.

"We all got calls from Rex, who told us to come for interviews. We met at The Pit, and he never showed. We were pissed, but ended up spending the night shooting the shit and playing pool. Apparently, the 'interview' was pretty much just seeing how well we all got on together, because we got calls offering us jobs afterward."

"And you've never met Rex, all this time?" Everly asked.

She still had hold of his arms, and Ball still had his hands on her waist. He knew he wasn't in any hurry to leave; he was enjoying this little time alone with her. "Nope."

"And how did your friends meet their girlfriends?"

Ball chuckled. "Those are all *really* long stories, and I'll leave it to them to tell you."

"Can I ask something?"

"Of course."

"It's just that . . . I don't understand how you can be so opposed to women, yet seem so happy for your friends that they're dating."

"I'm not opposed to women," Ball said.

She raised her eyebrows at him.

"I'm not," he insisted. "I love Allye, Chloe, Morgan, and Harlow as if they were my own sisters. I'd do anything for them. They're brave and smart, and they deserve men as awesome as my teammates."

"But?" Everly said.

"I love that they've found someone who completes them, but I haven't wanted that for myself because of my past. My ex, Holly, really did a number on me, and the last thing I ever wanted was to be put in that kind of vulnerable position again."

"I see."

"I don't think you do," Ball said, tightening his hold on Everly when she started to pull away. "Intellectually, I knew all women weren't like my former partner or my ex-girlfriend. But I still didn't want to put myself out there and get hurt again. So I kept women at an arm's length, including telling myself I wasn't going to purposely work with a female again. But then Rex threw that curveball at us, and I didn't have a choice."

Everly frowned and tried to step away once more. This time, Ball pulled her close and wrapped an arm around her waist, plastering her to his front.

"But in one week, you've shown me how flawed my thinking's been for years. Riley and Holly were also flawed, but that doesn't mean I should make other women suffer for it for the rest of my life . . . and it doesn't mean that I shouldn't try to find a bit of happiness for myself either."

She stared up at him with big eyes.

Ball continued. "I love my friends' women. I'd do anything for them, simply because they make my friends happy. But it wasn't until the last couple of days that I truly understood how my friends felt about them."

"Ball—"

"No pressure, Everly," Ball said before she could continue. "I want to take you out, get to know you better. I want to get to know Elise better. If things progress, great. If we decide we're better off as friends, fine. But, regardless of how things turn out for us personally, you should know that I'd welcome you at my side on any future mission, no questions asked."

She blinked rapidly at his words, then swallowed hard. "I . . . Thank you."

"You're welcome." Then Ball took a chance. Leaning down slowly, giving her time to reject his advance, he paused with his lips hovering above hers.

She stood on her tiptoes and closed the distance between them.

The brush of her lips against his was the best feeling ever.

The second they touched, something changed inside him.

Mine.

The word echoed through his head, but Ball was smart enough to keep it to himself. He knew without a doubt that Everly wouldn't take too kindly to such a possessive statement this early in their relationship, if ever. That wasn't who she was.

But that didn't change what Ball felt.

One hand moved up to clasp the back of her head and hold her to him as he changed the kiss from a short, exploratory meeting of their lips to a claiming.

Her mouth opened as soon as his tongue brushed along the seam of her lips, and he surged inside. Everly moaned as he took possession of her mouth. His head tipped one way, and hers went the other. Her hands gripped his biceps hard enough that he had a feeling she was leaving little half-moon marks on his skin even through his T-shirt.

Ending the kiss way before he wanted to, Ball pulled back and licked his lips, savoring the taste of her. It took a moment for Everly to open her eyes, but when she did, Ball was rewarded by a look of such desire in her green gaze that he had to force himself to not devour her again.

"I need to get you back to your sister," Ball said quietly.

Everly nodded.

"It's been a while since I've done this," he told her.

"Done what?" she asked.

"This," he said.

"Dated?" she said with a small smile.

"Yeah. I've gone out with women, but I did so knowing nothing would come of it. But this . . . this means something." He held his breath, waiting for her response.

"Yeah," she said softly.

It was enough. Untangling his fingers from her hair, he smoothed it away from her face before stepping back and giving her some breathing room. "Ready to get back to Elise?"

Everly nodded.

"If there's anything you need, will you please let me know? Even if that's just space. You haven't had even a minute to yourself since we left Colorado Springs. I'm happy to entertain your grandparents, or watch over Elise, if you need an hour to just sit in a quiet room by yourself."

"Thanks. I appreciate that. Seriously. It's been tough, as I'm used to being by myself a lot, but right now, I know if I had the time to think too much about what's been going on, I'd just freak myself out more than I already am."

"Okay. But anything you need, let me know, and I'll do what I can to get it for you."

"Like a pint of Ben and Jerry's ice cream?" she teased somewhat shyly.

"Just tell me what flavor, and it's yours," Ball said seriously. He took her hand in his and ran his thumb over the ring on her finger as they walked toward the car. "And that goes for when we're back in Colorado Springs too. It's going to be a big change for both you and your sister, and the last thing I want is for your relationship to suffer because of those changes."

"We'll be okay."

Ball nodded. "The offer is always open. And . . . hopefully you'll be seeing me a lot anyway."

She smiled. He waited while she seated herself in the car, then closed the door behind her.

When they were on their way back to Me-Maw's house, Everly asked, "Do you really think this was a trafficking thing?"

Ball was a little disappointed that their talk had turned back to business, but maybe it was for the best. "It's likely. The FBI will be looking into it, as well as Ramirez and the other detectives. Hopefully they'll be able to find something that'll lead to taking down the rest of the ring."

"I hope so."

"Me too."

The rest of the ride was quiet. Ball was as lost in his thoughts as Everly was. It had been a weird week. He'd had a lot of epiphanies that had changed everything about how he saw his future.

And try as he might, he couldn't get that kiss out of his head.

As much as he'd been irritated at Rex for pushing Everly on him and involving her in the mission, he couldn't deny that it had been the best thing for him.

Chapter Eight

Five days later, Ball wondered if he'd dreamed that intimate moment with Everly in LA. From the moment they'd arrived back at her memaw's house, she'd been all business. Elise sat between them on the flights back to Colorado Springs, and Everly had barely even remembered to say goodbye when he'd dropped them off at her apartment.

He'd called and talked to her a couple of times, but she'd seemed distant and somewhat irritated by his calls. He'd resorted to texting so he wouldn't interrupt her, but her return texts were short and almost rude.

He got the message.

He'd thought they'd connected while in Los Angeles, but obviously he'd been mistaken. She'd been overwhelmed while her sister was missing, and now that she'd been found, Everly was overwhelmed in a different way.

Feeling let down and irritated, even as he understood her position, Ball did his best to pretend everything was fine when he was around his friends, but when he was at home, alone, he was grumpy, and the smallest things annoyed him.

So when his phone vibrated with a text in the late afternoon, he almost ignored it. He was putting the final touches on a website and didn't want to be bothered by one of his friends trying to cheer him up.

As much as he'd tried to hide his piss-poor mood from his teammates, they'd picked up on it anyway.

When the phone vibrated for the fourth time, Ball sighed and picked it up.

Elise: Are you there?

Elise: I thought I saw something, and I'm scared.

Elise: Ball?

Elise: I don't know what to do!

Ball's heart rate shot up, and he typed as he headed for the door.

Ball: On my way. Stay inside. Don't open the door. Where's Ev?

Elise: She got stuck at work. I didn't want to bother her.

Ball shook his head in frustration. He didn't even know Everly had gone back to work. He'd thought she still had a couple of days off before she started her shifts again.

Ball: Be there in 5 min. Hang on.

Elise: OK.

Ball drove his Mustang like a bat out of hell. Luckily, Everly's apartment complex wasn't too far from his place. He pulled into a parking space and headed for Everly's apartment. He texted Elise as he went.

Ball: I'm here. Put your hand on the door so you can feel the vibrations of my knock. I'll knock 2 times. Then pause. Then 2 more times so you'll know it's me.

Elise: OK.

He took the stairs two at a time and was in front of Everly's door in seconds. He knocked twice, then two more times. The door opened immediately, and Elise flew into his arms.

Ball moved them into the apartment and closed the door behind him. He held on to Elise for a moment before taking her shoulders in his hands and backing her up so he could see her.

She had tear tracks on her face, but otherwise looked fine. "Are you okay?" he asked slowly, so she could read his lips.

She nodded.

Hating that he couldn't talk to her, he pulled out his phone. Without Everly to translate for them, they had to resort to texting to communicate, but he had to hand it to the teenager: she could text just as fast as she could sign.

Ball: Tell me what happened.

Elise: I was doing my homework when I thought I saw something out the window from the corner of my eye. I looked out, and someone was running through the parking lot. He went behind a few trees, and I swear he stopped and was staring up at the window.

Ball: I'm going to go look around. You stay here.

Elise shook her head violently and grabbed his arm.

Ball gathered her into his embrace again, and when she stopped shaking, he released her and signed, *You're safe.* Then he typed into his phone again.

Ball: I promise, I'm not leaving, and I'll do everything in my power to keep you safe. I need to look around and see if I can find anything. I'll be right back.

Elise read the text, then reluctantly nodded.

Ball squeezed her shoulder and headed out. He walked the property all around the apartment and didn't see anything out of the ordinary. Nothing that screamed danger. He had no idea if Elise had really seen something, or if she was experiencing a bit of PTSD. He wouldn't be surprised if she was.

He knew Everly had gotten her in to see a psychologist and was doing her best to make sure Elise felt safe, but often, time was the best healer.

He went back upstairs and texted Elise when he was there. The door opened immediately, and she raised her eyebrows while signing something.

Assuming she was asking if he'd found anything, Ball shook his head.

Elise's shoulders slumped, and she turned away from him, dejected. She picked up her phone.

Elise: I'm sorry I bothered you.

Ball: You are NOT a bother. Ever. You did exactly what you were supposed to. You reached out for help. Never be ashamed of that.

Ball: If it's all right with you, I'd like to stay until Ev gets home.

Elise: I'd like that.

The next two hours went by fairly quickly. Ball helped Elise with her math homework, then they spent the rest of the time working on his signing. He'd learned a bunch of new signs, and Elise had lost the haunted look in her eyes by the time he heard a key in the lock.

Standing, Ball motioned to the door and signed, *Everly*.

Ball watched as several emotions flitted over Everly's face in quick succession upon seeing him. Surprise, pleasure, irritation, then concern.

"What's wrong? Why are you here?" she asked.

"Elise texted me, said she thought she saw someone outside. She was scared."

Everly ran a hand over her face, and Ball saw the utter exhaustion there. His irritation that she hadn't called or gotten ahold of him for the last week disappeared in an instant. He took her arm and steered her to the couch next to Elise.

"Sit. Relax. I'll make you a cup of tea."

She didn't argue, which told him even more about how tired she was.

Standing in her kitchen, waiting for the water to heat up, he watched as Everly and her sister "talked."

Their hands moved a mile a minute, and the progress Ball thought he'd made in being able to speak to Elise seemed like a joke. He knew it required more than a couple of hours to be proficient in sign language, but seeing them talking made him realize exactly how long it was going to take.

Everly was still wearing her uniform. He'd once thought that seeing her wearing it would remind him too much of Riley, and his dislike of working with women, but that didn't happen.

Instead, his mind immediately went to how much he'd like to help her remove it, piece by piece. Like unwrapping a present.

Shaking his head—because the fact they hadn't had any meaningful conversations since they'd returned to Colorado Springs didn't bode well for any kind of disrobing in the near or distant future—Ball steeped her tea, then walked into the other room with the mug.

She accepted it with a small smile, took a sip, then put it on the coffee table in front of her and continued her conversation with Elise.

He had no idea what they were saying, but neither woman looked freaked out, so he was going to take that as a good sign. He stayed quiet and sat on a nearby chair. It was interesting to observe the sisters so close together. They both had red hair and green eyes, but where Elise was petite, Everly was not. She was quite a bit taller than her sister, and was filled out, as a woman should be. Elise was pretty, but in his eyes, Everly was beautiful.

He was brought out of his reflection when Everly turned to him. "Will you bring me Elise's phone? She said it's on the table."

"Of course. Something wrong?" Ball asked as he stood to collect the phone.

"No. I check it every day to make sure she hasn't been talking to someone she shouldn't be."

It made sense, but Ball hated that for both of them.

"She has to have a phone, for safety's sake, but I'm terrified whoever she was talking to before, whoever snatched her, will try to get in contact with her again. She swears she hasn't downloaded any of the apps she'd used, but I'm still paranoid."

He handed the phone to Everly. "I don't blame you." He knew he was being rude to Elise, but he turned so she couldn't see his face as he said, "If you want, I could get Meat or Rex to put a tracker on it. They could also monitor it to make sure."

Everly looked up at him. "You'd do that for her?"

"No."

She blinked in surprise. "But you just said—"

"I'd do it for you."

"Ball—" she started, but then Elise touched her arm and signed something.

Everly nodded and clicked on a few buttons on her sister's phone. Elise didn't seem to care that her sister was checking up on her. She simply waited patiently until Everly was satisfied that Elise hadn't been talking to someone she shouldn't.

They signed for a bit longer, then Elise stood up. She came over to Ball, who was still standing near the couch, and signed slowly so he could understand her. *Thank you for coming.*

You're welcome, Ball said. *Call me anytime.* He couldn't wait until he learned the signs for more words. Spelling out words was annoying and took forever.

Elise smiled and reached out to hug him.

Ball returned the hug, then watched as she headed down a short hallway and disappeared into a room near the end.

He turned to Everly. She was staring at him with an expression he couldn't read. "What?"

"Why are you being so nice?"

Ball frowned. "I don't understand."

"I haven't seen you since you dropped us off. I've been ignoring you . . . basically been a bitch when you didn't do anything to deserve it."

"I'd say we're even, then," Ball said calmly. "Because that's how I acted toward you when we first met."

Everly closed her eyes and let her head plunk onto the cushion behind her.

Ball walked over and stared down at her for the longest moment. Then he held out his hand. "Come on."

Her eyes opened, and she looked at his face, then his hand. Without question, she reached up and put her hand in his. He pulled her to her feet, then turned her around. With his hands on her shoulders, he pushed her down the hall to the other bedroom. "Change. Put on something comfortable. Then come back out, and we'll talk. Or not. Or watch TV. Whatever you want to do."

"What I really want to do is be able to sleep more than two hours a night," Everly muttered.

"Change, Ev," Ball ordered.

"Bossy," she protested, but she smiled slightly when she said it.

Ball returned her smile and backed out of the room.

Twenty minutes later, she reappeared in the living area. She had on a pair of black leggings and an oversize T-shirt that covered her down to midthigh. Her hair was brushed out of the bun it had been in, and the waves, having been confined all day, now curled around her face in abandon. She'd scrubbed her face, and it was still a little pink. But even after changing and freshening up, she still looked stressed.

"Come here," Ball said from the couch, and held out an arm. Surprisingly, she did. Everly plopped down, leaned into him, and brought her knees up. Ball tightened his arm around her, and they sat in silence for a few minutes.

"You hungry?"

She shook her head. "I grabbed something on the way home. I figured Elise would've eaten."

"She did."

"Did you find anything?" Everly asked.

Ball knew what she was talking about. "No."

"Do you think she was making it up?"

"No. She was really shaken when I got here. It could've been her imagination, but you tell me, is she prone to exaggeration?"

"She hasn't been, but then again, that was before she was kidnapped by someone who probably wanted to sell her into sexual slavery."

"I heard from Rex yesterday. He said the FBI hasn't been able to find any additional information yet."

Everly sighed. "But they do still think it's a sex-trafficking ring?"

"Yeah. The MO fits. Kidnapping all those girls around the same time, who all look very different, isn't something a run-of-the-mill kidnapper would normally do."

"So we just wait?" Everly asked.

"We just wait," Ball confirmed.

"Waiting sucks."

He couldn't help it, he chuckled. "Yeah, Ev, it does." Then his tone turned somber. "What was it?"

"What was what?" she asked.

"What was it I did that made you change your mind about us?"

He wasn't sure she was going to answer, but finally, she said softly, "My life is so screwed up. The last thing you need is to get involved with me and my issues. I don't want to fuck with your head the way your ex did."

He turned to look at her. "How do you figure you'll do that?"

Everly shrugged. "I'm probably going to have my teenage sister living with me for the foreseeable future. She's deaf, and while that means little to me, I know how much she'll have to struggle in today's society. Employers will assume she's stupid simply because she can't hear. She'll be made fun of and mocked. My grandparents aren't getting any younger, and they're living in a city I hate. My mom is a bitch. And I have to figure out how to help Elise get through what happened to her, keep her safe, *and* go to work so I can keep a roof over our heads. I have no idea how to do all of that *and* have a boyfriend at the same time. I just figured it would be easier for both of us if we let it go."

"You want to know how you do all that and have a boyfriend at the same time?" Ball asked.

Everly looked up at him, but didn't respond.

"You let your boyfriend help. You don't have to do everything on your own, Ev."

"I don't want to take advantage of you," she replied.

"Letting me help you isn't taking advantage. Let me put it this way . . . if something happened to me during one of my missions, and I had to be in a wheelchair for a few months, what would you do?"

"It's not the same thing," she protested.

"Isn't it?" Ball countered.

She stubbornly shook her head.

"Let me help you," Ball pleaded. "We don't have to date. Believe it or not, I understand your reluctance. But let me help you get Elise settled. As I suggested before, she can come over to my house after school and continue to help me with signing. I'll make sure she does her homework and that she stays off the internet. If I have to go on a mission, I'll get Allye, Chloe, or one of the others to stay with her."

"But I don't even know them," Everly protested.

"Then I'll introduce you. Allye's pregnant, and she's already in that mothering stage where she loves everyone. She's going to adore Elise . . . not that the others won't."

Everly closed her eyes and put her head back on Ball's shoulder. "I'm scared."

"Me too."

"Are you?"

"Yeah, Ev. My last relationship crashed and burned, and what do I know about teenage girls? Nothing. But I'm willing to give this a try. If you're hesitating because of me, all you have to do is say so. The last thing I want is to find out in a few months that the chemistry I'm feeling is one-sided. I'll still introduce you to the other women, and they'll still do what they can to help. Rex will still bend over backward to get to the bottom of what happened and take down whoever's responsible. Accepting help from me doesn't come with strings."

She sat up . . . and then boldly straddled his lap.

Surprised, Ball gripped her hips to steady her.

"I'm not hesitating because of you . . . Well, not in the way you mean. I just . . . I was scared by how much I came to rely on you when we were in LA. I've never been that way with anyone else in my life, and it worried me. I don't want to become one of those women who can't do anything without checking with her boyfriend first. Who can't make decisions on her own."

Ball couldn't help it. He laughed.

Everly glared at him. "I'm being serious here."

"I know, and I'm sorry. But Ev, I have no doubt you'll never be *that* kind of woman. One of the things I admire most about you is the fact that you *don't* need me. Holly rarely made decisions on her own. I had to decide what we would eat for dinner, when to go to the grocery store, where we were going on dates, who was driving anywhere. It was exhausting."

Everly studied him for a moment longer, then sagged into him.

Ball held her close to his chest and shifted to put his feet up on the coffee table in front of him. He couldn't believe how well they fit together. "Give me a chance, Ev," he said quietly. "Give *us* a chance."

She nodded, and Ball felt as if he'd just won the lottery.

They sat in silence on her couch, just enjoying each other's company for a long while. So long that Ball felt the moment when Everly became deadweight in his arms. She'd fallen asleep.

Shifting as slowly as possible so he didn't wake her up, Ball shoved a pillow under his head and relaxed into the couch. He had no idea how long she'd sleep that way, but he wasn't going to do anything to wake her up. She needed rest, and he'd do whatever he could to help her get it.

Closing his eyes, Ball sent up a silent prayer that things would work out. Elise would heal, Everly would learn to trust him, and Rex would figure out if there was still a threat against Elise. For now, he was going to treasure the trust Everly had given him by letting down her guard enough to fall asleep in his arms.

~

In her room, Elise covered her head with her blankets and turned on her phone. It was new. Everly had bought it for her the day they'd arrived in Colorado Springs. It was also a newer version than her old one, so that was cool.

She clicked on the app store and downloaded a calculator app.

But it wasn't a calculator at all. Rob had told her about the secret app so they could talk without worrying about anyone sticking their noses into their business. At the time, she'd thought it sweet and somewhat daring. Now, it just seemed creepy.

But she couldn't help but wonder if what happened didn't have anything to do with Rob. The boy she'd thought she knew was sweet, and he'd always been ultraconcerned about her.

Trapped in that house, she'd been convinced Rob didn't exist. She knew Everly and Ball were also sure the person she'd been talking to for all those months was the same one who'd kidnapped her.

Now, safe in Colorado Springs . . . Elise couldn't help but hope they were all wrong.

She had to know one way or another.

Trusting Everly was either asleep or still talking to Ball, she clicked on the icon for the messaging app and logged in.

What she saw horrified her.

Not only were the last messages she and Rob had sent to each other still there, but he'd written to her after she'd been rescued as well.

Rob: I'm excited about meeting u 2day.

Elise: Me 2.

Rob: Meet me across from that gas station near your school.

Elise: OK.

Rob: Elise?

Elise: Yeah?

Rob: I love you.

Elise: I love you too.

Rob: C u soon.

That had been the last message she'd seen before she'd been kidnapped. The next ones were dated the day *after* she'd been rescued.

Rob: You're the one.

Rob: My favorite.

Rob: We're meant to be together.

Rob: The other girls didn't compare to you.

Rob: No one will love you like I will. I'll never leave you. We'll make a beautiful family.

The cops and Everly were right. Rob didn't exist. She'd been talking to the old guy the entire time. Not the beautiful boy she'd dreamed about.

Without thinking about the consequences, Elise quickly typed a response.

Elise: You're sick! You're not 17, you're old. You hurt me! You lied to me just like my mom always does. Leave me alone!!!

As if he'd been sitting around waiting for her response, his answer popped up immediately.

Rob: Never. You're mine.

Terrified, Elise clicked out of the app and immediately deleted it from her phone. She sat up and threw the phone on the floor, not even caring if she broke it. Then she lay back down, covered her head once more, and sobbed.

Chapter Nine

Five days later, Everly paused outside the run-down-looking bar/pool hall. The sign was crooked and looked like it would be knocked down with one strong windstorm. The wood panels on the outside of the building gave it a rustic feel.

As if he could read her mind, Ball said, "It's not as bad as it looks."

Everly raised an eyebrow. "I've been here, remember?"

He chuckled. "Right. Come on."

She felt his hand on the small of her back as she dutifully headed for the door. It was around noon, and Elise was at school. Everly had the day off, and Ball had decided it was time for her to reacquaint herself with his team and meet their women. He'd arranged for everyone to gather here at The Pit.

Everly was nervous. These were Ball's friends. The men and women he'd move heaven and earth for, if required. If they didn't like her, she had a feeling the relationship between her and Ball was screwed.

And it definitely felt as if she *was* in a relationship. How it had happened, Everly wasn't sure. It wasn't so long ago that she'd walked into this bar and overheard Ball bad-mouthing her. She'd been pissed and a little hurt.

But he'd managed to crawl under her defenses. Not a day went by now when she didn't see him, even if it was just for thirty minutes or so. A few days ago, he'd popped over to her apartment right after she'd finished her shift just to drop off a lasagna that he'd made for her and Elise. Another day, he came over after Elise had gone to bed, and they'd sat around and talked until she'd looked down at her watch and realized it was one in the morning.

He'd asked about Me-Maw and Pop and kept her up to date on the trafficking investigation being done back in LA. And then there had been the texts. He was constantly sending her messages, just letting her know he was thinking about her, or telling her what Rex had found, or sending her a silly joke.

Not only that, but he'd been texting Elise as well. Everly'd had a long talk with her sister about internet safety, and even though it was a little late, she figured it was better than never. Every morning, Everly checked Elise's phone. She wasn't happy about having to do it, just as Elise wasn't happy that her sister was checking up on her, but she understood why.

And every morning, Everly scrolled through pages and pages of texts between Ball and Elise. Her little sister was slowly opening up more and more to Ball, and not surprisingly, he was extremely sensitive in his responses. He listened to her worries about finding friends, fitting in at school . . . they'd even had a fairly in-depth conversation about sex and relationships. Topics Elise wouldn't discuss with Everly. Particularly, what men like the guy who'd kidnapped her got out of hurting women, and how Elise should never have sex if someone was pressuring her. One comment really stood out for Everly:

Ball: Sex can be many things . . . passionate, quick, slow, hilarious, playful, and serious. But one thing it should never be is painful. Or manipulative. On your part or his.

Everly had never had playful sex. Or even sex that was all that passionate. But he was right on the money in saying it shouldn't be manipulative or painful.

Ball was insightful, and sensitive to what Elise had been through, and it made Everly like him all the more.

But their conversations weren't all emotional land mines. He'd also sent short videos of him signing. He was getting better, but was still pretty rough. Elise was extremely patient as she corrected him, and she'd even sent some videos back of herself, demonstrating signs.

Everly loved seeing the relationship blossom between her sister and Ball, but it also worried her. She didn't think Ball was the kind of man who would drop out of Elise's life if things between him and Everly didn't work out, but that didn't stop her from at least thinking about it.

Ball was almost everything she'd ever wanted in a partner—and that scared the shit out of her. Her life was crazy enough as it was. She wasn't sure she wanted to—or could—fit a man into everything else she had going on. But she couldn't deny that it felt good being with him.

They entered the bar, and it was just as Everly remembered it. A little dark, the smell of alcohol prominent, and music coming out of a jukebox in the corner of the front room. She assumed the music would be turned up as the place got busier and the hour got later, but for now, it was simply quiet background noise. Ball led her over to the bar.

"Everly, this is Noah Ganter. There are several bartenders, but Noah and Dave are here the most."

She held out her hand. "Hi, it's good to meet you." The bartender was probably in his late twenties, and he had that boy-next-door look about him. His brown hair was tousled, and his hazel eyes sparkled with humor. He looked happy, as if he didn't have a care in the world.

"Same," Noah said. "Can I get you something to drink?"

It was still early, and even though she wasn't driving, Everly wasn't much of a drinker. "A Coke?"

"You asking me or telling me?" Noah responded with a grin.

Everly smiled back. "Telling."

Noah reached for a can of Coke and put it on the bar in front of her. "And before you ask, women at The Pit always get bottled water, and they always get canned soda. This is a pretty safe bar, but shit happens. Though it's *not* going to happen if we can help it."

Everly liked that. She took the can with a nod. "Appreciate it."

"Anytime."

Noah reached for a glass and poured Ball a ginger ale. He put a lime and a lemon in the glass and scooted it over the bar toward him. "You know, you could just order a Sprite. It would be the same thing."

"I like this," Ball said.

Throughout the short conversation, Ball's hand had been resting on her lower back, and now he put a little pressure on his hand to steer her away from the bar.

But before they got too far away, Noah called out, "Everly?"

She turned. "Yeah?"

"If you ever get tired of Ball, I'm single."

Everly laughed. She had a feeling Noah would be a fun person to date, but when push came to shove, she much preferred Ball's intensity.

"Seriously?" Ball growled from next to her.

Everly put her arm around Ball's waist and hugged him to her side. "Thanks!" she told Noah. "I'll keep that in mind."

"You will not," Ball muttered as he turned to the door that led to the back.

Everly heard the din of a large group of people talking before they went through the door. The second they stepped into the room, the talking stopped, and everyone turned toward them.

She'd seen them all before, but the circumstances were different. She'd been there to get details on how the Mountain Mercenaries were going to help find her sister. Now she was there for a social visit.

Normally she didn't care what people thought about her. As a cop, she was used to snide comments and people hating her on sight. But she wasn't here as an officer of the law. She was with Ball, and she knew without a doubt she was going to be judged.

He led them over to the group standing around two pool tables. Without leaving her side, he greeted the men with a chin lift.

"About time you got here," one of the women said.

Ball smiled. "Sorry to keep you waiting, Allye."

So this was the infamous Allye. Everly had heard a lot about her, and Ball had even mentioned that maybe she'd be willing to talk to Elise, since she'd also been kidnapped.

The pregnant woman came up to them and gave Ball a brief hug. She turned to Everly. "Hi, I'm Allye. I'm with Gray. I'm so glad your sister is all right."

And with that short introduction, Allye solidified a place in Everly's heart. Concern for her sister's welfare right off the bat made Everly like the woman immediately.

"Me too," Everly said.

"What's really scary is that it could happen to anyone," said a woman about the same height as Elise. "I mean, teenagers are so vulnerable, and assholes like whoever took her know that. Oh, and I'm Chloe."

"Hi," Everly said.

Another woman came up next and hugged Everly tightly. She had blonde hair with the ends dyed purple. Everly generally didn't like people she didn't know touching her, but knowing these were Ball's friends made it tolerable, and the other woman pulled back quickly. "I'm Harlow. I'm sorry about what happened to your sister, but I admire you for bringing her back here to live with you. And with our men on the case, I know she's gonna be safe."

"Thanks."

Everly recognized the next woman who stepped forward. She blinked in surprise. If she'd been there the last time she was at The Pit, Everly hadn't realized it. She'd know this woman anywhere . . . Morgan Byrd. Possibly the most famous missing person the United States had seen in years.

"Hi, Everly. I'm Morgan," the petite woman said.

"I know," Everly replied.

She gave her a small smile. "Yeah, it feels weird to be famous because I was kidnapped. Anyway, I just wanted to say, welcome to the crazy. We're all probably a bit too forthcoming, and we tend to say whatever pops into our heads, but no matter what, we stand by our men and each other. And if you're with Ball, that means you're one of us. This feels weird to say to a cop, because, well . . . you're a *cop*. But if you need anything, all you have to do is ask, and we're there. You need a place for Elise to go while you're working, one of us will be happy to entertain her for you."

Everly wasn't a crier, but she felt tears well up at Morgan's words. Here was a woman who had been through absolute hell. But she hadn't let it beat her. She wanted Elise to meet *her* too. To see that the bad things that happened to her didn't have to define her. That she could move forward without fear and be happy. "Thanks," she croaked out.

She felt Ball's thumb brushing back and forth over the small of her back in silent support. She'd always felt a part of the "brotherhood." The comradery she shared with her fellow police officers was bone deep. But it wasn't like this.

These women had opened up to her as if it was a foregone conclusion that she and Ball would be together forever. They were acting as if she was a permanent part of their little group, when she and Ball hadn't even known each other a month ago.

"And of course, my teammates," Ball said, helping her push back her emotions by moving on with the introductions. "You met most of them already and have talked to some on the phone briefly, but in case you forgot, this is Gray. He knocked up Allye."

Everyone chuckled, and Everly appreciated the reduction in tension.

"And this is Ro. He likes to pretend he's American, but you can tell by his accent that he's a Brit through and through."

"Sod off," Ro said with a smirk. "I've lived here in heathen territory long enough that I can call Sam my uncle too."

"Sam?" Everly asked, looking up at Ball.

"Uncle Sam?" he teased.

"Oh! Duh," Everly said with a smile. "Hi, Ro. It's nice to meet you again."

"And this is Arrow, and Black," Ball said, reintroducing the next two men. Then he turned to the only man not standing with a woman. "Ev, meet Meat. Meat, Everly."

She had the same thought she'd had upon first meeting him—he didn't look anything like what she thought the team's resident computer expert should look like. He was probably around six feet tall, with brown hair and eyes that seemed to switch from gray to stormy blue, then back to gray. He was lean, but with very broad shoulders. He reminded Everly of some of the swimmers she saw in the Olympics.

"What? Don't tell me—I don't look like a computer nerd, do I?" Meat asked.

Everly shrugged and gave him a small smile of apology. "Nope. But honestly, I think it's probably good that you don't look like Charlie Eppes, from that old TV show *Numb3rs*, or Spencer Reid from *Criminal Minds*. I'd never believe that you were former Delta Force, if that was the case. No offense."

Everyone was silent for a second, and Everly thought maybe she'd put her foot in it. Not everyone got her humor.

But then they all burst into laughter. Meat reached forward and gave her a bear hug. Everly almost dropped her can of Coke, but managed to keep hold of it, even when Meat bent her backward dramatically.

"Cut it out," Ball groused.

Everyone laughed harder, Everly included.

When Meat brought her upright, he looked briefly into her eyes—and Everly saw a glimpse of something she hadn't expected to see.

Sadness.

What this amazing man had to be sad about, she had no idea. But the emotion was gone almost as soon as she recognized it.

"It's good to meet you. I've read so many of your texts and messages to your sister over the last few weeks, I feel as if I know you."

Everly rolled her eyes.

"And I'm considering how much trouble I'll get into if I try to blackmail an officer of the law by threatening to let all her cop buddies know how much she loves the Backstreet Boys."

Everly moved without thought. She shoved her Coke at Ball and launched herself at Meat. He laughed and easily deflected her half-hearted attempt to take him to the floor. They playfully grappled for a second, with the women cheering her on, until she ended up with her back to Meat's chest, his arms successfully securing her so she couldn't escape his hold.

He leaned forward and whispered in her ear, "Don't worry, your secret's safe with me."

She didn't have time to respond before Ball smacked Meat on the back of the head. "Get your own girl. Leave mine alone."

Meat grinned and released her. Everly let Ball grab hold of her hand and pull her into his embrace. She rested against him and turned to the girls. "I heard the Backstreet Boys and New Kids on the Block are touring together. Anyone want to go with me to see them?"

All four of the women immediately yelled, "Yes!" at the same time.

Everly stuck her tongue out at Meat. "It's a requirement to love the Backstreet Boys. It's a girl thing, you wouldn't understand."

"That's it," Chloe declared. "We're keeping her." Then she came over to Ball and pulled Everly out of his arms. "Go talk amongst yourselves. We're taking Everly." She tried to pull her away, but Ball didn't let go.

Everly felt his finger rub over her ring, then he leaned forward and kissed her forehead. "If they want you to lead a raid on one of the local chocolate shops, don't let them talk you into it."

She smiled. "I won't."

"Good." Then he slowly let go of her hand, his fingers trailing along her palm for as long as possible before they lost contact.

Chloe pulled her over to a table against a wall while the guys leaned against one of the nearby pool tables.

"Is Elise truly okay?" Morgan asked once they were settled.

Everly nodded. "I think so, but it's hard to tell. I've got her seeing a psychologist every other day to talk about what happened. She doesn't really talk to *me* much about it, though, which I hate."

"She doesn't want to worry you," Allye said. "The people you love the most are the ones you try the hardest to keep your shit from touching."

Everly thought about that. It was true. "She's been talking to Ball about some things, though. About how she thought this Rob person really loved her for who she was. That he didn't care about the fact she was deaf. It just sucks so hard that 'Rob' was some psycho who was using her vulnerabilities against her."

"Yeah. What's the latest on the search for the culprit? Have the other girls been able to shed any light on what happened?" Harlow asked.

"Not really. They had more information than Elise, simply because they could hear, but so far, every lead has been a dead end. It's maddening." Everly sighed. "Not to be rude . . . but do you think we could talk about something else? Not that I don't want you guys to know stuff about my sister and what's going on, but I've literally not thought about anything else in way too long."

"Of course!" Chloe exclaimed. "How rude of us. How about this . . . what are you and Elise doing this weekend? Harlow is using us as guinea pigs for her next cooking class. She runs through recipes with us first, before going into local women's shelters and helping teach the residents how to cook quick, healthy meals."

"I'd love that," Everly said, then turned to Harlow. "How'd you get into that?"

Harlow went into the story about how she'd been hired to be one of two full-time chefs at a women's shelter that had burned to the ground, and now she was doing what she could to help women trying to get back on their feet, teaching them how to cook on a limited budget.

"I know Morgan's story," Everly said after Harlow was done explaining how she and Black had gotten together. "But I don't really know the rest of yours."

"I'm a dancer," Allye said. "Some weirdo got it in his head that he wanted me for his personal collection because of my hair and eyes. I had left town, but he started kidnapping my friends, so I went back."

"Oh shit!" Everly breathed. "And Gray let you?"

Allye winced. "Well . . ."

The others chuckled.

"Not exactly. I kinda left town without him knowing. Yes, that was stupid, and yes, the bad guy got me . . . I think you know that."

Everly nodded.

"But the Mountain Mercenaries came and found me. I still dance for a troupe in Denver now and then, but my passion is teaching kids, especially special-needs kids, right here in Colorado Springs."

"My brother had me doing taxes for the Mob, and he held me hostage in our dead parents' home because he wanted to get his hands on my mom's money," Chloe said matter-of-factly. "The Mob got involved, and they took me, but then they actually let me just walk out of their compound up in Denver. Ro and the others were all ready to storm the castle, so to speak, and then there I was, walking out. It was surreal."

"And your brother?" Everly asked.

"Not a problem anymore," Chloe said succinctly. "Anyway, I don't work full-time now, but I used to be a financial adviser. I still have my official certifications and everything. I'm sure you probably have your shit together, but if you ever want any financial advice, I'm happy to help."

"Thanks. I was good, but now with Elise living with me, I probably should rethink some of my investment strategy," Everly said.

"I'm no good with money, and I probably couldn't fight my way out of a paper bag," Morgan said, "but if you want a nice jar of fresh honey, I've got you covered."

Everly laughed. "I'd love that."

"Arrow and I are building a house up in Black Forest, and I went ahead and got a hive going—a good distance away from the construction, of course. I can't wait for the house to be done so we can truly settle in."

"Morgan is a motivational speaker," Allye said. "She goes around to schools and conferences and things and talks about overcoming obstacles and making the most of your life."

Everly was impressed. She'd seen her share of women who never got over the things that happened to them. They let their attacker, abuser, or crappy situation get the better of them, often repeatedly. They turned to drugs to self-medicate and turned off their emotions. From where she was sitting, Morgan was one hell of a woman.

"What happened to me sucked," Morgan said. "There's no getting around that. But I only have one life to live. If I let one year ruin the next forty, what does that say about me? Besides, I have a hell of a lot to live for."

"You certainly do," Allye said emphatically.

Morgan smiled at her friend. "I mean, outside of the *normal* lot to live for." Her hand went to her belly. "I'm pregnant," she whispered.

Her announcement set up a flurry of congratulations and excitement from the others at the table. So much so that the guys came over to make sure everything was all right. After much assurance, and more congratulations from the men, things calmed down, and the women were alone once again.

"I guess that means you were able to get over your mental roadblock when it came to sex," Chloe quipped.

Everly thought it was kind of an insensitive thing to say, but since Morgan just grinned, clearly she didn't think so.

"Obviously. And it took way too long for my peace of mind. I hated not being able to make love to Arrow. *Hated* it. But he never pressured me. There were times I wished he would push me harder, as a matter of fact. But once we were actually doing the deed, I realized that there was absolutely nothing similar about making love with Arrow and what happened to me before. And the rest, as they say, is history. I jumped him every chance possible, and lo and behold, now I'm about seven weeks along."

"I'm so happy for you," Allye said. "And me. I'm scared to death about being a mother. I'm afraid I'm going to screw my kid up somehow. Knowing someone else will be having a kid not long after me is a relief."

"I feel the same way," Morgan reassured her. "I know I'm going to be super overprotective, and I'm going to need you guys to rein me in, okay?"

Everyone answered in the affirmative.

"What made you want to be a cop?" Harlow asked once the excitement over Morgan's big news was over.

Everly had been enjoying not being the center of attention. It was inspiring to watch the dynamics between the friends. They were supportive without being judgmental, and it was nice to see they were able to talk about their past experiences openly and honestly, without feeling as if they had to try to pretend they were perfectly okay after what they'd been through.

She was especially interested in Morgan's story. She made a mental note to see if she could find some of her speeches on the internet to show Elise.

"I'm not sure, really . . . No, that's a lie." Everly decided to be completely honest with these women. They'd made her feel more welcome than she'd ever felt before, and she knew without a doubt that they wouldn't judge her. "I was seven, I think. My mom had been gone for at least a day, maybe more. I was in our crappy apartment by myself after school. I was hungry, and there wasn't much to eat because Mom had spent what money she had on drugs. She burst into the apartment and slammed the door behind her. She was yelling for me to hide, and if someone knocked on the door, to stay quiet and not answer it. She shoved me into my bedroom and locked me in, for my own safety, she claimed.

"I didn't know what was happening, but instead of being scared, I got mad. That very day in school, one of the kids in my class had a birthday party. Her mom brought in these beautiful cupcakes. They were professionally decorated, and we all sang 'Happy Birthday.' And I realized my mom wasn't normal. I'd had my suspicions for a long time, but I guess that was the day it hit home more than ever. So instead of hiding under my bed like I usually did, I crept to the window and looked out.

"I stayed there for the next two hours, watching as the police did a raid on one of the apartments across the parking lot from ours. There were these two female officers . . . I'll never forget them. They were right there when the doors were bashed in, and I thought they were so brave. Two men and three women were brought out of the two apartments, and even though one of them was handcuffed, he decided to fight. Was probably high. And those two females brought him to the ground so fast, I couldn't believe it. They were so much smaller than he was, but it didn't matter. I decided right then and there I wanted to be just like them.

"I knew what drugs were, and I hated that my mom did them. She'd promise to stop, but she never did. After they took the adults out of the house, they brought out four kids. Probably around ages two to four. They looked scared to death, and again, those two policewomen took control of them, and within minutes, the kids were smiling and happy because they'd been given little stuffed animals and glow sticks.

"I sat at my window long after the cops left, and things got quiet again. My mom unlocked the door and tried to pretend like nothing happened. That it was normal for a drug bust to happen across the way. I knew it could've just as easily been our apartment. I wanted to be able to kick the butt of any guy or girl who dared make fun of me too. I wanted to make those policewomen proud, even if they never knew how much they'd changed my life."

There was silence after her story, and Everly thought for a second that she'd been too open. That she should've just gone with her original statement, letting them think she didn't really know. She'd just met these women—they didn't need to hear her sob story.

She opened her mouth to say something, anything, when an arm came around her diagonally from behind.

She recognized it immediately as belonging to Ball, so she didn't shove her chair backward and send him flying over her shoulder.

"You should've seen her out in LA," Ball said, the pride easy to hear in his voice. "She took on two assholes who'd jumped me as if they didn't outweigh her and weren't easily several inches taller. We also went to her sister's school a couple of times to try to see if we could get any leads on where Elise had gone, ultimately to no avail, but that's beside the point. Anyway, Everly was easily able to gain the kids' trust." He kissed her on the side of the head. "I'd say you more than made those policewomen proud, Ev. You about ready to go? Elise will be home from school in thirty minutes or so."

Surprised that so much time had passed, Everly looked down at her watch. "Shoot. Yeah, I'm ready."

It took quite a bit of time to say goodbye to everyone. Unlike on the rare occasion when she went out with fellow cops, everyone wanted to give her a hug and have just a few more words with her. To tell her how lucky Elise was to have Everly as a sister. And to express how glad they were that she was a cop in their city. That she'd better get used to hanging out because they were going to bug the crap out of her to join them whenever possible, and they were looking forward to meeting and getting to know Elise.

The entire experience had been overwhelming . . . in a good way. It was no wonder she liked Ball so much; he had friends like these to keep him grounded. And yeah, he'd been an ass when she'd first walked into The Pit and met him, but she'd seen the aggravated looks his buddies had given him that day. They hadn't condoned his behavior. Had probably even conned him somehow into going to LA with her . . . not that she was complaining.

When Meat hugged her goodbye, he told her that he'd been able to get a few conversations off of Elise's old phone, and that he'd send them over to her and Ball later.

Everly nodded. She wasn't sure she was ready to see how this "Rob" person had manipulated her sister, but she needed to know, to possibly figure out how to prevent it from happening to Elise, and other teens, in the future.

She waved bye to Noah as they left, and he cheekily held up a hand to his ear, mimicking a phone, and mouthed, "Call me." Ball scowled at him, but the bartender merely laughed and waved.

When they were outside, Ball shook his head. "Jeez. I swear I hadn't realized how obnoxious they were. If I had, I wouldn't have brought you here."

"I bet you were exactly the same way when you met their women," Everly said.

Ball put a hand on his chest in exaggerated surprise. "Me?"

She could only laugh. When they got to his Mustang, he turned her before opening the door, trapping her against the warm metal. "You okay?"

"Yeah, why?"

"I didn't mean to eavesdrop, but I didn't want to interrupt you. That was kinda intense."

"Ball, compared to what the others went through, my story isn't the least bit intense. I wasn't beaten. Me-Maw and Pop made sure to see me at least once a week and stuff me full of healthy food."

Ball shook his head. "Don't compare what you went through with what the others did. They were different circumstances, and you were only a kid. Your mother should've protected you. Made sure you were safe and fed. She did none of that. If she'd done the best she could, she would've gotten off the drugs and done everything in her power to protect you. And for the record, Ev, I don't want to meet her. Ever. I don't think I'd be able to keep my mouth shut."

"I wasn't planning on introducing you to her. Ever," she said, intentionally repeating his proclamation.

"Good." He brushed a lock of hair off her forehead and stared into her eyes. "Every time I think to myself that you're too good to be true and I should take a step back, be more cautious with whatever it is that's happening between us, you knock my feet out from under me."

"I'm sorry?"

He chuckled. "Don't be sorry. I feel as if I've waited my whole life for you. That I had to go through all the other shit in my life just to appreciate you."

Wow. That was . . . Everly didn't know *what* that was. But Ball didn't give her a chance to respond.

"I don't know the first thing about teenage girls, but I *do* know that Elise is going to be okay. She's got you as a role model. How could she be anything but?"

Then he kissed her on the forehead and leaned over to open the passenger door.

Everly sat, not sure what to say. But he obviously didn't expect her to say *anything*. He simply climbed into the driver's side and headed for her apartment.

~

That night, Everly watched as Ball and Elise both made fun of his latest attempts to communicate. He never seemed to get frustrated, and he no longer relied on Everly to translate for him. He and Elise muddled through, and if either of them got stuck, they picked up their phones sitting nearby and texted each other.

Everly had never dated anyone who'd gotten along with her sister like Ball did. Granted, not many of her boyfriends had even met Elise, but the few who did were uncomfortable when she and Elise had a conversation they couldn't understand, and they hadn't made even the smallest effort to learn any signs.

She might've thought Ball was trying too hard to impress her, except when he and Elise started "talking," Everly may as well have not even existed.

It was after dinner, and Elise and Ball had been at it for at least an hour, when Everly heard a sound she hadn't heard in more than a decade.

Her eyes whipped up, and she stared at her sister in surprise.

She was *laughing*. Out loud. Hard. Her head was thrown back, and she was holding her stomach, laughing so much that tears were coming out of her eyes.

When Elise finally recovered enough to talk, she nodded and repeated the sign for *bullshit*. She made horns with her pinkie and pointer finger on one hand, holding that arm up, and formed a fist with the other, touching it to the opposite elbow, opening and closing her hand quickly. Like crap coming out of the back end of a bull.

Ball laughed and repeated the sign.

Everly had no idea how long her sister had been teaching Ball dirty words. She stood and walked over to the pair. She didn't want to end their fun, but felt somewhat obligated to break it up. "What are you guys doing?" she asked, even though it was pretty obvious.

Without guile, Ball said, "Elise is teaching me how to swear. Look." He made a circle with the fingers of one hand and slammed the middle finger of the other inside. "Asshole."

Everly rolled her eyes. "I know what it means. I'm not sure my little sister should be teaching you that stuff. *She* shouldn't even know it." Everly was signing as she spoke so Elise wouldn't feel left out of the conversation.

Everly, seriously? I'm fifteen. I'm not a nun. Of course I know how to swear.

How about you say good night to Ball and get ready for bed? You've got school in the morning, and I have to work.

Elise pouted, but couldn't hold it for long. She smiled immediately, signed *good night*, and beamed at Ball when he returned it. She hugged Everly and headed for her room.

"She's a good kid," Ball said when her door shut behind her.

"Yeah. I can't take credit for that, though. It was all Me-Maw and Pop."

"Now *that* I don't believe," Ball told her, yanking on her hand and pulling her down to sit next to him. "I had a long talk with your grandmother while I was there, and she told me how you called and Skyped all the time, and also how you got your mother to let Elise go when she went to live with them full-time."

Everly shrugged. After Elise had made her way to Me-Maw and Pop's on her own, Ella wasn't too happy when she'd found out. And she *did* try to take her back. She wanted to keep control over Elise for some reason, and she couldn't do that if she moved out.

Everly didn't want to remember the way she'd threatened her own mother. In the end, Ella had been more concerned about not being turned in to the cops than keeping her daughter. That had been the last time Everly had seen her mother, and she didn't much care.

"She also said you sent money so Elise could attend her deaf school, and you visited as often as you could."

"It wasn't enough," Everly said sadly. "She still fell prey to someone because of her insecurities."

"That's not your fault. I think all teenagers feel lost at one point or another."

Just then, both Everly's and Ball's phones vibrated.

Ball got to his first. "It's Meat. He sent over the conversations he's been able to recover from her old phone. They're from an app called Omegle. Essentially, it's a free online chat app that lets people talk to each other without registering or putting in their identifying details."

Everly still wasn't sure she wanted to see them.

"I don't understand why there are all these apps that make it so easy for pedophiles and complete assholes to prey on teenagers and other vulnerable people," Everly grumbled.

"Me either. Come here," Ball said, and held up his arm. Everly snuggled into his side on the couch and pushed a hand behind his back to hug him. Being next to him like this felt so right. As if being close to Ball would protect her from all the bad things in the world.

~

Having Everly against him like this made him feel ten feet tall. As if he could protect her from all the evils in the world. He knew she wasn't thrilled about seeing the proof of how Elise had been duped, but they both needed to see what she'd written, to make sure she wasn't ever that vulnerable again.

"Ready?" Ball asked before clicking on the file Meat had sent.

Everly took a deep breath, then nodded.

"Okay. Remember, Rob is 'Stranger 1,' and Elise is 'You' in the conversation."

She nodded once more before they read the conversations in silence.

Stranger 1: Hey, beautiful.

You: Hi, Rob.

Stranger 1: How was school?

You: Boring.

Stranger 1: That's because ur so smart.

You: Whatever.

Stranger 1: It's true. Ur the smartest person I know.

Stranger 1: Why someone like u is talking to me, I don't know.

You: Because I like you.

Stranger 1: I like you too.

Stranger 1: Sometimes I get so lonely.

You: Me 2.

Stranger 1: Do you feel as if no one knows what u r thinking or feeling?

You: All the time.

Stranger 1: U r the only 1 I feel I can talk to.

You: Really?

Stranger 1: Yeah. U get me like no one else does.

You: I feel the same.

Stranger 1: When r u gonna send me a picture?

You: I don't know about that.

Stranger 1: Why not? Here, I'll send 1 of me.

Stranger 1: There. See? I'm harmless.

Stranger 1: Please?

You: Fine. Here.

Stranger 1: Beautiful. Inside and out.

Ball wanted to throw up at the way the guy had reeled in Elise. Making her feel important. Making her feel as if they shared something special. And the picture he'd sent was definitely that of a teenage boy, probably taken off someone's social media account. He kept reading.

Stranger 1: I love seeing ur smiling face.

You: Same.

Stranger 1: Im sorry ur mom didn't message u back.

You: Me too. I mean, I know she doesn't really care, but I hoped since it was my bday she would.

Stranger 1: I know, baby. U deserve more. I wish I could c u and say HB in person.

You: Me too.

Stranger 1: Maybe we should meet.

Stranger 1: Elise?

You: I'm here.

Stranger 1: I want to c u. Be with u. I wouldn't ignore u on ur bday.

You: I just don't know.

Stranger 1: Think about it.

"Notice how he's always the first to message her?" Everly asked quietly.

"Yeah. Although Meat said he wasn't able to recover all of the messages from all the apps. For all we know, Elise was messaging him elsewhere first," Ball said.

"I don't know. He's playing her. Complimenting her, bringing up things he knows will upset her so he can comfort her."

"Yeah," Ball said. It was classic predator behavior, and Elise had played right into his hands.

Stranger 1: I miss u so much. I hated not talking 2 u this morning. But it's ur fault.

You: I know.

Stranger 1: If u had messaged me when I told u 2 then we wouldn't have fought.

You: I'm sorry.

Stranger 1: It's OK. I love u. Do u love me?

You: U know I do.

Stranger 1: Have u thought more about meeting me?

You: Yeah.

Stranger 1: And?

You: I'm scared u aren't going to like me if we do.

Stranger 1: Not like you? Elise, I love u.

Stranger 1: I'm the only one who says u r pretty.

Stranger 1: I'm starting to think u might be seeing someone else.

You: I'm not.

Stranger 1: Then why don't u want to meet me?

Stranger 1: Maybe you should have time to think about it.

Stranger 1: I'll talk 2 u later. Maybe.

You: No! I'm sorry.

You: Rob?

You: Come back!

You: I don't have to think about it. I love u.

"Bastard," Ball muttered. He could feel the way Everly held herself tense against him, and knew she was just as angry.

Stranger 1: I'm so excited.

You: Me 2.

Stranger 1: I can't wait to meet you.

You: Me too.

Stranger 1: I love u.

You: I love u 2.

Ball clicked out of the document, put his phone down, and wrapped both arms around Everly. She hadn't said much, but it was obvious she was affected.

"Are they going to find him?" she asked after a while.

"I don't know. If it's a trafficker, you know how these groups are organized. There are layers upon layers of players. Whoever was playing the role of Rob online could be on the other side of the country, or even outside it. The person who picked Elise up is probably a low-level player who was allowed to do what he wanted with the girls until they were picked up by someone else. Most likely, arrangements were being made for different people to take them out of that house. It's so hard to catch these guys, but the FBI is doing what they can to track down their trail."

"I'm just scared for her. I check her phone every morning and don't see that she's downloaded any of the apps that were on her other phone, but I know she's way more tech savvy than I am. And every day, there are more apps developed for teenagers that will help them talk to whoever they want without their parents knowing. It's creepy as hell," Everly said.

"I know. But I honestly think Elise has learned her lesson. She was shaken to the core by what happened. She's not stupid. She knows she had a very close call. She's not going to make the same mistake again," Ball tried to reassure her.

"Ball?"

"Yeah?"

"Thanks."

"For what?"

"For being here for me. For being so awesome with Elise and trying to learn sign language. You have no idea how much that means to her. Thank you for introducing me to your friends, they're awesome. Just . . . thank you."

"You absolutely don't have to thank me," Ball said. "I have no doubt even if I wasn't around, you and Elise would've gotten your feet under you again. I should be thanking *you* for giving me a second chance."

He tipped her chin up and brushed his lips against hers. The second they touched, he shivered. The electricity between them was hot, and getting more and more demanding every day. But Ball refused to rush them. Things had already moved fast enough, and the last thing he wanted to do was something that might make Everly think twice about a relationship.

Besides, Elise was in the other room. She couldn't hear them, but she could come out of her room to ask her sister something at any time.

He respected both Everly and Elise enough not to put any of them in an awkward situation.

They made out for a while, and when Ball felt Everly's hand cover his hard cock, he forced himself to pull back. He didn't reach for her hand, because it felt absolutely perfect where it was. "We should stop," he murmured, even as he leaned forward and nuzzled the skin on her neck.

Everly chuckled. "You think?"

For a split second, Ball wanted to pick her up and carry her into her room, but he forced himself to take a deep breath, even though that made it even harder to pull back, since her scent filled his nostrils. "We have plenty of time to go there," he told her, not able to endure the feel of her hand on his dick any longer. He picked up her hand and kissed each of her fingers before doing the same to her palm.

"I'm thirty-four, Ball. I'm not a teenager who doesn't know what she wants."

"And I'm forty, old enough to know what I want too. And that isn't some quickie orgasm on your couch, all the while worrying if your teenage sister is going to come out and bust us. I like you. A hell of a lot. And I want to see where this relationship between us can go. But I don't think slowing down will hurt either of us. I never want you to think I'm only with you because I want some. You're the first woman I've wanted to actually have a real relationship with since the fiasco with Holly. I don't want to do anything to fuck this up."

She stared at him for a long moment, and Ball was afraid she might be pissed. But then she nodded and snuggled into his side once more. Her hand came to rest on his belly, instead of his dick, which was both a relief and a disappointment at the same time. "We can still make out here and there, right?" she asked.

Ball chuckled. "Absolutely. In fact, I think I might insist on it. Our time will come, Everly. And I don't mean that as a bad pun."

She giggled.

"For the first time in my life, I'm enjoying simply being with a woman without sex being held over my head. Not to say I don't want to make love to you—I do—but for now, I'm just enjoying getting to know you better. Does that make sense?"

"Yeah. I feel the same way."

Ball exhaled in relief. "Want me to stay? I know you have to work in the morning."

"Just for a little bit longer," Everly said.

Ball reached over, grabbed the remote, and turned to the Science Channel. There was a show on about Chernobyl and the effects on the land around it, even after all this time.

Within thirty minutes, Everly was snoozing in his arms, and Ball couldn't think of anything he enjoyed more than watching her sleep.

Chapter Ten

We're going to be late! Elise signed.

No we're not, Everly told her sister. *Calm down.*

Ball's driving like Pop!

Everly translated for Ball, and he laughed.

"I can't exactly drive eighty miles an hour through the Broadmoor neighborhood," he said, and smiled as Everly translated for her sister.

The hike's supposed to start at ten. It's nine forty-five. We're going to be late! Elise signed again in agitation.

A month had passed since Everly had met Ball's friends and they'd gotten the transcript of the messages between Elise and the mysterious Rob. Elise had met twice with Morgan, and each time, Everly could see some of the tension Elise had held close to her chest dissipate. Through an interpreter, she and Morgan had talked about how it felt to be scared and alone and wonder if anyone would ever find you. They'd discussed Elise's anger that someone had tried to manipulate and deceive her, and how frustrated she was that the people who'd done it hadn't been caught.

Elise had also gone into the Colorado Springs Police Department and met with their sketch artist. The completed drawing of the man who'd claimed to be Rob's father had been sent off to the FBI and the LAPD—but interestingly enough, there weren't too many similarities between the seven sketches done with each of the seven victims. Because the van that had picked up all the girls had been the same—a boxy, nondescript white van—but the sketches of the suspect weren't, the police determined that it was almost impossible to narrow down what the kidnapper really looked like, except that he was a white male with brown hair.

Elise still had the occasional nightmare, but spending time with Allye, Chloe, Morgan, and Harlow seemed to be good for her. It helped her improve her social skills around hearing people, and because the other women were so down-to-earth and accepting, she never felt awkward or uncomfortable with them.

Everly and her sister had also figured out an easy routine in their new lives together in Colorado Springs, and Everly kicked herself daily for not bringing Elise out earlier. Yes, the school in Los Angeles had a better overall academic program, but when it came to her sister, Everly realized she should've concentrated more on her mental well-being than her academic concerns.

Me-Maw and Pop were thrilled by how well Elise was doing and wanted to make a trip to Colorado to see both their grandchildren. They hadn't heard from their daughter, but what Ella did was on her. Plain and simple.

Everly and Ball had dialed down their physical relationship, and she definitely knew him much better now because of all the time they'd spent together, just talking. She knew that he was the best driver of all the Mountain Mercenaries, and that he'd never let anyone but *her* drive his Mustang. Not even his friends. He'd told her one night that if he couldn't trust a cop with his "baby," who could he trust? She'd laughed—and enjoyed getting it up to one hundred miles an hour on the interstate, just to see what he'd do. He hadn't panicked, just lifted one eyebrow at her.

Everly knew that when Ball put his mind to something, like learning sign language, he didn't do it halfway. He'd spent hours and hours watching videos online to try to teach himself, and he and Elise had spent many a night working together as well. He still wasn't fluent, but he could pretty much hold his own when conversing with Elise and her friends. He had to resort to finger spelling sometimes, but everyone was always patient with him.

Elise seemed to blossom in her new school. She'd made some new friends and joined the Outdoor Club. There were a ton of excellent hiking spots in Colorado Springs, and she'd gotten the bug after one short after-school orientation hike.

This was the third hike she'd done with the group, and this time Everly and Ball had signed up to chaperone. As a surprise, they'd asked Meat to join them. Elise had taken an immediate liking to the man, and the feeling was mutual. He'd learned a few signs, but the two of them mostly communicated via texting.

Everly always shook her head at the exchanges between the two when she checked Elise's phone. She'd backed off to only checking her sister's phone once or twice a week. Elise had sworn up and down that she was done with all the apps she'd been using. That she didn't ever want to talk to a boy online again, and she definitely wasn't going to meet up with someone she didn't personally know—ever. And Everly believed her. It had been a hard lesson, but it seemed like Elise had definitely learned it.

While Ball and Elise's conversations were sweet, the ones between her and Meat were hilarious. The man never seemed to say anything serious, and was always joking with Elise. Everly was glad her sister was seeing how good men should act around women. Between Meat and Ball and the other men, she was getting a real education, and learning to trust again.

Seven Bridges Trail was located at the top of the prestigious Broadmoor neighborhood. The trail itself wasn't too strenuous and was shaded pretty much throughout. There were supposed to be ten kids coming today, and Everly was looking forward to getting to know a few more of Elise's new friends.

Ball found a place to park a bit down from the actual trailhead. It looked like a lot of other people had also thought going hiking today was a good idea. Elise bolted from the car the second it was parked and jogged up to where a group of kids from her school had gathered.

"Looks like she's anxious to get going," Ball said dryly.

Everly laughed. "It's good to see her excited about something. For a while I was afraid she wouldn't bounce back."

"It's because of you," Ball said.

She looked up at him. He'd taken her hand in his while they headed for the trailhead a little more sedately. Everly shook her head. "I honestly haven't done much."

"Haven't done much? Ev, you've changed your entire life around for her. You brought your sister here to *live* with you. You're paying for the private school, and you've made sure Elise has gotten all the counseling she needs to deal with what happened."

His praise felt good, but it still didn't feel as if she'd done anything special. "She's my sister. I'd do anything for her. As Me-Maw told me, she's the one person I'll know the longest in my entire life. If I didn't do everything I could, what kind of person would that make me?"

"I think you know better than most that blood isn't always thicker than water. You're supposed to be able to rely on your relatives, but that isn't always the case."

She knew what he meant. Her mother was a prime example.

Meat waved as they approached. Ball squeezed her hand before letting go and shaking his friend's hand. "Hey. You ready for this?" he asked.

"Hell yeah. It'll be fun. Everly, I'd like to teach them a couple of our signs. Think that'd be okay?"

"Your signs?"

"Ones we've used in the military."

"Oh, sure. I don't see why not."

"Will you translate for me?" Meat asked.

"Of course." Everly stepped over to Elise and tapped her on the shoulder. She quickly signed that Meat wanted to talk to everyone, and Elise helped gather the group. Everly signed as Meat spoke.

"I don't expect any trouble on today's hike, but just in case, I thought I would share a couple signs that I might use today." Meat held up his arm with his fist clenched. "This means freeze. I'll be walking in front, and if you see me do this, immediately stop right where you are." He held his hand up to his brow next. "This means watch, or that I see something. And if I pump my fist up and down like this, it means hurry up."

Everly smiled as the kids excitedly nodded. A few asked to know more.

"Meat, they want to know more."

"I can see that, but those are probably the only ones we'll need today," he said.

Everly shrugged. "Doesn't matter. Now they're curious."

For the next ten minutes or so, Meat shared more signs that he'd used while he'd been in the Army, and that he probably still used while with the Mountain Mercenaries on missions: cover this area, enemy, hostage, sniper, vehicle, and crouch. Many of the signs were similar to American Sign Language.

Everly walked around and made sure everyone had water and didn't need to use the restroom, and finally they were ready to go. Meat led the way, with Everly and Ball bringing up the rear.

They'd been walking for about ten minutes when Ball turned to her and said, "I hadn't thought about it before we set off, but it's kinda weird to see kids so quiet."

Everly laughed. "They're not talking, but they're not quiet." She pointed to the boy and girl who were walking right in front of them. They hadn't shut up the entire way so far. Their hands were moving a mile a minute, and it was obvious they were more interested in each other than the beautiful area they were walking through.

Ball chuckled. "Good point."

They walked for another mile or so, then took a break off to the side so others could pass without issue. Everly saw a boy named Carl talking to two other kids.

Did you guys see that dude about a half mile back?

What guy?

No.

I didn't get a good look at him. He was wearing a black shirt and jeans. He was off to our right in the woods. I saw him out of the corner of my eye.

"Ball," she said, not looking away from Carl.

"Yeah? What's wrong?"

"Carl said he saw someone in the woods."

"Where? When?"

"He estimated about a half mile behind us." She looked up at him. "Should we be worried?"

Ball didn't look freaked out, which settled Everly's nerves a little bit. "Ev, this is public property. There are a ton of people out and about hiking today. Just because someone was in the woods doesn't mean they're stalking us. Okay?"

She nodded. But she obviously didn't look convinced, because he took her head in his hands and leaned close. "I'll talk to Meat, and we'll be on the lookout, but don't overthink this. We haven't heard anything from the cops out in LA, and even the FBI said that they hadn't found anything that suggested this was a huge trafficking operation. Even if it was, they aren't going to send someone all the way out here to the Springs to track Elise down. It's too risky. They're all about doing things the easy way. Okay?"

"What if it wasn't trafficking?" Everly asked the thought that had been haunting her since they'd found out the FBI was moving on to other cases because of a lack of evidence in Elise's and the other girls' kidnappings.

"The same logic applies. Colorado Springs is a long way from Los Angeles. No one in their right mind would come all the way out here to look for Elise. It's just not logical."

"And a psycho who kidnaps girls uses logic?" she asked with a raised brow.

"Okay, good point. But it's been a month. She hasn't heard from the mysterious Rob, so he's probably moved on. Just in case, like I said, I'll talk to Meat, and we'll be on the lookout."

Everly nodded. The kids were getting restless, so Ball jogged over to Meat to tell him what Carl had seen before they headed back out.

It took another hour to get to the point where they were going to turn around. There were a few strategically placed rocks that the kids sat on to eat their lunches. One boy and girl started to walk off the trail toward a large rock that they obviously wanted to climb.

Ball yelled, "Don't go off the trail!" forgetting that he was with a group of deaf children. He swore under his breath at his stupidity when the pair didn't even flinch and kept going. Before Everly could do anything, he was jogging toward them. He came back toward the group with the couple and asked Everly, "Will you translate?"

She nodded.

"It's not safe to go off the trail."

But there are, like, a million people around here, one of the kids signed.

"Right, and what happens if a million people all decide they want to wander to look at a bush off the trail? A rock? A bug?" Ball didn't wait for an answer. "Then this place becomes less of a nature trail than a tromped-down piece of dirt. Staying on the trail is as much for your own safety as it is to preserve nature."

But I've seen that guy going on and off the trail all day, a boy named Scott said as he pointed off to their left.

Meat was moving before Everly could even focus on what Scott had pointed at. She saw Meat heading for a man in his midforties.

He was wearing black jeans and a dark-red T-shirt. The uneasy feeling returned, and she stepped closer to where her sister was talking with a girl named Ruby.

Meat had a short discussion with the man, then started back toward their group. He smiled and gave them a thumbs-up as he came back toward them.

"Breathe, Ev," Ball said from beside her. She felt his hand brush against her shoulder blades before he stepped away. That was something he did all the time. Ball was always touching her. Light caresses that were never inappropriate and always made her think about Me-Maw and Pop. Her grandfather once told Everly that touching his wife was a way to make sure she knew he was thinking about her, and to remind himself how lucky he was to have her in his life.

"It's okay," Meat said, and Everly quickly stepped in front of the group to translate. "I mean, it's not okay that he's not on the trail, Ball already covered why, but he's geocaching."

Of course all the kids wanted to know what that was.

"It's like treasure hunting with a GPS. Someone hides a box, or a film canister, or any kind of container, and puts the coordinates online to where it is. Then anyone can look them up on a website and go find it. The finder signs the log inside and puts it back for the next person to find."

Immediately the kids wanted to know if there was an app, and when they found there was, they were all downloading it and checking it out.

Meat walked over to Ball and Everly. "Are you sure that's all it was?" she asked.

"I'm sure. I saw the compass open on his phone screen. No one's touching one hair on these kids' heads, Everly. Relax."

She nodded. Easier said than done. As a cop, it was pretty much ingrained in her to see the boogeyman behind every rock and tree. She wasn't sure she'd ever relax her guard when it came to Elise. The days when she'd been missing had been pure hell. She couldn't go through that again.

After lunch, the kids were excited to hike back to the cars because there were three geocaches along the way. The more enthusiastic kids walked at the front of the line, and the others who didn't care as much were in the back, closer to Ball and Everly.

They'd been walking for a while when Ball turned to Everly and asked, "Is your sister discussing Meat's ass?"

Everly watched Elise and Ruby talk for a second, then laughed out loud. "As a matter of fact, yes. They're impressed with all his . . . attributes," she told Ball.

"Better him than me," Ball muttered.

"Don't worry. They're actually comparing the two of you now."

"Shit! I don't want to know," Ball said, covering his eyes in mock embarrassment.

Everly nudged him with her shoulder. "Thanks for coming today, Ball."

"Any chance to spend time with my favorite cop," he quipped. "How's work going?"

They started talking about her job and which websites Ball had designed that week. There were no more encounters with any strange men in the woods, and the kids were thrilled to have found all three geocaches on the way back to the cars.

The parking area was even more packed by the time they arrived around two in the afternoon. Everly vaguely noticed that there were cars from all different price ranges, representing every level of income, which wasn't unusual for a Colorado Springs hiking trail. There was a Mercedes parked next to a Kia, as well as Fords, pickup trucks, a Beetle, a few minivans . . . even a Tesla and somebody's work van.

She pointed it out to Ball and Elise, commenting on how nice it was that hiking was truly an activity anyone could do, no matter their social status or how much money they had.

I love being out here, Elise said. *There aren't any places like this in LA.*

There were, but to get to them meant driving quite a distance away from where Me-Maw and Pop lived. Everly didn't bother to point that out.

Elise kept talking as they walked back to Ball's Mustang. *When I was in that basement, I never thought I'd be able to do something like this again.*

Do what? Everly asked.

This. Smell the pine trees. Hike. Be free.

Everly had been all ready to tease her sister and say something to the effect that she'd never been hiking a day in her life before she'd joined the club here in Colorado, but the last two words hit her hard.

Ball's hand curled around her waist and squeezed her for a second, before he let go to respond to her sister.

Are you interested in learning some self-defense?

Really? Elise asked eagerly.

Yes. Allye and Morgan have backed out because they're pregnant, but Chloe and Harlow are still interested.

I'd love to! Elise signed. *Everly has already taught me some basic stuff, but I'd love to learn how to really kick ass. Can Ruby come too?*

Ball looked over to Everly. She gave him a small nod.

Yes. That will make the numbers even.

Cool!

Elise rushed away to tell her friend about the upcoming training.

It was Everly's turn to put her hands on Ball. She hooked her thumb in the belt loop at the back of his waist and leaned her head on his biceps. She watched as her sister ran over to Carl's car. He'd obviously driven a bunch of the other kids there. Elise eagerly began a conversation with Ruby about the self-defense class Ball had invited them to.

"You didn't have a class already set up, did you?" she asked quietly.

Ball chuckled. "No. But I have no doubt Chloe and Harlow will be eager to join in. I wanted to take her mind off what happened to her, and that was the first thing I thought of."

"It's perfect," Everly told him. "Thank you. I should've thought about it before now. Maybe it'll give her more confidence in the future."

"You'll come too, won't you?" Ball asked.

"Sure. Why?"

"I just . . . I don't want to do anything that might cause her to have a flashback. I mean, you've already taught her the basics, but that was before she got kidnapped. You know as well as I do that when we start out, we'll go back over the simple stuff, like how to knee someone in the groin and how to break away if someone grabs ahold of her arm. But eventually we might work up to how to escape and defend yourself if someone's got you pinned to the floor."

Everly loved that Ball was always thinking about how Elise might feel or react about different things.

Then she froze and almost stopped walking altogether.

Loved? That was just a figure of speech . . . wasn't it?

She'd almost convinced herself when Elise returned and flung herself into Ball's arms.

He laughed and hugged her back. Then she started an animated conversation with Ball about how excited she was, and Ruby too, and how they were going to be ninja warriors by the time he was done with them.

It was obvious to Everly that Ball was missing most of what her sister was saying, but he didn't get frustrated and was able to catch enough to get the gist.

Loved.

Did she love Ball? What did she know of love?

Everly loved Me-Maw and Pop. She loved Elise. She loved her job and loved Mexican food. But when it came to the opposite sex, she didn't think she'd ever loved a man before.

She liked Ball. Enjoyed being with him. Looked forward to his texts and phone calls. She appreciated his help with Elise and admired his relationship with his friends and their girlfriends. She respected him, valued their relationship, and thought he was as smart as anyone she'd ever met.

But loved?

She continued to watch her sister and Ball chat. She hadn't seen Elise act so carefree since she'd brought her to Colorado Springs. Everly watched as she hugged Ball once more and climbed into the back seat of his car.

Putting all thoughts of whether or not she loved Ball to the back of her mind, Everly got into the car and turned around to smile at her sister. Then, without thought, after Ball had backed out and was on the way to her apartment, Everly reached out and grabbed hold of his hand. They always held hands in the car, and it was as natural as breathing for her.

Chapter Eleven

Ball knocked on Everly's apartment door with a heavy heart. He hated the feeling. He'd never had a sense of reluctance about going on a mission in the past. In fact, he'd relished the challenge of using the skills he'd learned in the Coast Guard and looked forward to getting someone out of the desperate situation they'd found themselves in.

But he hadn't been dating Everly in the past.

A week had passed since they'd gone hiking in the wilderness above the Broadmoor neighborhood, and he was supposed to be teaching Elise and her friend some self-defense in a few days.

But now he had to leave town. Rex had called and told them about a two-year-old who'd been taken out of the country by her noncustodial father. Rescuing little kids always made missions more stressful. They didn't understand what was happening or why, and typically they were terrified when the Mountain Mercenaries made entry to where they were being kept.

The door in front of him opened, and Ball couldn't help but smile at seeing Everly. The last six weeks had been amazing. He'd gotten to know her extremely well, and he couldn't think of one thing he didn't like. She was an amazing sister, and watching her take care of Elise gave him a glimpse of what she'd be like as a mother.

The thought should've scared him, but instead it made him feel settled. Content.

"Hey," she said as she opened the door wider, "I thought you weren't coming over until later this afternoon."

"I know. I hadn't planned on it. Can I come in?"

"Oh! Of course. Sorry." She stepped back from the door and held it open for him. Ball entered her apartment and immediately felt his anxiety ease. He felt like that every time he came over. Just being in her space somehow made him settle. Many a night he'd worked late, sitting at her table. He'd played marathon games of Monopoly with Elise and Everly, and he'd fallen asleep with her in his arms too many evenings to count.

But he hadn't slept in a bed with her since Los Angeles. He wasn't sure what he was waiting for, but he somehow knew he needed to move slowly. He couldn't just move himself in, or move them into his house . . . as much as he might want to.

Once upon a time, he'd sworn not to be like his friends. They'd declared their women "taken" and had practically moved them in a few weeks later. But now here he was, wishing he knew an easy way to move their relationship along. To hold Everly in his arms every night.

Telling her that he had to leave for an undetermined period of time, knowing he wouldn't be there if she needed anything, and wouldn't see her and her sister for who knew how long, wasn't sitting well. At all.

"I was about to go and run some errands. Lord, I forgot how much teenagers can eat. I used to nap on my days off. Now I've got to go to the grocery store, the dry cleaner's, go visit the school and talk with Elise's teachers, and, if I have time, I wanted to go check out the next hiking area the club wants to do."

Ball turned, leaned his ass against her table, and smiled.

"What? What's wrong?"

Deciding not to drag it out—not that he really had the time to drag it out—he said, "I'm headed out in a couple hours for a mission."

"Oh."

That was all she said. *Oh.*

Ball waited for her to ask where they were going, when they would be back . . . something. But she just stared at him.

Not able to stand it any longer, he took a step toward her and pulled her into his embrace. She went willingly, and he felt a little better about her reaction when she grabbed hold of his shirt and held on for dear life.

They stood like that for a moment, then he gently pulled back. "No questions?" he asked softly.

"I only have a million of them, but I know you probably can't answer any," Everly said.

"It's not that we *can't* tell you. We don't work for the military anymore. But we're used to not talking to anyone about our missions. It's potentially safer that way. And I never know for sure how long we'll be gone. It depends on whether the intel we have is good or not. But all things considered, this *shouldn't* be long and drawn out."

"You'll be careful?" she asked, then cringed, as if she knew how silly her words sounded.

"Of course. I didn't get it before."

"Get what?"

"When the other guys mentioned the excitement of getting a new mission had waned for them. I couldn't imagine it. I mean, we used to live to get out and do something. To make a difference. To take down the bad guys. I didn't understand how they could go from being all gung ho about using the skills they'd learned as soldiers, to being reluctant to leave. But I understand it now."

Everly looked up at him, but didn't say a word.

"Leaving means I don't get to see you. I don't get to text you and see how your day has gone. I don't get to hear your crazy stories about the men and women you've met on your shift. I don't get to practice my signing with Elise. I don't get to touch you, hold your hand, and have you fall asleep on me. And I can't do this . . ."

Ball leaned forward and kissed Everly's forehead. Then he brushed a kiss against her cheek, then the other one. And finally, he lightly kissed her lips. When he did, she stood on her tiptoes and put her hands behind his neck, pulling him down to her.

She kissed him so carnally, Ball immediately got hard. All the blood went from his head straight to his dick. He pulled her closer, until they were touching from chests to thighs. And still she kissed him as if for the last time, tilting her head one way, then the other. Their tongues dueled, and he'd never felt anything better in all his life.

Knowing they didn't have time for anything but kissing, he tried to slow her down, to ease up the intensity of the kiss, but Everly was having none of that. She moaned into his mouth and clutched at him harder.

"Easy, Ev." His lips brushed against hers as he spoke, and that seemed to break her out of whatever trance she'd been in. She moved her hands to his back and buried her face in his neck.

"I'm gonna miss you," she said softly.

"Same," Ball told her.

"And I'm gonna worry about you."

"Just like I worry about you every time you're on shift," Ball said dryly.

She looked up at that. "You do?"

"Of course I do. But I know you're a damn good cop, and you'd never do something stupid that would risk your life."

She stared at him for a beat. "You're trying to tell me that you're good at what you do, aren't you?" she asked.

He smiled. "Would I tell you how to think?"

She chuckled. "Uh . . . yeah, you would."

"Then I'm good at what I do. And I've got five of the most competent and capable men at my back. You know about us, Ev. I've told you how they're former Delta Force, SAS, and SEALs. It's why the whole *team* is so good at what we do."

"I know. But it's different hearing about it, and having the reality of you leaving to go out and do something dangerous right in front of me."

Not wanting to promise her something that he couldn't positively deliver—like promising he'd come home safe and sound—Ball changed the subject. "You'll explain to Elise why we can't do the self-defense thing this weekend?"

"Of course. She'll be disappointed, but she'll understand."

"I'll let you know the second we land back in the States," Ball told her.

"Okay."

"If I can, I'll text while I'm gone, but sometimes we don't have reliable cell service."

"I figured. I can text *you*, though, right? I mean, your phone's not going to chime with an incoming text and blow your cover right before you break into the bad guy's house, is it?"

Ball chuckled. "No. You can text. Elise too. When I land, I'd love to catch up with what happened while I was gone."

"Okay. We'll do that, then."

"Everly, I've done my best to give us both time to be sure this is what we want. But it's taken me leaving on this assignment to realize how much you mean to me. You *and* Elise. I want to be a permanent part of your lives. I want to wake up in the middle of the night and not feel guilty that we've fallen asleep on the couch again. I want to let Elise pick out furniture that she might like for a room in my house.

I want to sleep cuddled up to your back like we did in California. I want it all.

"I know this is a lot, and I know it's coming out of left field, but I don't want a casual relationship anymore. I want to make you mine in every way a man can make a woman his . . . starting with being inside you so deeply, neither of us knows where one starts and the other begins."

Ball took a breath and licked his lips. She hadn't interrupted him, hadn't torn herself out of his arms, so he was taking both as good signs. But then, she also hadn't said anything at all.

"You done?" she asked.

"Yes. No, wait. No, I'm not. I swear that I'm over whatever issues I had when we met. I've done a lot of thinking, and as awful as my situation with Riley was, I shouldn't use what she did to paint all women with the same brush. I've also figured out that Holly and I were never going to last. She was all about herself. She liked the fact that I was in the military more than she liked me. I should've figured it out and shaken off her rejection, but instead I wallowed in my misery. I've changed, and I promise if you give me a chance, you'll see how much I care about you."

Ball swallowed and waited for her response, barely breathing in the process.

"Okay."

Then he waited for her to continue . . . and when she didn't, he asked, "Okay?"

"Yeah. I want all that too. So okay. When you get back, we'll have wild monkey sex, probably participate in way too many public displays of affection, and scar my sister for life. I'm not ready to move in permanently with you, but I wouldn't mind sleepovers. All that's fine—as long as you remember that Elise and I are a package deal. I'm not going to send her back to Los Angeles. She's better off here with me. We're better off together."

"I couldn't agree more," Ball said. Then he reached up and pantomimed wiping a bead of sweat off his brow. "You made me sweat there for a bit, woman," he complained.

Everly giggled. "You were the one who kept going on and on."

It was true. He had. "You're the best thing that's happened to me in a really long time. I'm not going to fuck this up. I know a good thing when I've got it."

"A relationship has two people in it, Ball."

"Meaning?"

"Just that you aren't the only one responsible for keeping us going. I know I'm not the easiest person to live with. To be with. And with both of us having jobs that put us in danger, well . . . that can put a lot of stress on a relationship."

"Point taken." He paused, then said, "When I get back, you'll spend the night at my house? Because so far, we've mostly hung out over here. I know this is Elise's home and all, but even though my house isn't huge, I do have that extra room we can fix up for your sister."

"I'd love to," Everly said shyly.

"Good." He glanced down at his watch and grimaced. "I have to go."

"Me too."

Ball kissed her once more. A long, tender kiss that neither of them let cross the line into passionate. He pulled back reluctantly. "Text me," he said.

"I will."

"Elise too."

"Her too."

"Be careful," Ball said, not wanting to go.

"I should be saying that to you," Everly said.

"I'll miss you."

"Ditto. Now go," she told him, shoving at his chest. "Before we both just stand here and find endless things to say to prolong the moment."

"I'm going. Ev?"

She huffed out a breath in exaggerated impatience. "Yeah?"

Ball opened his mouth to tell her he loved her, but closed it. Now wasn't the time to say that, and then leave. When he told her how much she meant to him, he wanted to have the time to show her as well. "Stay safe."

"I will. Now go and do your thing so you can come home."

"Home. Yes, ma'am," he told her. He caressed her cheek with the back of his fingers one more time, then turned and headed for her door.

~

Four days later, Everly and Elise were hanging out at Allye's house near Black Forest. It was quite the drive from her apartment, which was south of downtown and closer to the Broadmoor area. But it was a Friday, and both she and Elise were missing Ball way more than either of them had thought they would.

This was supposed to be the night Ball gave Elise and Ruby their first self-defense lessons, so instead of sitting around moping about it, she'd accepted Allye's invitation to come for a sleepover. They'd both packed pajamas and a change of clothes, deciding it would be fun to watch movies and hang with the other woman.

Elise was bundled up under a blanket on Allye's couch in the basement, totally engrossed in a Netflix movie, when Allye asked Everly, "How are you doing?"

"Me?"

"Yeah, you. I've talked to Elise about what happened to her, and I think it's great that you got her into therapy so quickly. Too many people think that not talking about things will somehow make them disappear, but it doesn't work like that. But you also went through a lot when Elise was missing. So how are *you* doing?"

"I'm okay."

Allye quirked an eyebrow.

"I'm scared to death to let her out of my sight. I hate it when she goes to school, and I want to tell her that she has to come right home the second school lets out and not do anything with anyone. That won't help her heal, but it's how I feel."

"Have you told her?"

Everly looked over at her sister and sighed. She looked completely at ease. Her eyes were glued to the television, reading the subtitles as they came across the screen. "No. The last thing I want is for her to think I'm not strong, or give her something else to worry about."

"Everly, I know you're a cop, and you're more than capable of handling a whole lot of things, but struggling to deal with the aftereffects of her kidnapping doesn't make you weak. And I think she probably should know. One, it'll show her exactly how much you love her, and two, if you're feeling that way, don't you think she is too?"

Everly thought about that. She absolutely didn't want to freak her sister out. But . . . hadn't she thought just the other day that Elise seemed a bit jumpy? Maybe if they talked about their fears, it would help them both.

"I had a long talk with Gray after I was taken. Yes, I was scared to death when that psycho had me, but Gray was dealing with his own hell. At first I didn't understand. I mean, *he* wasn't the one who was taken. But then I tried to put myself in his shoes, and I realized the terror he was feeling, while different, was just as valid as what I was going through. I think if you talk to Elise and explain how you felt when she disappeared, it'll help you both."

Everly nodded. She felt as if her fright and worry was somehow nothing compared to what Elise had gone through. It seemed silly to even bring it up, because what could be worse than what happened to

Elise? But hearing that Gray had gone through similar feelings made her feel better.

"I will. I think it's worse because the guy who took Elise is still out there. I have no idea if he's lurking around a corner waiting to strike again. I know it's unlikely. I mean, we're a long way from California, and I've done everything possible to make sure Elise knows not to download or log on to any of the apps she used before to talk to him, but I'm still scared for her. For me."

"I don't know what I'd do if Gray disappeared like that," Allye said. One hand went to her belly and rubbed as she talked. "I have such respect for single parents. I don't think I could do it. I'm scared to death to have this kid. I'm afraid it'll change everything about my relationship with Gray."

"It won't," Everly said.

Allye smiled. "No offense, but you don't really even know us, right?"

"You're right, I don't. But I've seen how he looks at you. He can't take his eyes off you. When we were at The Pit, every time I looked over at the guys, he was staring at you. And I may not be around you guys all that much, but men like the Mountain Mercenaries don't seem like the kind who do anything halfway. Not their soldiering, not their other jobs, and not loving the women they're with."

"They don't," Allye agreed. Then she tilted her head and asked point-blank, "Do you love Ball?"

Everly blinked. She hadn't expected Allye to be so blunt. But she should've. Ball was a respected and loved member of their tribe. If she was in the other woman's shoes, she'd want to know the same thing.

"I don't know." She saw Allye frown, and hurried on. "But the first thing I do in the morning is grab my phone to see if he texted while I was asleep. More and more often, though, I wake up in his arms on my couch. We fall asleep that way and don't wake up until morning.

He respects my sister and has gone out of his way to learn how to talk to her. *Really* talk to her, not just scribble shit on a piece of paper or do weird pantomimes. I see the worry in his eyes when I'm wearing my bulletproof vest for work, but he hasn't said anything to indicate that he thinks I should choose another safer profession. I've never felt my body tingle from merely a kiss before . . .

"Is that love? I'm probably the worst person in the world to ask about love. My own *mother* didn't love me. I can promise you this, though, I'm not interested in a casual fling with Ball. I'm too old for that shit. And if we get to that point, the first person who hears that I love him will be Ball, not you . . . sorry."

Everly held her breath, hoping like hell she hadn't offended Allye. When the other woman leaned back against the couch with a huge smile on her face, she figured she was all right.

"Good answer," Allye said, still grinning.

"Does this ever get any easier?" Everly asked.

"What? Waiting for them to get home? Wondering if they're okay and what they're doing? Not really."

"Not the answer I wanted to hear," Everly said dryly.

"But you know what does make it easier?" Allye asked.

"What?"

"Knowing that wherever they are, whatever they're doing, they've got each other at their backs. Those men know what they're doing. Yes, many times their missions aren't exactly safe, but I know without a doubt that they'll do whatever it takes to get home unharmed."

"Yeah, that helps," Everly admitted. It was a lot like the brotherhood she felt as a police officer. When a call for assistance got broadcast, every cop in a ten-mile radius dropped everything to get there to help.

"But more importantly—and you should understand this better than anyone—is knowing that what they're doing is helping other women and children get home to their families. It's hard to believe in today's day and age that human slavery still exists, but that's what trafficking is. It's ugly and perverse, and our men are making the world a better place, even if it's only one woman at a time, one kid at a time."

That Everly could definitely understand. It was why she'd contacted Rex in the first place. "You're right, that does make it easier."

"I thought it might," Allye said.

They fell silent as they turned their attention to the movie.

Half an hour later, Everly looked over at her sister and saw she was fast asleep.

"You want to wake her up and tell her to go to bed?" Allye asked quietly.

Everly shook her head. "If it's okay, I think we might both just sleep right here."

"That's more than okay. I'll leave the hall light on in case either of you wakes up disoriented."

"Thank you."

Allye pushed herself to her feet and shook her head. "No, thank *you.*"

"For what?"

"For being exactly the kind of woman Ball needs."

Everly chuckled. "I'm not sure you need to thank me for that. I'm the one who's wondering how I got so lucky."

"Good night, Everly. I'll see you in the morning. Maybe we'll *both* get lucky and hear that our men are back tomorrow."

"Hopefully."

And with that, Allye headed out of the room, leaving Everly alone with her sister.

The movie was still playing on the TV, giving off just enough light to see. For a long time, Everly watched Elise sleep.

It could be argued that the Mountain Mercenaries had had nothing to do with Elise being found, though Everly couldn't help but think that somehow they had. Rex and Meat had worked tirelessly to find any kind of clue in her sister's computer and phone, but more important, they were lifelines when she'd needed them most. Knowing she had the best of the best at her back had made the entire situation a little easier to endure.

Ball was out there somewhere, trying to save someone else's sister. Child. Friend. She vowed right then and there to never make him feel like he had to choose between her and his job. Besides, it wasn't as if her job was without risks. Every time she suited up with the SWAT team, there was a chance she could be shot. Every time she pulled a car over, the possibility existed that someone would whip out a gun and blow her away before she could do anything. But she loved what she did. Loved putting assholes behind bars where they belonged. Loved taking drugs off the street that could make their way into the hands of children. Loved making neglectful parents accountable for their actions . . . something her mom had never had to learn.

Reaching forward, Everly grabbed the remote and clicked off the television. The room went dark, but she could still see an outline of her sister because of the light Allye had left on in the hallway. Before she fell asleep, Everly grabbed her phone from the coffee table in front of the sofa. She typed out a heartfelt text to Ball, then placed it back on the table. She snuggled up under the fuzzy blanket and sighed in contentment.

Everly: In case I forget to tell you later, you have the best friends. I've never felt so welcomed and supported as I have since you left. I miss you. Terribly. But I know if it was Elise out there, lost, scared, and alone, I'd want you and your team on her case. Can't wait to see you when you get back.

~

"Wake up!"

Everly bolted straight up on the couch and reached for her firearm . . . which of course wasn't on her hip.

"Everly, are you up?" Allye asked urgently again from the hallway.

"We're up," Everly told her friend, nudging a still-sleeping Elise.

"The guys are back, but Ball and Gray were hurt."

Everything in Everly froze.

Hurt? Ball was *hurt*?

She had a million questions, but just one thing went through her head as she quickly signed what was happening to Elise. Allye had said *hurt*—not *killed*. It was a huge distinction.

Chapter Twelve

Ball winced as Elise flew into his arms. He rocked on his feet, but felt Everly's hand on his back, supporting him.

He hadn't wanted to worry Everly by telling her that he'd been grazed by a bullet, but Gray had let the cat out of the bag by texting Allye and telling her about their injuries. He'd had no idea that Everly and Elise were over at Gray's house until his friend told him.

The second he'd entered the house, Elise had thrown herself at him.

"I'm okay, Elise," he murmured, knowing she couldn't hear him.

Everly took a step to the side and touched her sister's shoulder. *Careful, hon. He's hurt.*

Elise let go of him so quickly, he tottered again on his feet. Everly was there once more, hand on his back to keep him steady.

Ball had read every one of her and her sister's texts probably ten times since he'd gotten back in cell tower range. They'd done as promised and sent him dozens of texts since he'd been gone. Elise's ranged from talking about what she was doing in school to sending him short little videos of her signing simple sentences to prevent him from forgetting what he'd already learned.

But it was Everly's texts that made him miss Colorado Springs more than he ever had before. It was weird because in the past when he'd been on a mission, he hadn't thought about anything *but* the mission.

But this time, it seemed that everywhere he looked, he saw things that reminded him of Everly.

A police officer standing on a street corner.

Someone gesturing wildly with their hands made him think about Everly signing to her sister.

Even seeing an older woman walking arm in arm with a younger female who was obviously related to her made him think of Me-Maw and Everly.

They'd found the missing child exactly where their intel had told them she would be, but unfortunately, the father was a paranoid son of a bitch who had holed up with a bunch of weapons. He'd started shooting when they'd made entry into his piece-of-shit, run-down house, and hadn't even cared that his daughter was right there next to him.

Ball had made a desperate grab for the little girl to get her out of harm's way, getting grazed by a bullet in the process. Gray had sustained a concussion when he'd tackled the father, smacking his head against the wall of the shack as he'd grabbed him.

Even though the little girl had screamed her head off throughout the entire rescue and most of the way home, the look of relief on both her and her mother's faces when they'd been reunited at the airport had made everything else fade into the background.

He'd reread Everly's last text several times on the way to Gray's house. He'd been planning on going straight to her apartment, but of course he changed his mind when he'd learned Everly and Elise had spent the night at his teammate's house.

Ignoring the twinge of pain in his side, Ball signed to Elise, *I'm okay.*

Her hands moved so fast there was no way Ball could possibly translate, but of course, Everly was right there. "She says that she was so worried. That you should've ducked or moved faster or something. She's mad at you, but also relieved that you're okay. She's ordering you to never be hurt again."

Ball smiled and brushed a lock of hair behind Elise's ear. *I will do my best,* he finger spelled slowly.

Elise nodded and hugged him once more, this time a bit more carefully. Out of the corner of his eye, he saw Gray greeting Allye. She was giving him the same third degree that he'd just received from Elise.

Everly's hand was still resting on the small of his back, and he'd never felt anything better. It wasn't a sexual touch, but he could still feel the emotion emanating from her. The second Elise stepped away, he turned to Everly.

Without a word, he gathered her into his arms and closed his eyes as he breathed out a huge sigh. This was what he needed. He hadn't had time to register the pain in his side in the heat of the moment. He'd been too concerned about making sure the little girl they'd been sent to rescue was safe. Then he'd been worried about getting her out of there without the rest of the neighborhood breaking out into a riot. *Then* he'd done his best to reassure and calm her during the flight.

Between his side, Gray's head, and trying to placate the toddler, the trip home on the plane hadn't been a relaxing time to decompress, as it sometimes was. Arrow had cleaned and bandaged his wound, reassuring him that it wasn't serious. Gray's concussion was slight, and he'd be fine after a day or so of rest.

But putting his arms around Everly seemed to be exactly what he needed to allow his body to shut down. Suddenly, he was exhausted. He wanted nothing more than to collapse in a heap . . . preferably on a comfortable mattress instead of the crap beds they'd been making do with over the last few days.

"You're more than welcome to stay here," Allye said from next to them.

Ball picked up his head and saw Gray and Allye standing with their arms around each other, sides plastered together. Gray narrowed his eyes and shook his head slightly. Ball laughed.

"Thanks, Allye, I appreciate it. But if it's all the same to you, I think I'll crash in my own bed tonight."

"Offer's always open," Allye said.

"I know. Thanks." Ball nodded at Gray when his friend mouthed, *"Thank you."*

"I know it's the middle of the night, but think you could drive me home?" Ball asked Everly. "I came here with Gray, and my car's back at my place."

"Of course." She turned to Elise and signed, *We're going to bring Ball home. Go change out of your pj's and pack our things. And don't forget our phones. Oh, and anything you've got in the bathroom.*

Elise nodded and rushed from the hallway to head down the stairs.

"Are you okay?" Everly asked Gray.

"Yeah. Just a little knock on the head."

She hesitated, then asked, "And the mission was successful?"

"Yep. There's a little two-year-old who's probably completely zonked out in her mother's arms tonight."

"Thank God," Allye breathed, and Ball didn't miss how her hand protectively rested on her belly as she said it.

"That's good," Everly said.

"Yeah," Gray agreed.

"Thank you for bringing Ball here," she added.

Gray chuckled. "As if I had a choice. The second he heard this was where *you* were, he demanded I hurry my ass up and drive faster."

Ball liked the blush that bloomed on Everly's cheeks.

"You shouldn't have been driving," Allye scolded. "I could've come and picked you both up."

Gray shook his head. "Kitten, it's two in the morning. There's no way I was going to have my pregnant fiancée drive all the way to the airport to pick me up."

"I'm not pregnant. I could've done it," Everly added.

"Not happening," Ball said.

Allye and Everly both rolled their eyes, and seeing it made every ache and pain in Ball's body fade away. He hated comparing Everly with Holly, even in his head, but damn, his ex wouldn't even bring him a damn pain pill from the other room if he asked.

They all heard Elise's feet pounding back up the stairs and turned to see her bounce into the room, two large flowery bags over her shoulders. She immediately looked in their direction, as if she was afraid they might have somehow disappeared in the few minutes she'd been gone.

Did you get everything? Everly asked.

Elise rolled her eyes exactly like her sister had moments before, and nodded.

"If I find anything, I'll put it aside until you're up here next, or I'll arrange to get it to you," Allye said.

"Thanks, I appreciate it."

Ball didn't want to take his hands off the woman by his side, but forced himself to let go. He reached for one of the bags on Elise's shoulders, but she jerked away from him.

No! she signed. *You're hurt. I've got them.*

Once again, a memory flashed in his head. It wasn't too long after he'd been discharged. He was still in a sling, and he hadn't started physical therapy for his shoulder yet. He was taking Holly out to try to . . . Well, he wasn't sure *what* he was trying to do. Save their relationship, he supposed, which was stupid because it was obvious now that he'd been the only one trying.

They were going to stop by her apartment on the way to the restaurant, because she wanted to drop off a bag of her things that had accumulated at his house. That was another huge fucking red flag that he hadn't heeded. She was literally cleaning her shit out of his place while he was injured, and he hadn't thought a thing about it.

She'd stood in front of his door like a princess waiting for her servant to do something she'd thought beneath her . . . like carry her own bag and open the door. She knew his shoulder hurt—and hello, he'd had a fucking sling on—but she'd still expected him to carry her bag.

Everly grabbed one of the bags and went into a bathroom. She reappeared two minutes later wearing jeans and a CSPD T-shirt. Ball sort of preferred her in her blue-and-white-striped pajama bottoms and the tank top she'd been wearing. She obviously hadn't bothered with a brush, because her bedhead was sticking up in several different directions, which made the differences between her and Holly—who had to look perfect at all times—even more striking.

Even while the memories of his ex ran through his brain, Ball watched as Everly hurried to the front door to open it for him. Between her and Elise, his past idiocy with Holly was losing its ability to hurt him.

"Thanks, Ev."

She nodded and turned to Allye. "Thanks for having us over. And for the talk."

"Anytime. And I mean that," Allye responded.

Elise signed, *Thank you*, and Allye signed, *You're welcome*, back.

Thankful for his friends, and how easily they took things in stride, Ball gave a chin lift to Gray, who returned it.

"Don't forget to clean that wound out in the morning," Gray said.

"He won't," Everly answered for him.

Smiling as she wound her arm around him, as if she was going to take his weight or something, Ball said goodbye once more and turned to head for Everly's white Jeep Cherokee. She hovered as he slid into the passenger seat and fretted over whether or not the seat belt would rub against his wound.

Ball took her face in his hands and kissed her. It wasn't long, but it wasn't short either. "I'm fine," he said firmly. "Stop worrying."

"Right. Stop worrying. Whatever," she mumbled as she shut his door and walked around to the driver's seat.

Ball grinned and turned to Elise in the back seat, who was also smiling. *Overprotective,* he finger spelled.

It's nice, isn't it?

Ball nodded. Yeah. It *was* nice.

The drive back to his house was peaceful. There weren't many cars on the road, and the trip through downtown was fast and easy. Before he knew it, Everly was pulling up to his house. She repeated the mothering, helping him out and walking slowly with him up to his door. Elise was still in the car, and he could feel her eyes on them.

"Stay here tonight," he said after he'd unlocked his door.

She hesitated, and he shamelessly used his injury to help persuade her. "I'll need help with cleaning my wound in the morning. It's the middle of the night, and you and Elise have to be exhausted. I don't have a bed for her yet, but she can sleep on the couch downstairs like you guys were doing at Gray's house. Are you on shift tomorrow?"

Everly shook her head.

"Right, and it's Saturday, so Elise doesn't have school. My feelings about what I want haven't changed. Spend the weekend with me. You and Elise. Please?"

She nodded quickly, and Ball felt ten feet tall. He knew her independence was important to her.

"I'm working on Sunday, though."

"It's okay. Elise can stay here with me. I'll take her home when you get off shift, or you can just come back here."

He couldn't read what she was thinking, but after a moment, she just nodded again. "Okay."

"If you don't want to, it's okay, I just—"

"I want to. I'm hesitating because I don't want to move too fast, too soon."

He couldn't help it. Ball laughed. "Too fast? Ev, if it was up to me, I'd call the guys and move all your shit into my house tomorrow."

"Um . . . maybe we can postpone that until the day *after* tomorrow."

Ball chuckled. "Go get your sister. I'm exhausted, and I figure you probably are too."

"Yeah. Ball?"

"Yeah?"

"I'm glad you're all right. I'm very proud of you. And even if that little girl never knows who you are or what you did for her, I do. Thank you."

Her praise meant the world to him. Ball kissed her on the forehead. "You're welcome. Now go get your sister. Her nose is practically glued to the window, watching us."

Everly laughed. "Okay, but no lifting anything!"

"Yes, ma'am."

Ball had no intention of going into his house and lifting a damn thing until Everly and Elise were by his side. He lived in a good neighborhood, but it was the middle of the damn night. "Get a move on. Nothing good ever happens after two a.m.," he told her. "Go tell Elise that you guys are staying, and let's all get inside."

She nodded, and he watched as Everly hurried back to the car, opened the back door, and told her sister they were staying. Elise was out of the SUV in two seconds flat. She grabbed their bags from the back and was skipping toward him before even a minute had passed.

She grinned as she passed him and disappeared up the stairs toward his room with Everly's bag.

Everly came up beside him, shaking her head. "Guess she's good."

"Guess so."

Everly wrapped her arm around him and pulled him toward the stairs. "Come on. You look dead on your feet."

He was, but not so dead that his dick didn't twitch in his pants at the thought they'd soon be lying together in his bed. Telling himself to chill out, Ball let her lead him up the stairs.

"Are you going to let me look at your wound?" she asked.

Ball immediately shook his head. If she saw it, she'd get worked up, and they'd never get any sleep. "Not tonight. It's fine for now. When we get up, you can help me clean it."

She sighed but didn't protest. That was another thing Ball liked about Everly. She didn't always insist on having her way all the time. Holly was the queen of getting her own way.

"I'm going to go find Elise and make sure she's good. Then I'll change," Everly said, gesturing to the bathroom. "Okay?"

"Of course," Ball told her. He wondered what she'd say if he requested she change right there in front of him, but decided not to push his luck. She disappeared out into the hall, and a few minutes later she returned and headed for the bathroom. Ball quickly removed his dirty jeans and shirt. He stripped off his boxers and put on a fresh pair, and then pulled on a T-shirt just as Everly came back into the room. He normally slept in nothing but his boxers, but he didn't want Everly to worry about his wound. And if she saw the bandage, she'd worry.

She looked adorable in her pajamas. Her hair was in disarray on her head, and he wanted nothing more than to muss it even further.

Telling himself to cool it, Ball strode toward her, kissed her on the forehead, and went into the bathroom behind her without a word.

He brushed his teeth and washed his face, not bothering to shave since he'd done so not too long ago.

The view that met his gaze when he went back into his bedroom made him stop in his tracks.

Everly had turned off all the lights except for the one on the nightstand next to his side of the bed. She was under the covers, and all he could see was her shoulders and her hair spread out on his pillow. She looked nervous, but so exactly right, he almost couldn't breathe for a second.

"Ball?"

Without a word, he came toward the bed. He lifted the covers and slid in. The sheets were cool against his skin, but the second he came in contact with her body, warmth engulfed him. He turned her and pressed his chest to her back.

They both sighed.

"I've missed this," he told her softly.

"Me too."

Ball kissed her shoulder and finally let himself fully relax. He'd been on alert for more than four days now. But the second he closed his eyes and inhaled Everly's familiar scent, he was a goner. He should've checked on Elise, made sure she was settled in all right and didn't need anything.

In the past, he'd also lie in bed after a mission and go over it in his head. But tonight . . . rather, this morning . . . his body immediately shut down after he gathered Everly into his arms.

She was here. With him. In his bed. All was right in his world.

Chapter Thirteen

Everly wasn't sure what woke her. She'd been sleeping like the dead. Hadn't slept as deep and as hard as she had the night before in years.

Something tickled her neck.

Her eyes popped open, and she was moving before she thought about what was going on. She heard a grunt but ignored it as she fought to get out from under the covers.

The morning light coming through the curtains made it easy enough to see where she was . . . and who she was with.

Panting, she stood next to the bed and stared down at Ball—who was lying there with one hand over his nose, staring back at her.

Awareness found her all at once. She was at Ball's house. In his room. In his bed.

And she'd just hit him in the face.

"Holy shit, I'm so sorry! Are you okay?" she asked, climbing back onto the mattress and reaching for him.

The second she did, he lunged, and before she knew it, Everly was flat on her back once again.

"Where was I?" he murmured.

"*Ball!* Did I hurt you?"

"No," he said, then lowered his head to nuzzle at her neck once more.

"Seriously, Ball. I'm so sorry. I woke up disoriented and felt you touching me and panicked."

"It's okay, Ev," he said.

She shivered as his lips caressed her vulnerable neck. Goose bumps broke out on her arms. "Ball?"

"Mmmm?" He didn't stop his exploration, and now his hand got into the action as well. Sliding under the sleeve of her T-shirt so he could touch her skin, he brushed his fingertips against her shoulder even as his lips closed around her earlobe.

"I should check on Elise," Everly said, holding back the moan that threatened to escape by sheer force of will.

"She's fine," Ball mumbled. "She'll still be sleeping."

"What time is it?"

"Don't know."

"Ball!"

"What?" he asked, lifting his head and raising an eyebrow. His fingers didn't stop their movement, and Everly shivered.

"I should look at your wound."

"I'm fine."

"But—"

"Everly, I'm fine. My side is fine. Elise is fine. This is the first time I've had you in my bed, and it's been four days since I last saw you. Touched you. If you don't want this . . . now's the time to say something. If you're just nervous, I can work with that. But if you truly don't want to make love, tell me. I'm not an asshole. I won't shrivel up and die if you want to wait."

She *was* nervous, but Everly still wanted him. She appreciated that he wasn't pressuring her.

Deciding to go for it, she reached down and grabbed hold of the hem of her shirt. Arching her back, she pulled it up and off, throwing it over the side of the mattress.

Leaving her arms above her head, she stared at Ball with an almost defiant look.

He didn't say a word, merely stared back, taking in every inch.

Shifting uncomfortably the longer he stayed silent, and regretting her impulsive action, Everly moved to pull the sheet over her naked chest.

But before she could even lower her arms, her wrists were caught in Ball's hands. His hold was firm, though it didn't hurt in the least. Everly felt her nipples harden, but didn't take her eyes from Ball's face. He let go of her wrists, and she kept still as he devoured her with his gaze.

His eyes were wide, as if he couldn't bear to even blink because he might miss something, and he licked his lips several times.

Then he slowly, ever so slowly, leaned forward.

An involuntary moan escaped her throat before he even touched her, but the second his lips closed around one of her nipples, it grew in intensity. She reached down and palmed the back of his head with one hand, and the other gripped his thick biceps. Her back arched as she pressed herself harder against him.

"Ball!" she exclaimed.

He didn't answer her, merely continued to suck and tease her nipple. His mouth was warm, and when he used his teeth to gently nip, she nearly came out of her skin. She felt him smile against her, then he moved his head to tease her other nipple.

If Everly hadn't opened her eyes at just the right moment, she would've missed the way he winced as he moved.

The last thing she wanted was him being in pain the first time they made love.

Knowing if she said something about it, he'd deny anything was wrong, she pushed against him gently until he was on his back, then Everly straddled him.

He didn't miss a beat at the change of position. He reached up and grabbed behind her neck, tugging her down to him. He lifted his head and took one of her tits in his mouth, even as his hand lightly pinched the other nipple.

Everly wasn't a newbie to sex. She was thirty-four, and she'd had her share of partners, but somehow, hovering over a man on all fours while he suckled her breasts was something she'd never experienced before. It was somewhat raunchy, and sexy as hell. She felt every suck on her nipple as a spark of desire shooting straight to her pussy.

Without thought, she began to rock back and forth slightly, the movement making her boobs sway and adding another dimension to the sensations.

Ball let his head plop back down on the pillow. He stared up at her, watching as she continued to sway above him.

"Fuck, you're sexy," he said, his eyes glued to her tits.

She sat up, forcing him to let go of her neck or risk hurting her. Both of his hands now rested on her thighs, caressing her. She waited until his eyes came up to meet hers.

"Here's how this is gonna go," she said as sternly as possible. Inside, she felt like a submissive puppy, wanting nothing more than to roll over on her back and let Ball have his way with her. But she summoned the take-no-shit cop from deep within and said, "You're hurt. You're gonna lie there and let *me* do this. The last thing I want is your wound to open and for you to bleed all over me. Got it?"

"Yes, ma'am," Ball said seriously. His hands smoothed higher up her thighs, until his thumbs brushed against the creases of her legs.

She seriously wished she hadn't worn a pair of leggings to bed now.

"You're so beautiful," Ball said in an awed tone.

A denial was on the tip of her tongue, but Everly pushed it back. She'd never thought of herself that way before, but she couldn't deny that the look in Ball's eyes made her rethink her image of herself. Why *shouldn't* she be beautiful? Just because she didn't like the small pooch she couldn't seem to get rid of, or thought her boobs were a little too saggy, didn't mean she wasn't beautiful. Women were way too quick to put themselves down, and if the look on Ball's face was anything to go by, he wasn't seeing anything he didn't like.

She sat up straighter and arched her back a little bit more.

"Fuck," Ball muttered, his eyes immediately zeroing in on her chest again. Wanting to see him too, Everly pushed her hands under the hem of his own T-shirt, and he immediately did what he could to help her remove it. The material sailed behind her when she threw it, her attention centered on the perfection beneath her.

Ball had very broad shoulders, which wasn't a surprise. His biceps flexed as he replaced his hands on her thighs. He had a very prominent happy trail leading under his boxers. His abs looked as if they were chiseled out of granite, and Everly couldn't stop her hands from exploring.

She kept her hands away from the bandage on his side, refusing to let the sight of it ruin the mood. She hated that he'd been hurt, wanted to see exactly how badly, but she needed him inside her more.

Flattening her palms on his stomach, she leaned forward, feeling his belly contract as she caressed him. His nipples beaded under her hands as she rubbed her palms over them. She curled her fingers around his shoulders and leaned down even farther. Her nipples brushed over his chest, the slight hair tickling as she explored.

She deliberately moved up, then back, dragging her nipples over him once more.

"Enough," Ball groaned. His hands gripped her waist, and he adjusted her so her pussy was directly over his cock. He was hard, and Everly couldn't stop herself from grinding down on him. Her underwear and leggings, and his boxers, prevented either of them from getting maximum enjoyment out of the sensation.

Ball shoved his hands under her waistband and palmed her ass, even as he pressed her harder against him. He didn't say anything, but the way his eyes dilated and his legs shifted told her everything she needed to know.

He was just as desperate for her as she was for him.

Moving quickly, dislodging his hands in the process, she stood up next to the bed and shoved her underwear and leggings off in one quick movement.

"Condom?" she asked, even as Ball was shoving his boxers down his legs.

He gestured to the table next to the bed. Everly wrenched open the drawer and grabbed the box. It was sealed, and it was taking precious seconds to try to open it.

Ball took it from her hand and ripped. Condoms went flying everywhere.

For a second, Everly could only stare, then she giggled. Her giggles turned into a full-blown laugh. She quickly bent down and picked up one of the packets off the floor and climbed back onto the bed. Not thinking about how much more intimate the position would be when she wasn't wearing anything, Everly straddled Ball once more.

It wasn't until she was settled on his thighs, staring at his hard cock, that she realized how open she was to Ball.

Her eyes whipped up to his, and predictably, he was staring straight at her pussy.

Her muscles clenched, and Everly had to make a conscious decision not to fall over on her side and grab the sheet to cover up.

Ball's hands went back to her thighs, and this time, when his thumbs caressed the creases of her legs, she squirmed. He was so close to where she needed him.

"Stay still and let me look at you for a second," Ball ordered in a gruff tone.

It was an almost-impossible task. Between her embarrassment and desire, she wanted to do anything but just sit there with her legs spread open and let him stare, but she did. To distract herself, she examined him just as eagerly.

His cock was thick, and arched upward toward his belly button. The veins seemed to pulse, and even as she stared, it twitched, and a bead of precome appeared on the head.

But her perusal of his manhood was forgotten when the sight of the bandage on his side registered once more.

Everly had no way of telling how bad the wound was, since it was covered, but the longer she stared at it, the more she second-guessed what they were doing. Her brows furrowed in concern, and she started to climb off him.

"Oh no," Ball said. "Don't get distracted." He grabbed her around the waist and pulled her upward.

Not wanting to squirm away and hurt him any more than he already was, Everly assisted by scooting forward on her knees.

His cock brushed against her open folds, making her hesitate yet again.

Ball growled something under his breath and yanked her forward quickly.

Before she knew it, Everly was looking down her body at Ball's face. She was hovering over his chest, and he was staring between her legs as if he were a starving man who hadn't eaten in a week, and she was a juicy steak.

His gaze slowly worked its way up her body until he was looking into her eyes. "Come up here," he said softly.

Knowing what he wanted, and as eager to feel his mouth between her legs as he was to get it there, she forgot about his injury and shuffled forward a few more inches. Ball scooted his body down a bit and put a pillow behind him, shoving it under his head.

Everly could feel his hot breath against her now, and she closed her eyes in anticipation.

"Spread your legs a bit more," Ball instructed, helping by putting his hands on her inner thighs and lightly pressing.

She did, and before she could truly prepare herself, Ball was there. Licking and sucking as if she were his last meal.

Groaning, Everly jerked, but Ball held her still as he feasted on her folds. He used his tongue, his lips, and even his teeth to devour her. It was like nothing she'd ever experienced before. No lover had ever been this . . . *feral* with her. This demanding. And she fucking *loved* it.

At one point, Everly looked down and couldn't help the whimper that escaped. Ball's face was covered in her excitement. Even his nose glistened with her juices. He was reveling in turning her on and eating her out, and his excitement more than showed in his enthusiasm.

When he latched on to her clit and sucked hard, Everly tried to pull away, the sensations too much. But he must've anticipated that, because his hand palmed her ass, his pinkie brushing against her back hole.

"Ball!" she exclaimed.

He didn't answer with words, merely increased his suction on her little ball of nerves.

Everly couldn't think. Couldn't decide if she should pull away or press harder against him. And he didn't give her an option. He continued to love on her clit until her thighs began to shake in preparation for an orgasm.

Luckily his other hand grabbed hold of her waist to steady her, because a second later, she exploded. She jerked and writhed in his grip as he continued to lick her clit even as she was coming.

"Shit! Ball . . . oh my God . . . !" Everly knew she wasn't making sense, but she felt as if her world had just imploded. Her body was like a limp noodle, and she couldn't seem to hold a thought in her head.

When she came back to herself, she was somehow sitting on Ball's thighs. He was rolling the condom over his cock, then his hands were back at her hips.

"Fuck me, Ev," he said in a low, husky voice.

His face still glistened, and he licked his lips in anticipation.

Now that she was cognizant again, Everly realized she was still turned on. Her inner thighs were soaked, and she wanted him inside her more than she wanted to breathe. Quickly rising up on her knees, she moved forward and took hold of his dick in her hand.

He inhaled sharply and didn't take his eyes from where they were about to be joined. Everly wanted to put on a show for him. Wanted to take him extremely slowly so he could watch, but her body had other ideas.

As soon as she notched the head of his cock to her folds, she felt the need to have him buried deep inside her still-throbbing pussy.

She dropped down on him in one fell swoop. Not giving either of them time to adjust.

They both gasped for air as he bottomed out inside her.

"God *damn*," Ball whispered. "I can feel you gripping my cock as if you'll never let go."

He was big. And it had been so long since she'd made love that having him inside her was just a bit painful, but her orgasm had been so intense, it had eased his way.

"Ev?" he asked, his fingers digging into her so hard, she knew she'd probably bruise, but couldn't care less.

"Yeah?" she whispered.

"Move."

So she did. Slow at first, then faster and faster, until she was slamming her body down on Ball's, his wound forgotten. Her tits bounced up and down so hard, she had a feeling her chest was going to be sore later, but the way Ball's gaze was fixated on them made her feel sexy as hell.

"So beautiful," he murmured. One hand stayed on her hip, and the other rested on her belly. She almost complained, not wanting him to touch her there—then his thumb brushed against her clit. It threw off her rhythm, and he smiled. "Keep going."

"I can't think when you touch me like that," she complained.

"Good. Keep fucking me, Everly."

She did her best, but when he rubbed harder against her clit as she rode him, it was difficult to remember what she was doing. Looking down, she saw red blotches on Ball's upper chest, and she loved seeing the evidence that he wasn't as unaffected as he seemed to be.

"I'm close," she warned as the familiar feel of another orgasm rolled up within her.

"I want to feel you squeeze my cock," Ball said, the dirty words turning her on even more. "Force the come out of me, Ev. Do it. Fuck me and squeeze me dry."

It wasn't his words, so much as the way he used his fingernail against her extremely sensitive clit. It hurt, but in a good way. One hand braced on his chest, and the other grabbed hold of his biceps so hard, she knew she was leaving marks behind.

"That's it. Fuck yeah, so beautiful. God!"

She barely heard his words through the haze of euphoria that had taken over her body. She slammed her pelvis down and stayed there, more because she couldn't move any longer than for any erotic reason, and shook as she exploded.

She vaguely felt him grab hold of her hips and forcibly move her up and down twice before holding her to him and arching his back.

She couldn't feel him come because of the condom, but she watched as the red blotch on his chest spread, and he squeezed his eyes closed as he came. His hips jerked under hers, and a grunt escaped his mouth before every muscle in his body relaxed.

Easing herself down on top of him, Everly let herself go limp. Ball's arms came around her, holding her to him, and neither spoke for a long moment.

She felt his heart beating hard, just like hers. After a while, she felt his cock slip out of her body, and she shivered.

"I hate that," she whispered.

"Not any more than I do," Ball whispered back. Then he brought his hands up and held her face tenderly.

Somehow looking him in the eyes when she was still lying butt naked on top of him, and remembering how wanton she'd been, was harder than facing down a bad guy hyped up on meth.

"That. Was. Fucking. Perfect," he said, enunciating each word carefully. "*You* were perfect."

"I . . . uh . . . I'm not sure you should get used to me being like that."

"Like what?"

Everly bit her lip. "Um, so . . . enthusiastic?"

He smiled. "That's *exactly* how I want you. Every single time. If I can't get you to light up like that for me every time, then I'm doing something wrong."

His words made her melt. "Ball . . ."

"Kannon."

"What?"

"Next time you're coming on my tongue or my cock, I want you to say my real name."

"Okay," she said immediately, liking that.

He leaned up and kissed her lightly, then dropped his hands and said, "I hate to be the one to break up this tender cuddle time, but I have to deal with this condom."

"And maybe wash your face," Everly said with a chuckle.

He shook his head. "Nope. I'm gonna leave you there for as long as possible."

"Ball!" she exclaimed, propping herself up on his chest and lightly smacking his shoulder. "That's gross!"

"Nothing about you is gross," Ball said with a smile. "Now scoot over and let me up. I need to put on some boxers so you aren't tempted to jump me again when you help me clean my wound."

Shit! She'd truly forgotten all about it. Everly scrambled off him so fast, she would've fallen if he didn't put out a hand to steady her. "Damn! I forgot! Are you okay? I didn't hurt you, did I?"

He didn't answer, and Everly looked at him with concern.

Then she rolled her eyes. His gaze was glued once more to her boobs.

Leaning over, she grabbed his T-shirt, which was miraculously still clinging to the edge of the mattress. She pulled it over her head and barely resisted laughing when he blinked, as if coming out of a trance. She had a feeling flashing her boobs at him in the future would be a great way to distract him. "Ball? Are you okay?"

"I'm fine," he reassured her, then rolled off the mattress and stretched gingerly.

Everly devoured him with her eyes. Lying down naked, he was hot, but standing and displaying every inch of his rock-hard body? He was fucking phenomenal.

"Like what you see, Ev?"

"You know I do," she told him, staring at the way his thigh muscles bunched as he walked toward her.

"My eyes are up here," he quipped.

Everly didn't even feel guilty for taking her own sweet time in meeting his gaze. Even semihard and still covered in a condom, his cock was impressive. She licked her lips.

"Fuck, Everly. Cut me a break here, would ya? I'm trying my best not to jump you and fuck you so hard, you'll feel me every time you sit for a week."

His words made her shiver. As it was, she was already going to be sore, considering how hard she'd taken him, but thinking about him being in charge in bed was enough to make her nipples tighten under his shirt once more.

He grabbed the back of her neck and forced her up on her knees on the bed. She was still shorter than he was in this position, and the way she had to crane her head up and back to meet his mouth was fucking hot.

He kissed her hard, the taste of herself on his tongue only making the moment more carnal than it already was.

Then he let her go and turned to head into the bathroom. "Give me a minute, then you can come in and help me clean my wound."

Everly nodded, fell backward on the bed, and stared at his ass as he went. How she'd gotten so lucky, she had no idea, but she was going to hold on to him with both hands. Kannon "Ball" Black was *hers*. Period. Done. And she wasn't giving him back. No way. No how.

Chapter Fourteen

Elise: I'm headed home on the bus now.

Everly: Why? I thought you had an Outdoor Club meeting?

Elise: I quit.

Everly: What? Why?

Elise: Because. I don't want to talk about it.

Everly: Well, you're going to have to. I'll be home around five or so. We'll talk then.

Everly: Hear me?

Elise: Yeah, whatever.

Everly: Go straight to the apartment and lock the door behind you. I didn't arrange for anyone to come hang with you today because I thought you'd be at school until I got out of work.

Elise: I'm not a baby. I'm fine by myself. It's not like I'm not used to it.

Everly stared down at her phone in dismay. Something was up with her sister. It had been brewing for the last week or so. She'd seemed happy the morning after Ball had gotten home from his mission. They'd had a perfect day on Saturday, and she'd said that Ball had been "awesome" the following Sunday when Everly was at work.

But something had obviously happened at school, because Elise had been sullen and withdrawn when she'd gotten home Monday night. And now on Friday, only a few days later, she'd apparently quit the Outdoor Club, which she'd been so excited about. They were supposed to have gone on a short hike after school today, and then tomorrow, they had a long eight-mile hike planned.

Everly had been looking forward to it because that meant she and Ball had the entire day to themselves. And he'd already informed her that they were going to spend it in his bed.

They'd spent every night together over the last week, and Everly had never been so content. It wasn't the sex. All right, it wasn't *just* the sex. It was sharing her day with him. Talking about the people she'd met and helped, and even the ones who weren't so glad to have met her in her official capacity as a police officer.

He'd talked to her about the websites he was working on, and Everly had to admit she was always impressed. She hadn't truly understood what was so hard about putting a website together, but that was before she saw the work that Ball put into those he designed.

They laughed while cooking together. They watched television, and Everly loved how Ball and Elise got along and teased each other. The last week had been everything she'd ever wanted in a relationship.

But something was up with Elise, and Everly didn't have enough experience with teenagers to figure out what. Ball had told her to give her sister some time and she'd eventually talk about whatever was bugging her, but Everly wasn't so sure.

Sighing, Everly sent one last text to her sister.

Everly: I know you aren't a baby. I'm sorry. I'm just worried. I'll be home as soon as I can, and we'll talk.

Her sister didn't text back.

Not that Everly really expected her to. She was going to text Ball next, but dispatch radioed in about a disturbance, and Everly didn't get the chance.

As it turned out, she wasn't able to get home by five. It was more like six thirty, and that was because, after the disturbance call, she was busy nonstop. Then an accident with severe injuries happened right before the end of her shift, and it wasn't like she could just leave the scene because she was supposed to be off the clock.

Despite her busy day, she hadn't stopped thinking of Elise. She was frustrated that something seemed to be wrong, when she'd been doing so well. The last thing she wanted was for her sister to backslide. And Elise's current mood made Everly question if she'd done the right thing by taking Elise away from her friends and her school in LA. It wasn't like her to doubt herself, but her sister's abrupt decision to quit the club—and her refusal to discuss it—had added to an already difficult day.

By the time she got home, Everly was not only stressed and frustrated, but also a bit irritated with Elise. The more she thought about how her sister had blown off her concerns, and Elise's low blow about being left alone, the more upset Everly got. She was uncomfortable—the day had been hot, and the tank top she wore under her uniform was soaked with sweat—and she'd also sent a short text to Ball, letting him know she most likely wasn't going to be able to come over, and that she'd see him tomorrow, hopefully. Just one more thing piled on her shitty day . . . not getting to see Ball.

Everly unlocked the door to her apartment—and immediately panicked at seeing it was dark.

Elise should've been home. It was after dinnertime, so she'd expected to see her sister in the living room, watching TV.

Dropping her bag, Everly rushed down the hallway toward Elise's bedroom. She slammed the door open in her panic and stared.

Elise was lying on her bed, writing furiously in a journal that Ball had suggested Everly get for her sister.

Both relieved that she was all right and irritated that she'd been so scared, Everly stomped over to the bed and pounded on the mattress next to Elise's shoulder.

Her sister jerked in panic, then scowled at Everly when she saw her standing there.

What the hell? Elise signed.

Have you done your homework? Everly asked.

It's Friday. I don't have to have it done until Monday.

That was true. But Everly was upset, her dread upon walking into a dark apartment making her irrational. *I haven't asked a lot of you, but the apartment's a mess. You haven't taken the trash out yet, and your room is a pigsty.*

Elise glared. *Is that why you invited me here? To be a maid?*

Everly took a deep breath and tried to calm down. *No. I'm sorry. Did you eat?*

Of course. I was starving, and it's not like you were here. Was I supposed to wait? Yeah, not happening.

I'm sorry, Elise. There was a bad accident, and I had to stay late.

Whatever.

Everly clenched her teeth together, trying to keep her cool. Considering the last thing she'd seen at work that day, a surly teen should be nothing . . . The sight of the infant screaming her head off in her child's seat in the crumpled car still hadn't left her mind. She'd been cut by flying glass, and the fire department hadn't been able to get to her immediately. So she'd had to sit there, bawling, for about twenty minutes. It had been heart wrenching.

Perspective. With another deep breath, Everly tried again.

Can we talk about the Outdoor Club?

No.

Come on, Elise. Talk to me.

You're not my mom. You don't have to play one when we're alone.

Everly blinked. Wow. That had been harsh.

She knew she should stay and push to find out what was bothering her sister, but she was tired, not in the mood to try. That remark about not being her mom . . . yeah, that hurt. And the hurt actually made her feel guilty, considering what Elise had been through.

Without a word, she turned and left Elise's bedroom, shutting the door quietly behind her. She changed out of her uniform and into a pair of sweats and a T-shirt, not bothering with underwear or a bra, then she wandered through the living room and into the kitchen.

She opened the refrigerator and stared inside sightlessly. She wasn't actually hungry . . . all she really wanted to do was sit and cry.

She'd been so proud of how well she and Elise had been doing, but after the day from hell, and her sister's attitude, Everly wondered anew if she'd done the right thing, after all. Maybe she should've left Elise in Los Angeles with all her friends, in Me-Maw and Pop's stable home.

More than two months had passed since her abduction, and neither the cops nor the FBI had found out any more information about who'd been behind it. It was highly unlikely Elise was in any more danger. Yet Everly still felt a subtle paranoia lurking.

She knew she was blowing her tiff with Elise out of proportion, that things would look better in the morning, but at the moment, she couldn't help but doubt herself and all the decisions she'd made since bringing her sister to Colorado Springs.

Feeling tears well up, she closed the fridge and turned her back to it, sliding down until her ass was on the floor and she rested against the big stainless-steel appliance.

The phone in her hand vibrated with a text.

Ball: Hey, you home?

God. She couldn't deal with anything else right now.

Everly: Yeah.

Ball: Great. I'm downstairs. I'll be up in a few.

Wait, what? He was there?

Everly: Now's not a good time.

Ball: Why?

Everly: It's just not. Go home. I'll see you later.

Ball: No. I'm almost there.

Now she *was* crying. Maybe if she didn't answer the door, he'd just go away. Elise wouldn't hear him knocking, so he wouldn't disturb her. Her neighbors were kinda nosy, though. If he got obnoxious, they'd call the cops on him.

The first knock on the door sounded as soon as she had that thought.

Sighing in frustration, Everly got up off the floor. She'd never hear the end of it if her fellow cops were called for a disturbance at her address. Besides, she wouldn't do that to Ball. It wasn't his fault she was in a piss-poor mood.

She padded over to the door and unlocked it, but didn't bother opening it. She heard Ball turning the knob even as she walked away. She detoured into the living room instead of going back to the kitchen and sat on the end of the couch. She put her feet up on the cushion and wrapped her arms around her updrawn knees.

Within seconds, Ball was there. He gently wiped the tears from her cheeks. "What's wrong?"

Everly shrugged.

"Elise all right?"

She nodded.

"You're not hurt?"

She shook her head.

Ball slightly relaxed and sat down next to her. He hauled her into his lap, and Everly briefly resisted the comfort before giving in. He held her close without speaking. How long they sat like that, Everly had no idea. By the time she was ready to talk, she figured his legs had to be numb from her sitting on them, but he didn't seem to mind in the least.

"Ever have one of those days where nothing seems to go right?" she asked.

"Yeah."

"Well, today's been one of those days for me. Elise quit the Outdoor Club, which I thought she loved. She won't talk to me, and she's acting weird, lashing out. Work sucked. It was one crazy asshole after another today, and to top it off, I had to work an hour and a half past my shift because of an accident that happened right at five. No one was killed, thank God, but there were a ton of injuries, including a little, tiny baby. I'm hungry, afraid my sister hates me and I'm fucking up her life, and now I don't get to spend the day with you tomorrow."

To Ball's credit, he didn't immediately try to talk her out of her funk, he simply held her tighter and ran his fingers down her arm soothingly.

Finally, she sighed and sat up.

"Better?" he asked.

"Not really. But I can't exactly sit around like a moping teenager all night."

Ball took her hand in his. He led her to the kitchen and helped her sit on the counter. "Let me make you something. What are you in the mood for?" he asked.

Everly shrugged. "I don't know."

He opened the cabinets and looked at what she had. Then he looked inside the refrigerator. Turning to her, he asked, "How about cheese quesadillas? You've got tortillas and shredded cheese. There are a few tomatoes on your counter, and you've got sour cream as well."

Nodding, Everly put her hand over her stomach when it growled.

Smiling, Ball wisely didn't comment, simply got to work making her some dinner. He actually made two and, after he'd helped her down off the counter and gotten her seated at the table with a glass of lemonade and her meal, asked, "Do you mind if I take this one to Elise?"

"Of course not. But don't blame me when she bites your head off."

Ball hugged her with an arm around her shoulders and gently kissed her cheek. "For the record, you're doing an amazing job with her. She's fifteen. I'm not surprised her inner bitch finally came out. She's been here for two months, I was wondering when it would happen."

"Well, aren't you the smarty-pants," Everly said a bit snarkily.

He simply smiled at her. "Eat. You'll feel better once you get something in your belly."

Everly watched him grab the plate and head down the hall. Most men she knew would've turned around and gone the other way after getting her text. But not Ball. He ignored her bad mood, held her when she needed a hug more than a lecture, and was going to do his best to help Elise too.

Fuck, the man really was perfect.

~

Ball had no idea what he was going to say to Elise, but he had to try to talk to her. He hated seeing Everly so down. It wasn't in her nature to be grumpy, so he knew she had to have had a *really* bad day.

He also didn't like that Elise had quit something she'd seemed to love so much. Something must've happened. He hadn't known her all that long, but he hoped maybe she'd talk to him. That maybe she was just uncomfortable talking to her sister about whatever was bothering her. If nothing else, at least she'd know that he was worried.

Knocking on the door, he waited.

Then shook his head at himself. *Duh.* Elise couldn't hear him knocking.

He pushed open the door and paused, then peered inside.

Everly's sister was sitting on her bed, legs crossed, staring into space.

He pushed the door open all the way, and she looked up. She immediately smiled, and Ball took that as a good sign. He held up the plate with the quesadilla on it and raised his eyebrows.

She nodded and signed, *I'm hungry.*

He walked in and put the plate down on her nightstand. Elise gave him another small smile and reached for a wedge of the tortilla. He sat on the side of the bed, gave her a minute or two to chew, then signed, *Are you okay?*

She frowned. *You've been talking to Everly.*

She's upset. Not mad. But sad. Overwhelmed. She's worried about you. He had to resort to some finger spelling, but luckily, Elise seemed to understand him.

She looked down at her dinner.

Ball reached out and briefly touched her knee, getting her attention. When she was looking at him once more, he asked, *What happened with the Outdoor Club?*

The teenager lay back on the bed and pulled out her phone. She immediately began to type, her thumbs moving like lightning across the screen. Ball scooted until his back was against the footboard of her bed and waited for her to finish. When his phone vibrated, he looked down.

Elise: I didn't want to tell Everly because she already worries enough.

Ball: Tell her what? Talk to me.

Elise: It's just that every time we go on a hike, I feel weird.

Ball: Weird how?

Elise: Like someone is watching me. I know it's stupid, but I can't get the feeling out of my head. On the last hike we went on, it got so bad, I kinda freaked out. Everyone had to end the hike early and take me back to the school. I don't like being the weird kid. I mean, we're all already weird, but a deaf kid freaking out isn't a good thing, trust me.

Ball ignored her self-deprecation and concentrated on the main issue.

Ball: You did the right thing.

Elise: It doesn't feel like it. I like hiking. But I can't shake the feeling that someone's out there. Watching me. Have you heard from your guy about anything? Have they caught the guy who kidnapped me and the other girls?

Ball: I'm sorry, but no. You know the FBI had to drop the active investigation because of other cases. But they've still got their ear to the ground, just in case.

Elise huffed out a breath and let her arms fall to her sides. She stared up at the ceiling. Ball typed out a text and hit "Send." She didn't move when her phone vibrated in her hand. The flash on the camera was also blinking on and off, alerting her to the text, but she still didn't move.

Ball nudged her foot with his knee.

Finally, she sighed and looked at her phone.

Ball: What can I do to help you feel safer? Name it, I'll do it. Anything.

Elise took a deep breath before typing.

Elise: That's the thing. I don't know. I think I'm just being paranoid. I talked to my therapist about it, and she says that sometimes people imagine kidnappers around every corner after something like what happened to me. You and your friends are already pretty much babysitting me after school every day. I thought being out in the wilderness with friends would help make me feel freer, but instead it's made me more paranoid. I just want to go back to being the naive kid I was before. I'm scared to open any email from anyone I don't know, in case it's him. Every text I get, I feel the same way.

Ball: Do you want me to check your phone again?

Elise: What do you mean?

Ball: Check your phone. Make sure there aren't any tracker things on it.

Elise: I haven't been talking on those apps I was before.

Ball: I didn't say you have. But if someone knows what they're doing, they can send an email, and if you open it, even if you don't click on anything, it could put a tracker on your phone. A virus of sorts. I can plug your phone into my computer tomorrow, and Meat can log on and take a look.

Elise looked up and signed. *Really?*

Ball nodded and copied her sign. *Really.*

Elise: You wouldn't mind?

Ball: Absolutely not.

Elise: Will you check my sister's phone too? Part of me is scared that whoever took me will decide to go after Everly instead. I know it's silly, I mean, we're hundreds of miles away from Los Angeles, but she means everything to me. I know she's a cop, but I still worry.

Ball: I'll ask her. Elise?

Elise: Yeah?

Ball: Will you go out and talk to your sister? She was really upset when I got here tonight. Not mad, but just upset that she didn't know how to help you.

Elise: I can do that. Ball?

He smirked, but echoed her response anyway.

Ball: Yeah?

Elise: It's weird that we're talking this way. Hurry up and learn more signs, would ya?

Ball burst out laughing and lightly smacked her leg, then signed, *Go talk to your sister.*

I'm going. And Ball?

Yes?

Thanks. Since I'm not hiking tomorrow, can you have Meat look at my phone then?

I will. And we'll think of something fun to do tomorrow too.

Elise nodded and left the room.

Ball rested his elbow on a raised knee, put his chin on his hand, and stayed where he was, wanting to give the sisters time to clear the air. He hated that Elise had quit the club because she didn't feel safe. He had no idea if there was legitimately something to her feelings, or if it was a type of PTSD. Rex hadn't come up with any leads from her old cell phone. The people who designed the apps knew what they were doing. Most of the conversations were permanently deleted after a period of time had passed. Pictures, conversations, all of it. Poof. Gone.

The IP address on the stuff they did have led to a public library in Las Vegas, of all places. It was assumed the person had been rerouting and manipulating the IP addresses somehow, since the girls were all found in Los Angeles. Just to be safe, the authorities in Vegas had been notified, but after a few days of surveillance on the library, they hadn't seen anything out of the ordinary.

One thing was certain, though—Ball hadn't lied when he'd told Elise that he'd do whatever it took for her to feel safe. Over the last two months, he'd come to care about her almost as much as he cared about her sister.

She was funny and talented, and he knew without a doubt that she'd do something amazing with her life. Being kidnapped wouldn't define her, it would only make her stronger.

Ball shot off an email to Meat, letting him know that he needed him to look into Elise's new phone tomorrow, and he killed more time by checking out how the latest websites he'd designed looked on his mobile phone.

It wasn't long before he heard someone at the door. Looking up, he saw Everly standing there. She looked like a huge weight had been lifted from her shoulders, and he breathed out a sigh of relief.

"Feel better?" he asked.

She came toward him and crawled onto the bed, her knees resting on the mattress at his hips and her arms around his shoulders. "Yeah. Thanks."

"I didn't do anything."

"Whatever. You're like the teenager whisperer."

He chuckled. "Just wait until you see what I have in store for *you* tonight after she goes to bed."

As he hoped, Everly smiled. "Yeah?"

"Yeah."

"Your side's okay?"

"You know it is. You examined it in great detail this morning, if I recall. Right before you blew my mind . . . along with other things."

She smiled sexily, and Ball felt himself starting to get hard.

"I didn't hear you complaining."

"Fuck no. Why would I?"

"Come on, you. Elise is waiting in the other room for us to watch an episode of *Stranger Things*. Said she didn't want to burn her retinas by seeing us 'canoodling' . . . her word, not mine."

"Is there a sign for *canoodle*?" Ball asked, as he helped Everly stand.

"I doubt it. She spelled it out."

"I need to google that. Pick on her a bit," Ball said.

Everly pulled him to a stop and gazed at him with a serious look on her face.

"What?" he asked, concerned.

"Thank you for being so great," she said softly. "I know it's a lot, taking on a new girlfriend and her teenage sister."

Kissing her on the forehead, Ball said, "It's not a hardship. Especially not when both of you are so awesome. Come on . . . *Stranger Things* awaits."

She reached over and grabbed the plate with the half-eaten quesadilla and hooked her arm with his.

Later that night, as Ball lay replete and satisfied in Everly's bed and held her as she slept, he thanked his lucky stars that he and Everly hadn't gone through the shit his buddies and their women had. Yeah, they'd met because her sister had disappeared, but he was happy that their courtship had been relatively drama-free.

He fell asleep, content in the knowledge that the woman he was beginning to love and her sister were safe.

~

Tylor Tuttle sat in his work van across the street from the apartment his Elise was in. He watched as the light in her room went out, and he couldn't resist unzipping his pants and stroking himself while he thought about what their life together would be like . . . soon.

Out of all the girls he'd taken to test out, she was his favorite. He'd ultimately picked *her*. But he'd been stupid. Lax. And one of the second-string girls had gotten everyone rescued.

It didn't matter. He'd made sure not to leave any trace of himself in the house. He'd always worn gloves—and a condom, of course. The fact that the cops hadn't found him, or his house in Las Vegas, in the weeks since helped him relax a bit.

He'd been biding his time, watching his chosen bride for more than a month now. Memorizing her routines. Taking pictures of Elise and admiring how beautiful she was. Soon, she'd be his. His wife. His everything. She'd come to love him, just like the woman who was currently in the basement of his house in Las Vegas. But that one was old now. Used up. Had no spark left in her. He'd had her for fifteen years, and he needed someone newer. Younger.

He needed Elise.

The fact that she was deaf made her perfect.

She couldn't talk and annoy him.

She couldn't hear if anyone was in his house to call out for help.

He would be the center of her world.

She'd look to him for everything.

Food. Showers. Sex.

Unlike the woman in his basement, he'd let her bear his children. Lots of children.

They'd be a family. Forever.

Putting his head back, Tylor rubbed himself harder and faster and grunted when he came, thinking of Elise. Grabbing a tissue, he cleaned himself off and smiled.

Soon.

He picked up his phone and sent his Elise another message through their secret app. He'd been sending them to her for weeks. He knew she was reading them, she was just too shy to respond. That was okay. He liked that she was a good girl.

Rob: We'll be together soon, baby girl. Real soon.

Chapter Fifteen

Everly wasn't happy to hear the reason why her sister had quit the Outdoor Club, but she was also proud of her for being aware of her surroundings and not blowing off the weird feeling. As a cop, Everly had come to rely on those odd feelings. If she was approaching a car after pulling it over and felt weird vibes, she was always extremely cautious. Same when she was on a job as a SWAT officer. When the hair on the back of her neck stood up, she took extra precautions.

The weekend had actually turned out really fun. They'd all gone over to Ball's house Saturday morning, after he'd fixed them a huge breakfast of eggs, toast, bacon, and cinnamon rolls. There, he'd plugged Elise's phone into his computer and called Meat. After that was done, with Meat promising to get back to them as soon as he could, they'd all gone to the Cheyenne Mountain Zoo, which wasn't far from the Seven Bridges hike they'd all done together. At sixty-eight hundred feet above sea level, the mountainside conservation park was the highest zoo in America.

But more important, they had the world's largest giraffe herd. And babies. Lots and lots of giraffe babies.

Zoos weren't Everly's favorite thing. She always felt sorry for the animals being penned up, but she had to admit that feeding the giraffes and watching the babies totter around on their long legs had been amazing, and fun, and she'd loved seeing Elise relaxed and smiling.

She'd had to work on Sunday, but the feeling of coming "home" afterward was something she'd never had before. Ball had dinner waiting, had already helped Elise finish her homework, and they'd spent the evening relaxing, laughing, and helping Ball with his signing.

Everly hadn't been sure how spending nights at Ball's house would work out. She and Elise had finally gotten into a routine at her apartment. But she shouldn't have worried. Things were going extremely smoothly, and Everly couldn't have been happier. Ball didn't have any problem driving Elise in the mornings, and they all left at the same time . . . Everly for the police station, and Ball and Elise for the high school.

Somehow, instead of Elise and Everly's argument tearing them apart, it had helped bring the sisters closer together. Elise promised to do her best not to keep any more secrets about how she was feeling in regard to the kidnapping, and Everly promised not to treat her sister like she was a kid. Everly was more than aware that they'd been able to resolve things so quickly because of Ball. Elise liked him just as much as Everly did . . . well, maybe not *quite* as much.

Ball wasn't without his flaws. He was a perfectionist. Whether it was designing websites or trying to learn new signs, he wanted everything to be perfect, and he got somewhat moody when they weren't. He had a tendency to meddle, which had been a good thing that weekend, but Everly could see it being annoying under different circumstances. He'd been a bachelor for a very long time, and that showed in the way he burped freely and left his dirty dishes in the sink for days, and she didn't think he'd ever mopped a floor in his life.

But really, all that was superficial stuff. The things that mattered were that he always asked how her day had gone, then *listened* when she answered. He never got abrupt with her sister, and she had absolutely no doubt that whether she called him in the dead of night, or when he was in the middle of doing something, he'd drop everything to get to her.

It was that bone-deep belief that she and Elise came first in his life that was the clincher for Everly. He could suck at cooking (which he didn't), or be a slob (he wasn't), or do a hundred other petty little things, and it wouldn't matter. Not when she always felt as if she *mattered* to him.

Knowing she was quickly losing her heart to Ball, she was happy to receive a short text from him around lunchtime.

He'd heard back from Meat—who'd called and said he'd found something.

All the feel-good thoughts that had been flitting through her head all morning disappeared in a flash. She immediately called Ball.

"What's wrong?" she asked, instead of saying hello when he answered. "What'd he find?"

"I don't know yet. Meat just said that he wanted to talk to both of us at the same time. He had some more digging he needed to do first."

"Oh God. Has she still been talking to that Rob guy?"

"I don't know, but you need to stop panicking."

That was easy for him to say.

Just then, someone blew through a stop sign in front of her, and Everly knew she had to go. Frustrated because she really wanted to discuss more about her sister's phone and what Meat had found, but knowing she had to do her job, she quickly said, "I have to go. Are we coming to you tonight, or are you coming to us?"

She stilled at her own words. She'd just assumed they would be staying together. And she realized that it didn't matter where they slept. As long as she was with him, she was content.

"I'll come to you. We'll call Meat together. You get off at five, right?"

"Yeah."

"Okay. I'll come over around four thirty, maybe keep Elise company for a while until you get home. You want us to make anything in particular for dinner?"

All thoughts of the car that had run the stop sign gone, Everly closed her eyes at the comfort his words brought her. Talking about dinner and knowing he would be there for Elise made her want to cry. She was scared to find out what Meat had discovered, but they'd deal with it . . . together. "Whatever you make is fine," she managed.

"Okay, Ev. Try not to worry. Meat's good at what he does. If he found something, I can guarantee that he'll have suggestions as to how we should deal with it. And not only that, but if we need to worry about someone hurting Elise, the entire team will be on it. No one's gonna threaten one of our own and get away with it. Hear me?"

Yeah, she heard him. Loud and clear, and nothing had ever felt better in her life.

She'd always been the oddball. A female in a male-dominated profession. The girl with the deaf sister. The kid who had a druggie mom. But knowing she had the Mountain Mercenaries at her back if something happened to her sister was almost as comforting as one of Me-Maw's hugs.

"Yeah, I hear you," she said.

"You want me to text Elise and let her know the plan?"

Knowing she was pushing her luck already and needing to get her head back into work, Everly said, "Please. Thank you."

"Don't thank me for something that I love doing," Ball chastised. "I told you that last night after you tried to thank me for giving you an orgasm."

Everly grinned at the memory. He'd made her come harder than she'd ever come before, and she'd lain on the bed, a boneless mess, only able to say "Thank you." He'd laughed and told her that he should be the one thanking *her*, and if she ever tried to thank him for something he did for his own pleasure again, she'd be in trouble. He'd gone on to say that if she really wanted to show her appreciation, she could do so by fucking him like she had their first time together.

So she did.

They'd *both* been boneless messes by the time they were finally ready to go to sleep.

"Ball?"

"Right here."

"I . . . I don't know how I'd get through this without you."

His voice lowered, and she could hear the sincerity when he said, "You would've done it the same way you've kicked ass for the last thirty-four years of your life."

"I'm scared to death of letting you down like your partner and ex did," she admitted softly.

"Not happening," he said firmly. "Everly, you've already shown me in a million different ways that you are *nothing* like them. I held a grudge against all women because of the actions of two. That was stupid. I'm just glad you were able to forgive me and help me see the error of my ways."

"I—" Everly stopped herself from blurting out that she loved him just in time. It wasn't that she was ashamed to tell him, or even afraid, but the first time she said it, she wanted to be face-to-face with him. She wanted it to be special. It was crazy-early to even be thinking about love, but she'd never been one to hold back what she thought and felt.

"You what?" Ball asked.

"I'll see you later."

"Be safe," Ball told her.

"I will."

"Bye."

"Bye." Everly clicked off the phone and tried not to think about what Meat might've found on Elise's phone. Ball had told her the same thing he'd told Elise, that if she'd opened an attachment of any sort, it could've contained a virus that could lead a trafficking ring right to her. That wasn't likely, since those people liked to take girls no one was terribly concerned about . . . and with the publicity of the case and the fact that Elise wasn't even living in Los Angeles anymore, it made her a less-than-desirable target.

But that didn't make Everly feel any better.

Her radio crackled to life, the dispatcher calling for aid for a possible break-in in progress. Thoughts of her sister and Ball moved to the back of her mind as she switched gears to do her job.

~

Elise's head was down as she texted Kim, one of her friends back in Los Angeles. She kept in touch with a few girls, but not many. Most had seemed to forget about her the second she left.

Trudging up the stairs to the apartment, thumbs moving quickly over the screen of her phone as she texted, Elise wasn't in a hurry, because Everly wasn't home and Ball wouldn't be there for another hour and a half or so.

Smiling at the story her friend was telling about one of their old teachers, Elise told her to hang on a second, that she had to unlock her door. She put her phone under her arm so she had both hands free.

The second she'd turned the key in the lock and twisted the knob, someone shoved her inside so violently, Elise fell to her hands and knees just inside the door. Her phone fell to the floor, and Elise twisted to see who'd pushed her.

Gasping, she could only stare as the man she never thought she'd see again smiled down at her.

He'd shut the apartment door and was saying something, but she couldn't understand him. Scooting backward as fast as she could, Elise gasped again when her head hit a wall behind her.

The man who'd kidnapped her crouched, smiled, and, wearing gloves, badly signed *Hello* before standing up and reaching for something in his back pocket. He was tall and thin and extremely normal-looking. He had brown hair and extremely dark eyes . . . he didn't look threatening at all, which was why she'd gotten in the vehicle with him in the first place.

It wasn't until he'd grabbed her arm and yanked her purse away that she'd had an inkling he wasn't the mysterious Rob's father.

Not wanting to find out what he was reaching for, Elise leaped to her feet and ran for her room. Maybe if she could lock herself inside, she could open her window and yell for help.

But she didn't make it very far. The man, who definitely outweighed her and was almost a foot taller, tackled her from behind.

Elise went down like a sack of potatoes. The man's arms were around her, so she couldn't even put her hands out to stop her fall. She hit her chin on the carpet so hard she bit her lip and tongue. Blood welled up in her mouth, and she immediately spit it out.

A second later, the man's hand covered her mouth and nose.

Knowing she was probably making horrific noises, Elise fought. She did everything Ball had taught her, to no avail. The man was too heavy. His cologne reminded Elise of the night he'd nearly assaulted her in the dark.

Panicking, Elise realized that she was getting lightheaded. He was going to kill her. Right here in her own apartment. Ball was going to come over and find her dead body, and Everly would never forgive herself.

A moment later, Elise recognized that the man wasn't suffocating her. His gloved hand was wet . . . whatever chemical he'd put on his glove was making her pass out.

Her second-to-last thought was that she couldn't believe she was being kidnapped again.

Her very last thought, before she passed out, was thinking the odds of her being rescued this time were slim to none. He wasn't going to let her escape again. No way.

Everly parked her car and glanced at her watch. Ever since her talk with Ball, and learning that Meat had found something on Elise's phone, she couldn't concentrate. And not concentrating in her line of work wasn't a good thing. She'd requested to leave an hour early. Luckily the day had been slow as far as police work went, and her supervisor had granted the request.

Elise should've gotten home an hour before, but she wasn't answering any of the texts Everly had sent. Looking around, Everly didn't see Ball's Mustang, but wasn't really surprised; it was still early for him to be there. The lobby was empty when she entered, and Everly headed for the stairs.

Feeling oddly nervous, but thankful she'd been able to get off work early, Everly pushed open her apartment door. Knowing it would do no good to yell out for her sister, she put her bag on the floor just inside the door, and her purse and sunglasses on the kitchen counter. She headed for her bedroom to change for the night. Everly stripped off her bulletproof vest and uniform. She locked her weapon in her safe and changed into a pair of jeans and a T-shirt. Taking the time to brush her hair, she smiled as it fell in waves around her face, and studied herself in the mirror.

She felt different, but didn't *look* any different than she had a couple of months ago.

Had it really been just over two months since she'd met Ball? Since she'd been so furious with the way he'd disparaged her entire gender and assumed she would screw up the mission to find her sister?

Throughout her life, she'd never felt especially pretty. Even though Me-Maw had told her over and over that she was. Men liked to compliment her hair, but they'd usually follow that with some annoying comment about how hot she must be in bed because she was a redhead. It became easier to wear it in a bun or ponytail to try to curtail the rude comments. But knowing how much Ball liked to run his hand through her hair, she'd begun to leave it down more.

She still dressed the same, though, preferring comfortable clothes to the more trendy and fashionable duds. But inside, she felt more feminine. That was, of course, a direct result of how often Ball told her she was beautiful and spent hours showing her how much he liked looking at her body . . . both clothed and not.

Shaking off the thoughts, Everly turned to go find Elise. She pushed open her sister's door—and looked around in surprise.

She wasn't there. Her bed wasn't made, which was normal, and there were quite a few outfits lying around on the floor, not on hangers or in the dirty-clothes hamper, which wasn't out of character for her sister. She wasn't exactly a neat freak.

Confused, Everly turned and went back down the hallway. She peered into the half bath but still didn't find Elise. Standing in the doorway to the living area, Everly frowned deeply.

Elise wasn't there. And she had no idea where she could be. It wasn't like she'd made any friends in the apartment complex, because as far as Everly knew, there weren't any other teenagers living there.

Her book bag was lying next to a small table in the foyer of the apartment. Right next to where Everly had dropped her own bag minutes earlier.

Worried now, Everly pulled out her cell and shot off a quick text to Elise, asking where she was.

A flash of light caught her eye, and Everly turned to see Elise's cell phone on the floor halfway under one of the tables next to the couch, the blinking light indicating that a new text had arrived.

Dread filling her, Everly dove for the device. At the last second, she realized she probably shouldn't touch it, just in case there were fingerprints. Using the edge of a blanket hanging off the couch, she picked it up. The screen was cracked, but otherwise the phone seemed to be in working order. Everly used the bottom of her T-shirt to protect the device from her stray fingerprints and clicked the "Home" button. The text she'd just sent came up on the main screen. So did a few others from Kim, a girl Elise knew in LA.

It looked like the two of them had been in the middle of a conversation when Elise had suddenly stopped chatting.

Everly scrolled through the text conversation.

Kim: You should've seen Mr. Thompson. His face got all red, and I thought he was gonna lose it.

Elise: I bet that was hilarious! Hang on a sec . . . gotta open my door.

Kim: It was! I still laugh just thinking about it. I wish someone had gotten a picture.

Kim: Elise?

Kim: You there?

Kim: What happened?

Kim: Fine, I guess I'll talk to you later.

And that was it until her own text, telling her sister that she'd be home sooner than she'd planned.

A funny feeling welled up in her throat—and Everly suddenly felt lost. Even though she was a cop, for a second she had no idea what to do. Should she call 911? And tell them what? She couldn't find her sister? They'd just tell her what the police out in LA had . . . that she was a kid, she was probably visiting friends.

But no . . . her coworkers knew what had happened. They wouldn't do that, would they? They'd take her concerns seriously, especially after Elise had already been kidnapped.

Too many thoughts ran through her head, and Everly simply stood in the middle of her apartment, breathing way too hard, trying desperately not to panic.

Turning, she stared absently down at the floor in the hallway . . . and saw a small red spot.

Falling to her knees, Everly stared in disbelief at the patch of blood.

Bile came up her throat, and she forced it back down. She couldn't panic. Not right now. Elise needed her to be strong. To be smart.

And just like that, as if a switch had been flicked inside her, the fear that had almost overwhelmed her turned to fury. An anger like she'd never felt before covered her like a shroud. Thick, pulsing, and potent.

She'd been taught to be cautious and only use deadly force in cases of extreme danger, but Everly knew at that moment if the person responsible for hurting her sister had been standing in front of her, she'd have blown him away with absolutely no remorse and no hesitation. She was that angry.

She got to her feet and put Elise's phone on the kitchen counter. Then she reached for her own phone to call Ball, to get reinforcements, but before Everly even touched the screen, it rang.

Startled, Everly stared at the unknown number on the screen . . . and a strange calmness slipped over her. This was him. The asshole who'd stolen her sister. She *knew* it.

Clicking on the icon, she answered, "Hello?"

"If you want to see your sister again, you'll follow my directions to the letter. Are you listening?"

"Yes." This wasn't the time to be tough. Everly needed information. And she needed it now. There would be time to take this asshole down later. After Elise was safe.

"I'm watching you. Right now. I put a few cameras in your apartment so I could keep my eye on you."

Everly's head swiveled, trying to spot one of the cameras.

"You won't find them. Well, you would if you had the time to look, but you don't. My point is, don't do anything stupid. If you call anyone after we hang up, I'll kill her. Slowly and painfully, and I'll make sure she knows it's *your* fault. And I really hope you don't, because I don't want to kill Elise. She's so pretty. And quiet. That's calming. I can't stand when they scream. I plan on keeping her for a very long time."

Everly wanted to scream herself. She wanted to tell the man on the other end of the line to fucking drop dead and leave her sister alone. But the fact that he didn't want to kill Elise was good . . . *if* he was telling the truth. He could be lying, there was a chance he'd already killed her, but she didn't think he had. She'd learned to read people pretty well from her years on the job. And this guy sounded obsessed.

"I'm listening," she told the man.

"Good. I'm sure you're wondering why I'm bothering to call you, aren't you? Why I'm not already gone like the wind with my prize."

The thought *had* crossed her mind. "A little," she said.

"It's because you're a cop. A dirty, stinkin' *cop*. If you weren't, I'd already be starting my new life with my beautiful bride. But you aren't going to give up looking for her. I know it. You'll be a thorn in my side forever. And I can't have that. I have to take care of loose ends."

That didn't sound good, but he was absolutely right. There was no way Everly would ever stop looking for her sister. No matter how many years went by.

But . . . neither would Me-Maw and Pop. Or Ball. Or his friends. For that matter, neither would her friends and colleagues at the police department. This guy apparently hadn't factored in *any* of those people, which made no sense, but at the moment, she wasn't going to look a gift horse in the mouth. He'd called her. It could be traced. He was getting sloppy and leaving clues that would eventually lead right back to him.

"What do you want?" she asked.

"Once we're done talking, you need to put both phones in a drawer and leave. Lock the door behind you, and come outside like nothing is wrong. If you tell anyone what's happening on your way, I'll kill Elise. If you warn anyone, I'll kill her. If you even *look* like you're doing something that will draw attention to yourself, I'll kill her. Got it?"

"Yeah."

She got it. She wasn't sure she believed that he'd had time to wire her apartment, the hallway outside, the stairwell, *and* the parking lot. But then again, a lot of time had passed since Elise had moved to Colorado Springs. Everly had no idea what this guy looked like. She could've passed him in the hallway and not even known. She definitely wasn't going to do anything that might give him an excuse to kill her sister, that might put someone else at risk in the process. No, she'd have to play it safe and do what he said.

He continued. "You're going to get in your car and drive to the grocery store parking lot up the street. Park at the back of the lot. The surveillance cameras can't focus on what's going on all the way back here. I'll be waiting for you in a white van with a huge sign on the side that says *Tuttle Plumbing*. Don't fuck this up," the man warned. "You'd rather your sister be alive out in the world somewhere than dead, wouldn't you?"

"Don't hurt her," Everly said between clenched teeth.

"Of course I don't *want* to . . . she's my life," the man said. "But I will if you force me to."

"I won't."

"Remember, I'm watching you. And that red shirt you've got on will stand out a bit too much for my liking. You should go change. Put on a black T-shirt instead."

Chills ran up and down Everly's spine.

She hadn't fully believed the man when he'd said he could see her. She'd been planning on calling Ball the second she hung up. But she'd dug the red shirt out of the bottom of her drawer five minutes ago. There was no way the man on the phone could've guessed what she was wearing.

Dying to look for where he'd stashed the cameras, Everly forced herself to stand stock-still instead. "Okay. What else?"

"Flip-flops. You should put on a pair of sandals or flip-flops."

"Okay." She had no idea why in the world he wanted her in flip-flops, but at this point she didn't care. "How do I know Elise is okay, that you even have her at all?"

"You want proof?" the man asked.

"Yes."

Her phone vibrated in her hand. She took it away from her ear and stared at the picture that just came through.

Elise was sitting on the ground next to a tree, clearly in some wooded area. Her hands were bound behind her, and she was wearing the same clothes she'd worn to school that morning. Her eyes were red, and she had tear tracks through the dirt and dust on her face.

Everly heard the man talking and brought the phone back up to her ear.

". . . about thirty minutes ago. This will be your only chance to save your sister. Are you brave enough to take it, knowing I plan on killing you?"

Everly opened her mouth to answer, but the phone line went dead.

Furious that Elise was tied up in the middle of some damn forest somewhere, scared out of her mind, not able to hear anything that was going on around her, Everly could practically feel the hate in her soul festering.

She hurried to her bedroom and threw the red shirt she'd been wearing on the floor. Everly pulled on a Colorado Springs Police Department navy-blue shirt, just to be spiteful—and as a reminder to herself that no matter what happened, she could handle this jackass—then took off her tennis shoes and socks. She stuffed her feet into a pair of cheap flip-flops she'd bought to wear to and from the pool in the apartment complex and hurried back into the other room.

She grabbed Elise's phone from the counter and, thinking fast, took the time to go over to the sink. Assuming she was being watched, Everly pretended that she was crying—well, mostly pretended—and she stood there with her head bowed for a minute. Then she turned on the tap and threw some water on her face. Taking a deep breath, she pumped a large amount of soap into her hand. Lathering the fruity soap, she thoroughly washed her hands before drying them on a towel hanging on the handle of the refrigerator.

Then she went back to the phones and took a deep breath. She laid her hand over her sister's phone for just a second, taking a second deep, steadying breath.

By the time the sun rose the next morning, either *she'd* be dead, and Elise would be on her way to wherever the crazy asshole on the phone wanted to take her. Or she and Elise would both be home, safe and sound, and her *abductor* would be dead.

She grabbed both phones and placed them in one of the drawers in the kitchen. Then she turned and headed for her apartment door. If whoever had her sister thought she would be too cowardly to come for her, he was wrong. He'd flat-out said he was going to kill her, but Everly was trained for this shit.

And she had Ball. He'd realize that something was terribly wrong, and he'd do whatever it took to find both her and Elise. Of that, she had no doubt whatsoever. The reason he'd been so pissed at his former partner was because she hadn't *acted* like a true partner should. The same with his ex. Being a good partner meant everything to Ball.

He'd come for her. She knew it.

And she took comfort in the knowledge that, if the kidnapper did manage to kill her, Ball and his fellow Mountain Mercenaries wouldn't rest until they brought Elise home.

The kidnapper's mistake was not in thinking she'd never stop looking for her sister . . . he was exactly right, she wouldn't. His mistake was in thinking someone *else* wouldn't do the same. He obviously wasn't stupid, but for some reason, he was overlooking the obvious, that Ball wouldn't stop either. This asshole didn't understand honor and devotion, at least not in a way that wasn't obsessive and creepy. And Everly knew down to the very marrow of her bones that Ball wouldn't rest until he'd tracked down Elise and the kidnapper, and made him pay.

He'd told her the story about his mysterious handler's wife, how she'd disappeared more than a decade ago but Rex had never stopped looking for her. Never stopped believing she was out there somewhere.

That wasn't going to be Elise's fate, not if Everly had anything to say about it. But again, even if the kidnapper blew her away the second she got in his van—which she doubted, because the grocery store parking lot was usually fairly busy—Ball would succeed where she'd failed.

Her resolve kicking in, Everly did her best to look nonchalant as she approached the stairs to the lobby and parking lot.

She was a damn good cop. And it was going to take every bit of what she'd learned on the streets and in the academy to beat this asshole at his own game.

There were cameras throughout the building, and she knew the second Ball discovered she and Elise were missing, he'd have Meat or Rex get the tapes.

Taking a risk the man had only wired her apartment, Everly stopped in the stairwell before entering the lobby. She looked up at the camera in the corner and, not knowing if the kidnapper was watching, as quickly and surreptitiously as possible signed that Elise had been taken again and she was on her way to meet with the kidnapper.

She added one last thing that she hoped she'd get to tell him in person, but wasn't sure she'd have the chance to.

It wasn't a lot of information, but hopefully it would give Ball and his friends a heads-up that something was wrong and to start looking for them.

She took a deep breath, fortifying herself, and walked out of the stairwell, through the lobby, and out into the parking lot. As Everly climbed into her Cherokee, she prayed that Ball would get to her apartment sooner rather than later.

If he arrived and found the phones soon enough, they would alert him that something was wrong, that she and Elise weren't simply gone on an errand or something. The picture the kidnapper had sent her would also be a big fucking clue.

But she hoped he'd understand why she'd gone after Elise by herself, instead of contacting him first. She also hoped he'd figure out her clue when he saw what she'd left for him on top of her phone.

Chapter Sixteen

Ball took the stairs in Everly's apartment complex two at a time. He hadn't let on when he'd talked to her earlier, but he was extremely uneasy about whatever Meat had called to talk to them about.

He'd tried to get the man to tell him exactly what was up, but Meat had explained he didn't *have* much to tell him yet, just a suspicion, but he was working as fast as he could to figure it out, and when he did, he'd talk to both him and Everly at the same time.

Ball had meant to get to the apartment early, but one of his clients had called to talk about his website, and the conversation had gone on longer than Ball wanted. The second he hung up, he'd closed his laptop and left the house.

The sooner he could get both Everly and Elise to move into his place, the happier he'd be. It wasn't that he didn't like the apartment Everly was in. It was in a nice area, the security was good, there were cameras everywhere, and it was plenty big enough for the sisters. But he wanted her closer. At all times. Wanted her pictures on the walls of his home. Wanted her shit in his closet. Wanted her in his bed every night.

Granted, they were pretty much sleeping together every night as it was, but he wanted her with him. For some reason, she always seemed so much more relaxed at his house. He wanted that for Everly every night.

Ball rang the special bell Everly had installed over the last few weeks. It was attached to the door itself and connected via Wi-Fi to a flashing light inside. He waited—and frowned when several minutes went by and Elise didn't answer the door. He pressed the bell again, and when she still didn't come to the door, he idly reached out and tried the doorknob.

Shocked when it actually turned in his hand, Ball immediately went on high alert.

There was no way Elise would forget to lock the door when she got home.

He slowly pushed it open and listened for a moment.

Nothing.

It was completely silent.

Palming his phone, he pulled up Meat's number and was ready to call. But he didn't want to alert anyone that he was inside the apartment just yet. Ball walked silently through the living area and peered down the hallway. Dark and quiet. He peeked into the guest bath and saw it was empty. Elise's door was open, and he peered inside. Nothing seemed amiss.

Walking faster now, he listened at Everly's bedroom door and didn't hear anything. He silently pushed open the door and looked inside. Seeing no one, he walked in. There was a red T-shirt on the floor next to a pair of socks and her tennis shoes, and her work boots were near the closet. He quickly checked the closet, fingering the clothes hanging over the edge of the laundry basket. They were damp. Everly had been home, changed, and apparently she and Elise had gone somewhere. But why hadn't she called him? And why had they both left the door unlocked?

Things weren't adding up, and it left Ball feeling terribly uneasy. He wandered back out to the living room and simply soaked in the space. Something felt . . . off.

Nothing was out of place, everything as neat as usual. But Ball couldn't shake the feeling that Everly and Elise were in danger.

He went into the kitchen and saw that the sink had been used recently. It was still wet. Fingering the towel hanging on the refrigerator door, he noted that it, too, was damp.

"Where are you guys?" he muttered.

Then he noticed something that no one else would have given a second thought to.

One of the drawers was partly open.

Everly was meticulous about closing drawers. Whether they be in the kitchen, bathroom, or bedroom. She said it was a habit left over from her fucked-up childhood, when her mother always insisted on making sure every drawer was closed. Otherwise, if their house was raided by cops or some fellow desperate druggies, someone might know where to look for her stash if a drawer was open.

It didn't make sense to Ball, but then again, people who used drugs were known to be paranoid.

Seeing that drawer cracked open was a huge fucking neon sign that something wasn't right. He sidled up to it slowly, as if a dead body would somehow miraculously fit inside and spring up at him when he opened the drawer. Using one finger, he slid it all the way out. It was the silverware drawer, and the spoons, knives, and forks were all lined up neatly in their plastic thingamabob.

But the two cell phones sitting on top were *definitely* not in their proper place.

He recognized them immediately as belonging to Elise and Everly. But more alarming than the phones was the object sitting on top of Everly's cell.

Her ring.

The one Me-Maw had given her.

The one she never, *ever* took off.

She'd taken it off and left it behind for him to find.

Motherfucker!

His finger was clicking on Meat's name before his brain really had time to think about what he was doing. Ball stared down at the ring as the phone rang in his ear.

"Ball. I was seconds from calling you," Meat said.

"Everly and Elise are gone," Ball said.

"What?"

"They're gone. I got to the apartment, and even though Everly wasn't supposed to be home yet, she apparently got here early. But they're both gone."

"Shit!" Meat swore.

"Both their phones are here, so you can't track them that way." Ball didn't tell Meat about Everly's ring. He got her message loud and clear—Elise was in danger, so she'd gone with her, or *after* her. It didn't matter which had happened, just that they were gone. And he needed to find them.

"I was just going to call you and tell you to get your ass over there. I found an app on Elise's computer that I'd missed before. She had the same one on her phone."

"What kind of app?" Ball asked impatiently.

"It looks like a regular calculator app. When you click on it, a working calculator even comes up. But if you punch in numbers in a certain order, it opens a messaging app."

"Fuck!" It was Ball's turn to swear. "She's been talking to this Rob guy the whole time?"

"Actually, no, I don't think so. It looks like she downloaded the new app onto her phone a week or so after she got here, but she only messaged this fake Rob guy once."

"What'd she say?"

"She told him to leave her alone. But once was enough."

"For what?"

"Apparently for the bastard to find her. He got her IP address and followed her to Colorado Springs. According to the messages he's sent her, apparently he's been following her for weeks. But I don't think Elise even looked at his messages. If she had, I'd like to believe she would've said something."

"Why do you think so?"

"It's easier if I show you. Sending you an email . . . Okay, check it out," Meat said.

Ball knew he didn't really have time for this, but any information he could get might help him find his girls. Clicking on the speaker, he then went to his email and opened the one Meat had just sent.

His eyes scanned the screenshots in steadily growing horror.

Rob: I miss you.

Rob: Don't you miss me? Even a little?

Rob: Remember our talks? You told me you loved me, and I still love you, my Elise.

Rob: No one can love you like me. Not your grandparents, definitely not your mother, and not your sister. Everyone ignores you, just like you told me, but not me. I'll never ignore you.

Rob: I wanted to let you know that you look beautiful today.

Rob: That skirt looks fabulous.

Rob: Although you really shouldn't wear something so short out in public.

Rob: Your body is for me and me alone to look at.

Rob: To caress.

Rob: To love.

Rob: We're going to be happy, you and I. I'm going to take really good care of you . . . and as long as you behave, you'll get everything you need.

Rob: Elise? I'm not happy with you.

Rob: You haven't answered any of my messages.

Rob: That makes me sad. And mad. And jealous.

Rob: You're mine. You hear me?

Rob: Fine. I know what will make you happy.

Ball ran a hand over his face in dismay. It was hard to tell when the messages had been sent. They weren't dated, and they all ran together in the screenshots.

But he'd attached a picture to the next message. It was of an older woman with red hair. She was lying on a carpeted floor of what looked like a cheap motel. Her lipstick was smeared, and she had needles sticking out of both inner elbows. Her eyes stared sightlessly up at the ceiling.

Rob: Your mother never loved you. She hurt you. So I killed her for you. It was so easy. All I had to do was give her some drugs. After she took the first hit, she was putty in my hands. I told her that you hated her. That you ruined her life. That she didn't deserve such a beautiful daughter. She'll never hurt you again, my angel.

He'd then attached a few more pictures—of Ella Adams's armless, headless, and legless torso. Of a leg in a dumpster. An arm in someone's curbside trash can. Her head sitting on an unlit fire. And then ashes being thrown into the ocean.

Whoever was behind Elise's original kidnapping had murdered Elise and Everly's mother and scattered the body parts. It would be a miracle if all the pieces were ever found. And the fact that neither sister had been notified of their mother's death was telling as well. No one knew she was gone.

Everly had told him once that Ella tended to disappear for weeks at a time on benders of some sort. But she'd always eventually resurface, usually to call and ask for money. Crying to her parents and telling them she just needed a little money for groceries.

Ball wasn't sickened by the pictures, he'd seen worse, but he was out of his mind knowing the woman he loved, and her sister, were most likely at the mercy of this psychopath right now.

The messages continued after the pictures.

Rob: I thought for sure after seeing the lengths I'd gone to for you, you'd talk to me again.

Rob: But I can see now that you're really upset with me.

Rob: I'll have to make you love me again.

Rob: I saw you today. Hiking. You looked good in those shorts. But I want you to cover your legs next time, they're just for me to look at. To lick.

Rob: I like this area too. We'll have to come back. Soon.

Rob: You should be careful riding the bus. You never know who's watching.

Rob: I love that light-blue nightie you wore last night. I watched you through your apartment window. You should keep your curtains shut, Elise. Watching you sleep will be so much better when we're together.

The messages went on and on, and it was obvious that this man had been watching Elise while she'd been in Colorado Springs. Except for the time he'd had to spend to go back and kill Ella, he could have been right here in Colorado the whole time.

A thought struck Ball. Elise had been right. Someone *had* been watching her hike. She wasn't just being paranoid.

He was almost as proud of her as he was scared shitless.

"I'm so sorry I didn't find this until now," Meat told him.

"It's not your fault," Ball told him. "Finding those messages will help us prosecute this asshole when we locate him. Besides, I shouldn't have been so quick to dismiss her concerns. And I was late today."

"What?"

"I wanted to be here a while ago. But I was dealing with stupid shit that could've waited. Everly got off work early and beat me home. And now they're both gone. I need you to help me find them, Meat. There are cameras in the complex. Hack into them. No one can track down someone better than you."

"Consider it done. I'll also call the rest of the team."

"Thank you. Rex too?"

"Rex too. What are you going to do?"

"I'm going to start talking to the neighbors. She wasn't close to them, and some probably weren't home, but I have to start somewhere."

"Good. Don't be surprised if Rex calls soon."

"Later," Ball said, and clicked off the phone. He picked up both Elise's and Everly's cells and slipped the ring onto his pinkie finger. It fit perfectly.

Ball closed his eyes for a moment and said a silent prayer, then immediately headed for the door. Someone must've seen something.

Fifteen minutes later, Ball's phone rang.

"Ball."

"It's Rex," his handler said, the electronically altered voice grating on Ball's nerves for the first time.

"He got her," Ball said.

"I know. But we're gonna find her."

After questioning the neighbors, and learning nothing that would help him find Everly and Elise, Ball wanted to lash out in frustration. How was Rex going to find Elise and Everly when he couldn't even find his own wife?

Then he immediately felt bad for the thought. It wasn't fair. But Ball was feeling raw and uneasy. Knowing how easily the kidnapper had managed to dismember and dispose of Ella Adams's body made him realize that he could do the same thing to Everly and Elise. This was Colorado. There were thousands of wilderness acres where he could bury their bodies. It was definitely possible that they'd never be found.

"Meat and I have looked at the surveillance footage, and we know how he got Elise out of the building. He came up behind her as she was going into her apartment. She never heard him, obviously. He left the apartment with a full-size suitcase."

Ball turned and punched the hallway wall as hard as he could. "He put Elise into a goddamn suitcase?" he asked.

"Apparently. It was an effective way to get an unconscious person out without looking suspicious. She's small enough that he could've easily fit her in there, and she's light enough that it wasn't obvious the suitcase was overly heavy."

"How'd he get Everly?" Ball asked, extremely anxious. Everly was astute. It was hard for *him* to sneak up on her. There was no way a stranger would be able to shove her inside the apartment like he had Elise.

"As far as we can see . . . he didn't. She walked out of her apartment—without locking the door, by the way—and headed down the stairs. But she did send you a message."

Before Ball could ask Rex what he meant, his phone vibrated with a text.

He looked at the short video his handler had sent. It was Everly. She was in the stairwell, about to walk out into the lobby. She looked right up at the camera and signed something.

Swearing, Ball replayed the video. He concentrated, trying to remember his lessons. He missed a few words, but her meaning was loud and clear.

He kidnapped Elise again. He might be watching. I'm meeting him to try to get her back. Look in the woods. Maybe near Seven Bridges Trail. I love you.

She loved him. *Motherfucker.* She *loved* him.

Ball didn't deserve her, but that didn't mean he wasn't going to take her. She was *his*. She'd managed to look past his assholery when they'd met and had chipped away at his cold exterior piece by piece. She was exactly what he'd been looking for. As both a work partner *and* a life partner.

She'd left the apartment to go after her sister, *knowing* there was a chance she might not succeed and could possibly lose her life. But she'd done it also knowing without a doubt that he'd be right on her trail.

Fuck yeah, he was.

Pulling her phone out of his pocket, he put in her password. They'd shared them the other night, deciding that since he'd literally been inside her body, it was only fair that they knew each other's passwords. He'd laughed then, but he wasn't laughing now.

"What'd she say?" Rex asked.

"She thinks maybe her sister might've been taken into the woods near Seven Bridges Trail. I'm checking her phone now, hang on . . ."

Ball opened her texts and saw one from an unknown number. He audibly gasped when he saw the picture she'd been sent. There was no accompanying text, but then again, the picture spoke for itself.

He understood why she thought maybe Elise was up in the Broadmoor area. The trees around Elise in the picture looked familiar. Yeah, they were simply trees, but something about them reminded him of that hike. And if the kidnapper had been following her then, it was likely that he'd bring her back to somewhere familiar.

He forwarded the picture to both Rex and Meat, then clicked on her call history.

There. She'd accepted a call from an unknown number about half an hour ago. He wasn't too far behind her.

"Can I help you?" a woman asked from down the hall.

Ball turned and saw an irritated and frightened-looking middle-aged woman standing in her doorway. She hadn't answered when he'd knocked on her door earlier. Knowing Rex was still listening, Ball put Everly's phone back in his pocket and turned to her.

"Yes. I can't find my girlfriend and her sister. Everly and Elise Adams? They live right down there." He pointed to their door. "They weren't home when I got here. Have you seen or heard anything?"

The woman looked relieved. "I remember you now. You've been here quite a bit."

"Yes, ma'am."

"I didn't see Elise this afternoon, but I saw Everly. I only noticed her because I thought it was weird that she got home, then immediately left again. My apartment's on the parking-lot side, and my desk is right in front of a window. I work from home, you know, and I like the fresh air when it's cool outside. Anyway, I saw her come home and park. Then not ten minutes later, she was walking really fast toward her Jeep."

"Which way did she go?" Ball asked, the adrenaline pulsing through his veins.

"Right. She turned right. She even screeched her tires, which I thought was odd, because Everly is normally a very thoughtful and careful driver. You know, because she's a police officer and all."

"Thank you very much. I'll just go and see if I can't catch up with her then," Ball told the woman.

"So she's okay?"

"She will be. Thanks again." Ball turned and headed for the stairs and put his phone back up to his ear. "Got that?"

"Yeah. Going left would've taken her to the interstate, and there's no telling where she would go from there. But turning right means that she headed up toward the Broadmoor area. Not too many places to go up there."

"Right. I'm on it. Tell the others to meet me at the Seven Bridges trailhead. If I find something else on my way, I'll be in touch."

"Will do. Over and out."

Ball clicked off the phone and jogged through the lobby toward his Mustang. All sorts of scary scenarios went through his head as he headed for his car, but he forced them away. Everly wasn't a naive teenager. He wasn't happy that she willingly walked into danger, but he understood. Getting to Elise was her first concern, and she obviously thought she could hold her own against whoever had taken her . . . at least until he got there.

She was counting on him.

And he wasn't going to let her down like Riley Foster had let him down once upon a time.

Within two minutes, he was pulling out of the parking lot and heading in the same direction Everly had gone. He drove slowly, looking for anything and everything that might be a clue. Her car, a van like the one Elise was originally kidnapped in. Anything that would help him.

He almost missed it.

He had to do a U-turn and go back to the grocery store. It was busy, and cars were constantly pulling in and out. But at the back of the lot, he saw a white Jeep Grand Cherokee. Everly's car wasn't all that unique, but he had to stop and check it out.

As he got close, he saw that it *was* her car. And her kidnapper had chosen the meet spot well. It was as far away from the building as it could be, so any video that might've been taken would be practically useless. He shot off a quick text to Rex, letting him know that he'd found Everly's car and where, then made his way to the trailhead.

"Please let this be where he took them," Ball said, clenching the steering wheel so tightly his knuckles turned white. "I'm coming, Everly," he said. "Hang on, baby. Hang on."

Chapter Seventeen

Everly stumbled for what seemed like the thousandth time, but she didn't care. She wanted Tylor fucking Tuttle to underestimate her. Yeah, it sucked that she was hiking in flip-flops. And that she was still fighting the effects from the stun gun he'd used on her. But they were on their way to Elise, that was all she cared about. She needed to make sure her sister really was all right. Tylor was batshit crazy, and she wouldn't put it past him to have already killed her and not remembered doing so.

As she walked, the details of meeting Tylor played on a loop in her head.

Everly pulled into the parking lot and immediately saw the white van at the edge of the lot. It had a cheap **TUTTLE PLUMBING** *magnetic sign on the side, just like he'd said. She pulled up next to it and climbed out. She went to the passenger door, and the man behind the wheel motioned to the back door.*

Feeling as if she were a little kid accepting candy from the proverbial stranger, she opened the sliding side door and looked inside.

There were no seats in the back, just a lot of odd-looking tools hanging on hooks on either side. She did a double take, though, because in the back, a suitcase that looked suspiciously like the one that should've been in her apartment, in the back of her closet, sat open.

"Get in and shut the door behind you," the man said.

Without a choice, Everly did as he said, the sound of the closing door reminding her of a coffin lid slamming shut.

"It's nice to finally meet you," the man said. "I'm Tylor Tuttle. I'm going to be your new brother-in-law, but it's too bad we'll only be related for a short time."

She wasn't going to rise to that bait, but she couldn't stop the question. "Why?"

"Because as soon as you perform the ceremony that will make Elise and I husband and wife, I'm gonna kill you."

Everly blinked. "I'm performing the ceremony?" She was pissed at his assumption, but confused why he thought she would, or could, marry anyone.

"You're a cop. You have the authority to join us as man and wife."

There were so many things wrong with what he'd just said, Everly wasn't sure where to start. But she didn't have time, anyway, because he kept talking.

"And if you marry us, Elise will know you give your blessing for us to be together forever. She's scared, and she needs to know that her sister supports her. She's nervous."

"I bet she is," Everly said. "Maybe you should marry me instead?" She figured the suggestion was worth a shot.

Tylor wrinkled his nose. "You're old. I already have one old wife, I don't need another."

"If you already have a wife, how can you marry again?" She didn't care about his "old" comment. Thirty-four wasn't old, but if you were a pedophile, anything over twenty was ancient.

"Oh, I'll be getting rid of her as soon as I get home with Elise. I only have one appropriate room to keep her in, and I don't want Elise to be jealous."

Everly felt sick at the man's words. He looked normal and sane, but obviously wasn't. His brown hair was brushed neatly, and his clothes were relatively clean. He wasn't fat. In fact, he was a bit on the slender side, but not so much that it would make anyone look twice at him. He was absolutely ordinary. He could be anyone's next-door neighbor—and that was what made him so scary. If he was holding some other poor woman hostage, no one would suspect him.

She shivered. "Is Elise okay?"

"Of course she is. I don't want to hurt Elise. If I do, it's because she brought it on herself or because you did something stupid. She'll learn to obey me. She'll learn that she'll catch more flies with honey than vinegar. I've always loved that saying. It's cute, right?"

Everly clenched her teeth. The bastard had already hurt Elise once before, and he was blaming it on her? Besides being crazy, he was also an asshole. If he worked in management, he'd be the kind of man who'd blame losing an account on his female subordinate, just because he could. Misogynistic asshole.

"Although I appreciate you following my directions and doing as you're told, I'm actually shocked that you did. That wasn't very smart."

"I'm trying to make sure my sister is safe and unharmed," she told him.

"I already told you that she's going to live a long life with me," Tylor said with a frown.

"And you also told me if I didn't do what you said, you'd kill her," Everly reminded him.

He laughed. "As if I'd kill my beautiful Elise. I just told you that to make sure you'd come after her alone. I have to make sure you aren't around to mess things up and continue searching for her. When you're gone, we can live our lives in peace, without having to look over our shoulders."

Everly wanted to tell him he was wrong, that Ball and his friends would never stop looking for her, but she kept her mouth shut.

"I really do hope my Elise is smarter than you," Tylor said.

Then without warning, he lunged.

Everly put up an arm to block him, but he'd already stuck the stun gun into her left side.

She immediately fell over on her side. Tylor didn't take the prongs away, just kept stunning her. Everly had been tased before, and the effects of this stun gun weren't as severe as those of the weapon she carried for work, but it still did its job.

She was disoriented and couldn't get her muscles to work properly. She wasn't able to stop him when Tylor handcuffed one hand to a large ring on the side of the van, and secured her ankle with another pair of handcuffs dangling from a chain attached to the opposite wall of the vehicle.

Then he patted her on the cheek—more of a slap, really—and leaned over her.

"Pretty, but not that smart," he said, then turned and climbed back into the driver's seat.

Everly closed her eyes and let her head fall to the floor of the van. She ignored the pain in her side from the probes of the stun gun and did her best to get her body to cooperate with her brain. She needed to be at the top of her game.

Tylor Tuttle might've surprised her once, but he wasn't going to get a second chance.

He might think she was going to be an easy kill, but he was wrong. She had a lot more to live for—namely her sister, grandparents, and now Ball. And he was coming for her. She just hoped he'd find her in time.

They'd left the main trail a while back and were bushwhacking through the scrub brush. Everly was glad she was wearing jeans, as the branches and briars were doing their best to scratch her all to hell. Her feet were also taking a beating in the flip-flops, but she didn't feel the pain. Her hands were bound in front of her, allowing her to block some of the branches that came at her face. She did her best to break as many branches as possible as they walked, to leave a trail for Ball and the others.

Wherever Tylor had stashed Elise couldn't be too far away, because he wouldn't have had that much time to secure her, then get back to his van to meet Everly at the grocery store parking lot. The thought comforted her. Not that the parking area for the hiking trail was exactly civilization, but it was better than being in the middle of nowhere, like they were now.

They started going up a fairly steep hill—and Everly got a bad feeling in the pit of her stomach.

She could withstand a lot of things. Knife wounds, bad guys spitting at her, foot chases, even being shot, as long as it wasn't in the head . . . but one thing she definitely didn't like was heights. Never had. The longer they hiked uphill, the more anxious she got.

Swallowing the unease, she refused to let it get the better of her. She wasn't going to let Tylor win. No fucking way.

They trudged on, and suddenly they were in an open area on top of a bluff. It would've been beautiful, if Everly wasn't so fucking petrified.

"Beautiful, isn't it?" Tylor asked, as if reading her mind.

Everly nodded, her mouth dry, not able to speak.

"This is where you're going to do it."

"It?"

"Marry me and my Elise."

"Where is my sister?" she asked.

"This way," Tylor said, as he turned his back on her and headed down a small hill to their left.

She was so tempted to bum-rush him right then. Take him down. Kill him. But she didn't know where her sister was yet. Until she saw Elise, saw with her own eyes that she was all right, she wasn't going to do anything to antagonize their captor. She had to be patient.

Tylor led her down the hill and into a copse of trees.

And there, sitting on the ground, chained to a tree, was Elise.

Everly cried out from the sheer joy of seeing Elise alive and unharmed. She ran forward and fell to her knees next to her, throwing her bound arms over her sister's head and holding her tight. Everly felt Elise crying against her, but because her arms were behind her back, she couldn't touch her.

Closing her eyes for a second, Everly did her best to get her emotions under control. Then she took a deep breath. They weren't out of danger. Not by a long shot. She knew perfectly well that Tylor was going to kill her. Or at least try. It wasn't a matter of if, but when. Everly just needed to stall him long enough to give Ball and the others a chance to get to them.

Deciding to try being as submissive as possible, because that seemed to be what Tylor liked, she looked up at him. "Can I talk to her?"

Tylor eyed her for a moment before saying, "Yes, but you'll tell her what I tell you to. Nothing else. If you try any funny business, I'll kill you *and* her, got it?"

Everly nodded, even though she was pretty sure now the guy wasn't going to kill Elise. He had plans for her. He was either extremely stupid—she was unsure about that, since he'd managed to fly under the radar for this long—or he was too cocky and thought nothing could go wrong since he held all the cards.

"I need my hands to do it." Everly held her tied hands out to Tylor.

He came toward her and pulled out a pocketknife. "If you do anything to try to get away, I'll kill her," he said, nodding at her sister.

"I won't," Everly told him, lying through her teeth. The second she had an opening, she was going to use everything she'd ever learned about self-defense and from being a police officer to take him down. But for now, she needed her hands so she could talk to Elise.

Once her hands were loose, Everly turned back to Elise. She put her hands on her sister's cheeks and rubbed her thumbs under her eyes, wiping away her tears. Elise had a scrape on her temple, a split lip, and a black eye forming. All things considered, even though the sight of her injuries pissed her off, Everly knew she'd been lucky so far. If Tylor'd had more time between when he'd brought Elise here and when he'd had to pick up Everly, he could've hurt her a lot more.

"Tell her what my name is," Tylor ordered.

"How do you spell it?" she asked.

"Why does that matter?"

Everly resisted the urge to roll her eyes. "Because I have to finger spell it for her."

Tylor spelled his name, and Everly couldn't help the delirious thought that maybe he was so crazy because he'd had to spell out his name to every single person he'd ever come into contact with. She knew the thought was irrational, but she couldn't help hating every single thing about this man.

Turning to Everly, she signed, *His name is* T-y-l-o-r T-u-t-t-l-e. *Remember that, and tell Ball and the guys when they find us.*

"You sure did a lot of hand movements for just my name," Tylor said suspiciously.

"In sign language, it takes a lot more to say the same thing in hand motions than it does verbally." She was lying through her teeth, but this moron wouldn't know that.

"Okay. Tell her that I've missed her."

When I tell you to, you run. I mean it. Run like hell, and don't look back.

"And that she's beautiful and we're going to have a wonderful life together. But she has to obey me. If she doesn't, I'll have to punish her."

Everly's skin crawled, but she nodded at Tylor and turned to her sister. *We need to keep him calm until he unlocks that chain around your leg. Look up at him and nod.*

Elise did as her sister asked, and Tylor beamed. "Tell her I'm sorry it took so long for us to be together. I had to take care of some things back in LA."

Everly looked up at him. "What things?"

Without warning, his foot flew out, and he kicked Everly in the same side where he'd stun-gunned her. Wheezing in pain, she fell over, but immediately got back up on her knees. She didn't think he'd cracked a rib, thank God. She'd had those before, and while her side hurt, she felt okay.

From the corner of her eye, Everly saw Elise jerk in fear, but she kept her gaze on Tylor.

"You think I'm going to tell you?" he asked.

Everly nodded. She knew she was pushing things, but he wouldn't have brought it up if he didn't want them to know.

"Tell her what I told you to."

Everly turned to her sister. *I'm okay. Don't panic. Ball is going to come find us. We just have to be brave until then.*

Elise nodded. It was easy to see that her sister was frustrated at not being able to respond. Securing her hands behind her back was the same as gagging a speaking person.

"Now tell her that I took care of her good-for-nothing drug addict of a mother."

Everly's eyes went back to Tylor. "What? What'd you do?"

"I killed her. She was making my Elise sad. I couldn't have that. So she had to die."

His voice was monotone, and it was more than obvious he had not one iota of remorse over killing someone. Tears pricked the back of Everly's eyelids, but she refused to let them fall. She hadn't cared much about Ella, but she *was* still her mother. Even as horrible of a mom as she'd been, she didn't deserve to be killed by this asshole.

There was no way she was going to tell her sister right now what Tylor had done. Elise had to be thinking about escaping, and nothing else. *His plan is for me to perform some bullshit marriage ceremony. Just go with it until I tell you to run. No, don't look away, look up at him with wide eyes.*

Everly couldn't be prouder of her sister. She had to be scared to death, but she did what she'd told her to do.

Tylor preened. "That's my good girl." He stepped closer to them and ran his hand over her hair, petting her. He turned to Everly, but kept his hand on Elise's head. "It's time," he said. "Time to join us together for life."

~

Ball arrived at the entrance for the Seven Bridges Trail and parked in front of the white panel van so it couldn't simply pull out and leave. Tuttle Plumbing. Shaking his head, he was shocked to realize he recognized it. He'd seen it the day they came here to hike with the Outdoor Club—but it hadn't had the magnetic plumbing sign on it at the time. There had been so many vehicles in the parking lot that it hadn't particularly stood out, and he'd had no reason to associate it with the mysterious white van that had been used in Elise's abduction back in LA.

Peering into the back window, he saw a suitcase that he recognized as belonging to Everly. The thought of Elise being inside it made him see red. Taking a few deep breaths to control his anger, Ball waited impatiently for his teammates to arrive. He could've set off by himself, but he needed to organize a search pattern with the others.

It took another five minutes, but finally he saw a vehicle coming up the hill at a high rate of speed. Ball was the most skilled driver of the group, but the others could certainly hold their own. Within seconds, the best friends he'd ever had stood in front of him.

"You heard anything?" Gray asked.

"Meat said Elise is probably out here too?" Ro asked.

"Do we know this guy's name yet?" Arrow asked.

"My guess is Tuttle," Black said with a roll of his eyes and a nod to the van in front of them.

Just then, a Humvee came barreling up the road. Ball was surprised to see Meat, but he was thankful. He could use all the help he could get. And at this point, it didn't matter what was on the surveillance cameras or Elise's phone. He needed Meat *here* more than he needed him sitting at home behind a computer.

"You guys know what's up?" Ball asked.

"We know enough," Gray said. "What's the plan? Any ideas on where they are?"

"Not exactly. I'm thinking we walk the trail and see if we can find anything to tell us which way they went. Everly let him take her, so be on the lookout for clues from her."

"You think she knows we're coming?" Black asked.

"Not only knows, she's counting on it," Ball said.

The others all nodded.

"Anyone notify the cops?" Arrow asked.

"Rex suggested we wait until we have concrete information that they're out here," Gray said.

"Good call. The last thing we need is dozens of people tromping around and spooking this asshole," Ball said. "He's obsessed with Elise, and if someone tries to take her away from him, he's gonna lose his shit."

"Let's go," Ro said. "The sooner we find her, the sooner we can get her and Everly home."

Without another word, Ball headed for the trailhead. It would be dark soon, and the trail was closed at dusk. There weren't very many other cars in the lot. Every person they passed, Ball asked if they'd seen either Elise or Everly, or if they'd heard anything out of the ordinary. None had.

They'd been walking for ten minutes when Ball stopped on the trail. He tilted his head and studied the vegetation to his right.

Gray came up next to him. "What's up?"

"Does that look normal to you?" Ball asked his friend, his eyes glued to the right side of the trail.

"It looks like a couple people have been through there. Recently," Gray said.

"Let's hope there's not a geocache through here," Ball muttered. "If we're following some geo-trail for a bunch of hide-and-go-seekers, I'm gonna be pissed."

The six men fanned out and silently made their way through the underbrush. Every now and then, one of them would point out a broken branch or a scuff in the dirt.

"Good girl," Ball muttered under his breath. He had no doubt that Everly was behind the signs. She'd done everything she could think of to lead him right to her.

The climb wasn't difficult for the former Special Forces men, but it was quickly getting dark. They needed to hurry up and find Elise, Everly, and the asshole who'd taken them. Ball didn't want to think about what would happen when the sun went down.

He'd once told Everly that nothing good happened after two in the morning. It wasn't anywhere close to being that late, but he suspected the same train of thought applied here. Nothing good was going to happen once it got dark.

Chapter Eighteen

Everly tried not to hyperventilate. Tylor had unlocked the chain around Elise's ankles—but not her wrists—and carefully helped her up from the ground. He'd kissed her, and Everly's stomach felt as if it had a thousand angry bees inside at the sight. Elise was doing her best not to do anything that would make their captor lose his shit, but this was too much.

She shouldn't have to suffer his hands on her. Or his lips. Or any other part of him. The hatred welled up inside Everly so fast, she had to force herself not to attack Tylor right then and there. She had to wait. She had a plan. She had no weapon, other than herself. He was smart, making her wear flip-flops. The terrain was rough, and without proper footwear, she was at a disadvantage. While she and Tylor were around the same height, he outweighed her by quite a bit. And he was batshit crazy. In her experience, craziness oftentimes was the reason people could overpower someone bigger and heavier than they were. That and drugs.

Everly didn't think Tylor was on drugs. He wasn't acting like the men and women she'd dealt with while on duty. He was just obsessed.

Keeping his hand on Elise's upper arm, he half hauled, half guided her up the hill to the scenic bluff. Tylor hadn't bothered to re-tie Everly. He was one hundred percent sure she'd be compliant as long as he had his hands on her sister. And he was mostly correct.

Once at the top of the bluff, he raised his finger to point directly in front of him. "You stand there," he told Everly.

She didn't want to. He was pointing to a spot that would put her way too close to the edge of the cliff, and not only that . . . her back would be to it. She knew without question what his plan was. He was going to have her "marry" them, then push her over the edge.

She couldn't fault him, though, because that was her plan too, although it would be Tylor going over the side.

Swallowing her fear and trying not to look completely freaked out, Everly slowly went to stand where he pointed. The ground was rocky, and she took one glance over her shoulder before quickly turning her attention back to Tylor and Elise. The ground fell away about four feet from where she was standing. There were large boulders and scrub brush all the way down the slope. At the bottom was a small stream filled with more large rocks and forest debris. It was unlikely that she'd survive if Tylor managed to catch her off guard and push her over. But it was equally as unlikely that *he* would survive a fall. She kept that thought in her head.

Tylor twisted Elise and unlocked the handcuffs around her wrists. He then turned her to face him, and Everly almost had a heart attack when he reached for her hands once again. But she breathed out a sigh of relief when he merely cuffed her sister's hands together in front of her.

For a terrifying second, she'd thought he was going to cuff his own wrist to Elise's. That would've been a disaster.

"Okay, you can start," Tylor said, turning to look at Everly.

She had no idea what she was supposed to say. She'd only been to one wedding in her life, and she hadn't really paid much attention to the priest.

"I'm assuming you want me to sign as I'm talking?" she asked, trying to stall for time.

"Of course," Tylor said. "My Elise needs to know what's going on. Eventually I'll teach her our own special set of signs that only we understand."

Everly cleared her throat and spoke slowly as she signed. It was difficult to sign something different from what she was saying, but she did her best.

"We are gathered here today to witness the joining of this man and woman."

This is it. When I say, you turn and run as fast as you can.

"Marriage is a promise between two people who want to spend their lives together."

I have to finish this farce of a wedding, but I'm not going to let him touch you again.

"It allows two people to see each other through the trials and tribulations in their lives, as well as celebrate the happy times."

It'll be hard to run with those cuffs on, but you can do it. If you hear him behind you, hide. Do not come out, no matter what. I'll find you.

"To make a relationship work, it takes trust and dedication."

I love you. More than you'll ever know.

"You're taking too long!" Tylor complained. "Hurry up and get to the good part!"

Swallowing, Everly nodded and looked at her sister. "Do you take this man to be your husband, to love and cherish, in sickness and health, until death do you part?"

It's almost time. No matter what happens, remember that I love you. Now, look at him and nod.

Feeling sick, Everly watched as her sister bravely looked up at Tylor and nodded.

He beamed. "Now me," he demanded.

"Do you take this woman to be your wife, to love and cherish, in sickness and health, until death do you part?"

Everly knew Elise was watching her closely. *When he leans down to kiss you, I'm going to kick him in the balls. That's your cue. You run like hell, and don't look back.*

Elise was crying now, but Everly focused on her resolve and hate for Tylor.

"Say the rest!" Tylor insisted after he'd agreed enthusiastically to his part of the vows.

"You may now kiss the bride," Everly said dutifully.

Tylor smiled and leaned down to kiss Elise and seal their "marriage vows."

Everly took a deep breath, and even as her foot came up, she signed, *Now! Run!*

Elise spun on her heels and tore out of the clearing. She disappeared behind a bunch of trees, and Everly could hear her crashing and breaking tree limbs as she fled.

Tylor howled in pain and frustration. He'd fallen to his knees when Everly had kicked him, but in seconds he was up and reaching for her.

"Time to die, bitch!" he said in a voice she hadn't heard before. It was hard and dark, and for a split second, Everly thought he resembled a demon from one of the TV shows she liked to watch.

He lunged at her, and it took all of Everly's strength to grab hold of his wrist and prevent him from breaking all the bones in her face.

"She's mine! You just married us! She'll never get away from me! She's Elise Tuttle now. *Mine!* Once you're dead, I'll find her, and we'll live happily ever after!"

"Not a chance in hell," Everly muttered as she desperately fought to prevent his hands from getting around her throat, to no avail. His pupils were dilated, and his arms shook, probably from the adrenaline coursing through his body. He was trying to both choke her and push her backward at the same time.

Right toward the cliff.

One hand let go of her throat, and she gasped in a breath of air.

But she hadn't been prepared for his fist to fly back, then slam into the side of her head.

It hurt like a bitch, but Everly ducked beneath his arm and stepped away from the drop-off. But he was right there. His fists kept coming at her, some making contact and others missing completely. Everly used her knowledge of self-defense to land her own blows, but they didn't seem to faze him in the least.

He had anger, lust, and pure crazy on his side.

Everly began to tire too quickly. If she'd been wearing her steel-toe boots, she could've used those as weapons just as much as her fists. She'd lost the stupid flip-flops after her first kick. The soles of her feet were being torn to pieces by the sharp rocks on the bluff, but she barely felt it.

The pain from Tylor's blows was taking effect, however. He hadn't cracked any ribs with his earlier kick, but now the pain in her side was almost excruciating. Tylor had three scrape marks down his face from her fingernails, and he was limping from a blow he'd taken to the back of his knee, but he was still coming at her.

He mumbled something under his breath, but Everly didn't catch what it was. It didn't matter; she wasn't going to let him win. No fucking way.

Tylor bent and rushed her. He picked her up around the waist and fell to the ground on top of her. For a second, the air was pushed from her lungs, and Everly gasped.

The momentary loss of concentration cost her dearly. In a flash, Tylor had his hands around her throat. Squeezing tighter and tighter.

Everly looked up into his dark eyes and saw nothing but hate. She tried to pry his fingers off her throat, but nothing she did made a difference—even gouging her fingernails into his skin didn't faze him. She tried to push her thumbs into his eyes, but his arms were too long, and she couldn't reach.

As she desperately tried to loosen his hold on her, he hissed, "She's *mine*. She'll learn to serve me exactly how I want. I'm sure she'll be a handful at first, but eventually she'll do whatever I say. And the best thing? I can take her out in public and not have to worry about her telling anyone *anything*. I should've taken a retard for a wife a long time ago . . . I just hope that our babies won't be defective like her."

His words enraged her. First off, Elise was just as smart as anyone else, and being deaf wasn't a fucking defect. Second . . . babies?

Fuck no.

But Everly couldn't protest, because blackness was starting to creep in at the sides of her eyes. She looked frantically to her left, then her right, and finally realized where she was lying.

Tuning out Tylor's offensive and horrifying words about what her sister's future might hold, she tightened her grip on his wrists.

Taking a precious second to visualize exactly what she needed to do, Everly remembered lying on a mat on the floor when she'd been at the police academy. Her instructor had been taller than she was. And eighty-five pounds heavier. She'd been wearing her gear—bulletproof vest, equipment belt, the whole thing. She hadn't thought there was any way she'd be able to get him off her, but the instructor had walked her through exactly where to put her hands and feet and where to exert pressure, and before she knew it, she was free.

Wishing for the thousandth time that she had her boots on, Everly opened her eyes and looked up into the face of evil. Leaning his whole body forward, Tylor was smiling as he choked her, happy in the knowledge that he'd won.

Realizing there was a good chance he'd take her with him—and not caring—Everly planted her feet with her knees bent.

She suddenly slammed her knees against his ass with all the force she could muster.

He fell forward, immediately off-balance since he'd put all his weight into choking her.

Clutching his waist and using every last ounce of strength, she jerked him even farther forward and arched her back.

Then she prayed. Hard.

~

Ball held his fist in the air, indicating for the others to freeze. Everyone stopped, and Ball turned his head so he could hear better. Something or someone was coming straight for them, and not caring about how much noise they were making.

He motioned for the others to spread out. Gray and Ro pulled out their weapons and trained them steadily in the direction of the noise. Whatever, or whoever, it was got closer and closer, and Ball tensed.

One second they were all frozen in place, watching the area the noise was coming from, and the next, they saw Elise running full speed right toward them. She burst through a large patch of bushes as if the hounds of hell were after her. Her hair was in complete disarray, and she was covered in scratches and welts. Her hands were cuffed in front of her, and she weaved clumsily as she ran.

She ran into the small clearing and, when she saw the men standing there, stumbled and pitched forward to her knees. The terror on her face had Ball moving before he even thought about it. The sounds coming from her throat made his blood run cold.

He'd never heard the teenager do more than laugh, but at the moment, she was moaning and crying with enough desperation to make Black call out, "Jesus Christ, is she all right?"

Ball went to his knees in front of her and grabbed Elise's face in his hands. He forced her to look at him. He murmured, "Easy, girl. I've got you, you're safe," even though he knew she couldn't hear him.

It took a minute or so for her to calm down, but eventually she did enough to bring her hands up and try to sign.

Ball took her hands in his and stopped her before turning to the others. "Anyone have a cuff key?" It was a stupid question, because they all carried the damn things. Arrow got to him first. Ball held Elise's hands up, and the other man deftly and quickly unlocked the cuffs. Then he picked them up with the edge of his shirt and stuffed them into his pocket. They were all more than aware that they'd need to preserve any fingerprints to make sure there was no possibility of blame for any wrongdoing falling on their shoulders.

Ball let go of Elise's hands and asked, *Are you okay?*

Yes. He's got Everly.

Where?

Elise pointed behind her.

More. What was around you?

A cliff at the top of a big hill. The trees are thicker there. Everly told me to run.

Ball was both proud of his Everly and worried as fuck at the same time. He turned to Arrow. "Take her back to the parking area, and call the cops."

"Shouldn't we get her to show us where that asshole is?" Arrow asked.

"Fuck no," Ball returned immediately. "I don't want her anywhere near him ever again."

"Right."

"I'll go with you," Black told Arrow.

Ball turned to Elise. *I'm going to get Everly.*

He's crazy. He had her marry us.

Ball frowned. *You are* not *married to that asshole.*

Amazingly, Elise grinned. *It's weird to see you swearing.*

Thanking God that the girl in front of him wasn't broken, and feeling prouder of her than he could put into words, Ball hugged her fiercely.

She clung tightly for a second, then pushed him away. *Go get Everly.*

Ball nodded and got to his feet. He pulled Elise upright and turned to his friends. "She can text like a fucking phenom. Give her your phone and talk to her that way. Get her to tell you everything she can remember, and text the rest of us with the details."

"Will do," Arrow said.

Ball turned to her. *Go with Arrow and Black. Tell them everything you can remember. I'm going to bring your sister back to you.*

She nodded, and while tears sprang to her eyes, she didn't let them fall. She was as strong as her sister.

Ball watched until Elise and the others were out of sight. Then he turned and headed in the direction she'd come from at a fast clip. Now that Elise was out of the picture, Tylor was going to be pissed. And while Ball knew Everly could hold her own, that didn't mean she was invincible.

Following the broken branches and using his intuition, Ball led the other three men in the direction Elise had said she'd come from. The sun had disappeared behind the mountain, and the shadows made the trek more and more difficult.

After five minutes, Ball was afraid that they'd turned in the wrong direction at some point—until he heard what sounded like a voice ahead.

Running, he saw the large hill Elise must've been talking about. Off to the left, there was a chain lying on the ground, one end attached to a big tree. Turning his attention back to the hill, he saw that it went practically straight up. Ball's stomach clenched.

What goes up must come down.

For the first time in years, he was scared. And he was never scared on a mission. In fact, he could count on one hand the times he'd been truly terrified in his life, and one of those was when he'd been hanging off the side of the Coast Guard boat and couldn't get his arm untangled from the rope. He'd seen his life flash in front of his eyes that day.

But the thought of Everly being killed was more terrifying than anything he'd ever experienced. He couldn't lose her. Not when he'd finally found the woman he wanted to spend the rest of his life with. She was perfect for him. Beautiful, brave, and loyal as hell. He needed that. He needed *her*.

Meat, Ro, Gray, and Ball moved at the same time, and their muscular legs carried them up the hill with ease.

They burst onto the plateau, not one of the men slowing down a fraction, even as they saw what was waiting for them up there.

Tylor Tuttle on top of Everly.

She was on her back, he had his hands around her throat, and her head was literally hanging off the side of the cliff.

Ball didn't even have time to scream at Tuttle to get off her. Before he or his men could get to the pair, Tuttle was flying through the air.

His scream echoed around them, abruptly cutting off when he landed hundreds of feet below.

~

The reality that she was practically hanging over the edge of a cliff barely registered in Everly's mind. She felt somewhat numb at the moment.

But in the next second, a pair of hands latched on to her ankles.

Everly screamed in terror and tried to kick out.

"It's me! Ball! You're safe. He's gone."

Her eyes had popped open when her ankles had been grabbed, but upon hearing Ball's voice, her eyes slid closed once more. Her fingernails tried to dig into the sand and rocks, but she couldn't get a firm hold. "Get me off this ledge," she whispered. Her throat hurt like hell, and she couldn't avoid rehearing the thud Tylor's body made as it hit the ground far beneath her, and how his scream had stopped suddenly.

Instead of dragging her backward, Ball eased his arms under her back and knees, and he lifted her.

Everly latched on to him as if her life depended on it. "Don't drop me!" she croaked.

"Never," Ball vowed.

She counted his steps, and didn't open her eyes until she reached twenty and felt him lowering her to the ground.

"Elise?" she rasped as he hovered over her.

"Safe. She ran into us on the path. Black and Arrow took her back to the parking area and are calling in the cavalry."

Everly sighed and smiled. "I knew you'd come."

"Shhh, don't speak." Ball turned his head and yelled, "Meat!"

In seconds, the other man was there, opening a backpack. Everly swallowed, wincing at the pain that tiny movement caused.

"Where else are you hurt?" Ball asked.

"Honestly?"

"Always."

"Everywhere. Is he dead?"

"Yeah, Everly, he's dead," Gray said from above them.

Everly looked up into the other man's eyes. "You sure?"

"We're sure," Ro added.

"He could be faking it," Everly mumbled. "He has to be dead. He killed my mom and wants Elise. He's not going to give up."

Ro crouched next to her and said gently, "He's dead, Everly. You want me to carry you over so you can see?"

"No!" Everly gasped. "I hate heights!"

The men all stared at her in disbelief for a moment before Meat chuckled. "Tough as hell. You willingly let yourself get kidnapped so you could save your sister and flipped a man over a cliff when you're scared of heights?"

"Fuck off," Everly choked out.

"He's gone," Gray repeated. "His head obviously hit a rock on the way down. His brain is about twenty feet from where his body landed.

He's definitely dead, and he won't be coming after you or your sister again. You're safe."

Hearing that Tylor Tuttle would definitely not be a problem anymore made the adrenaline that was still coursing through Everly's body dissipate, leaving her weak and in more pain. Her throat felt like it was on fire, and every muscle in her body hurt, not to mention her ribs. Everly groaned, and her eyes closed again.

Something cool was placed on her throat, and she reached up to take it off, but her hand was caught in Ball's. "Leave it. I know it hurts, but it'll bring down the swelling."

At first the chemical ice pack *did* hurt, but the longer it was on her throat, the better it felt.

Everly felt her right hand being lifted . . . and smiled when she figured out what Ball was doing. The feel of the ring Me-Maw had given her being slipped back on her finger was a huge relief.

Ball had found it and had come for her.

The words she'd held back rushed to the surface. Opening her eyes, she blurted, "I love you."

Ball smiled, leaned forward, and kissed her forehead. "It's a good thing, because I love you too."

Everly heard the other men talking about the best way to carry her out, and the need to notify the authorities to recover Tylor's body, but she didn't care. In other circumstances, she'd be the one taking charge, but she trusted Ball's friends to do what needed to be done.

She stared up at Ball and couldn't look away from his gaze. Elise was safe. Her stalker/kidnapper was dead. And Ball loved her. She couldn't ask for anything else.

Chapter Nineteen

"Hey, Ball," Everly said as she entered the house.

Ball looked up to see his sexy girlfriend in her equally sexy uniform. She was still on half days at the police department, doing light desk duty until the doctor cleared her to go back to her regular routine. She'd healed remarkably fast, even though her fractured ribs had been very painful for a few weeks.

It had now been a month and a half since the incident with Tylor Tuttle, and when Ball had brought both her and Elise back to his house after Everly had been discharged from the hospital, they'd simply never left. They hadn't had a big involved conversation about them staying, it had just happened, and he was fucking thrilled.

Luckily, Elise hadn't been injured much at all. She had a few cuts and bruises from where Tuttle had hit her, and tackled her at their apartment. But Everly had to stay in the hospital for two days for observation. She had a few cracked ribs, her feet were a mess from the sharp rocks, and her larynx had been bruised when Tuttle had tried to strangle her.

Ball had wanted to kill him all over again after the doctor had finished telling them both how lucky Everly had been. The sight of that asshole strangling her was one he'd never forget. He'd been steps away from the fucker, from planting his knife in the back of his neck and paralyzing him for life, when Everly had kicked him over her head as if he'd weighed little more than a child.

He'd slept at the hospital with Everly, and Allye had taken Elise to her house. She'd called Elise's therapist to the house at two in the morning to see her, and the two had talked until dawn, only stopping when Elise couldn't keep her eyes open anymore.

Even though it seemed like ages ago now that Everly had almost died, and she was mostly healed, Ball couldn't help but get upset every time he thought about the bruises she'd had around her throat for way too fucking long. He had no idea what he would've done if Tuttle had succeeded in choking her, or had pulled her with him over the side of the cliff.

"What did you find out?" Everly asked as she dropped her stuff on the floor and came over to where he was sitting on the couch.

Earlier that morning, Ball had a phone call with the rest of the Mountain Mercenaries and Rex. Their handler had updated them on what was happening with the case. It had taken a while for everything Tuttle had done to come to light, but now that it had, Ball knew they'd been lucky. Very lucky.

He wanted to spare Everly the terrible details about Tuttle, but she was a cop, she dealt with awful things all the time. Although this time was a little different, considering it was her sister who'd almost fallen prey to this psychopath. But he respected her enough not to prevaricate.

"After his death, the cops went to his apartment in Las Vegas and didn't find much. Apparently that was his cover residence. There weren't many personal items, and it looked a lot like a motel room. But they did manage to salvage his cell phone from his pocket after he fell from the cliff. *That* was a treasure trove of information. He'd been communicating with someone named Jean, giving her explicit instructions about when to eat, when she could shower."

"That was his wife, right?" Everly asked.

"If you want to call her that, yes. More like his slave. Rex dug through years of missing children reports and found a twelve-year-old named Jean Sherry, who disappeared from Henderson, Nevada, fifteen years ago."

Everly gasped and put a hand to her mouth. "Holy crap! She's been missing for that long? And was with him the whole time? She's twenty-seven now?"

"Yes to all three questions. Rex was able to find an address for a house in a shitty part of Vegas. It was run-down, and no one in the neighborhood ever suspected Tuttle of being anything other than slightly weird. Cops went to the home to search it."

"And Jean was there? Alive?"

"Yeah. In the basement. And she's completely and utterly traumatized. Her parents couldn't believe she'd been found alive, but so far, she's not receptive to seeing them. Psychologists say it could take years for her to come to terms with what happened to her. Tuttle abused her so badly, she was afraid to do anything to irritate him. She wouldn't even eat without him telling her it was all right, never left the basement where she's been living for fifteen years without him with her.

"Rex sent me the interview transcripts . . . it's a miracle she's still alive, Ev. Every time she got pregnant, Tuttle beat the shit out of her, making her abort her child. He played countless mental games with her. Letting her shower only if she had sex with him first. He didn't celebrate her birthday, but instead bought a huge cake and gave her presents on the anniversary of her kidnapping. He'd regularly beat her to within an inch of her life, then lovingly nurse her back to health, telling her no one loved her like he did."

Everly gagged and put a hand over her mouth again.

Ball immediately felt horrible. He shouldn't have told her so much. He was an idiot. Of course that was what Tuttle had planned for Elise. She would've been just like Jean, living a life of hell until Tuttle either killed her or decided he needed a younger "wife."

He rubbed her back until she said, "Sorry. I'm okay."

"No, *I'm* sorry," he said immediately. "I shouldn't have said anything."

"Yes, you should've," Everly insisted. "I just . . . I feel awful for Jean. Is there anything we can do for her? Start a fund-raising campaign or something?"

"I'll talk to Rex."

"I just . . . That could've been Elise. And with her not being able to hear, I can't imagine the hell it would've been. I can't believe no one figured out how crazy Tylor was. No one suspected?"

"Apparently not. He'd received a few reprimands over the years for acting inappropriately, especially to women, but nothing serious enough to warrant being fired or jailed. Of course, his boss recently had him taken off the payroll since he basically disappeared for a month to come here and stalk Elise, but generally, he was just a normal-looking guy living a normal life, by all appearances."

"Boss?" Everly asked. "I thought he owned his own business, what with the *Tuttle Plumbing* sign on his van and all."

"It was fake. He just bought a magnetic sign to give him a legitimate reason to be in some neighborhoods when he was casing them. It also explained why none of the girls who'd been kidnapped ever mentioned a business name on the van. He could put it on and take it off whenever it suited him."

"God," Everly breathed. "We got so lucky."

"You are the most amazing woman I know," Ball told her.

Everly's brows came down, and she shook her head in denial.

"You are. He flat-out told you he was going to kill you, and you still climbed into that van. He could've pulled out a gun and shot you right there. Or while you were hiking to where he had Elise. Or a hundred other times." They'd talked about this a few times, but it still freaked the hell out of Ball.

Everly shook her head. "No. He wanted me to know what he'd planned for Elise. Wanted me to marry them, thinking, I guess, that Elise would believe I approved of them being together, probably so he could throw it in her face later that I'd willingly married them. Who knows what was going through his head? I knew you'd find us, and that if he did succeed in killing me, you'd never stop looking for Elise."

"Can we agree not to talk about you being killed anymore?" Ball asked, feeling the pain and terror he'd felt all those weeks ago surging inside him once more. He'd thought that Everly would be the one waking up in the middle of the night with nightmares, but instead it had been *him*. Even sleeping with her in his arms hadn't banished the bad dreams. Of him walking onto the bluff and looking over the edge and seeing Everly, lying broken and dead at the bottom of the cliff. Of seeing her turn blue while Tuttle strangled her.

As if she knew what he was thinking, Everly placed her hand on his arm. "It's over," she said softly. "I'm fine."

Ball pulled her onto his lap and held her gently. He'd been afraid to do more than gingerly hug her for fear of hurting her for a long time after she'd gotten out of the hospital, but she'd been telling him for a while now that she felt fine. That she *was* fine.

Elise was currently at school. She'd hung out with him and her sister for the first week after the kidnapping, and Ball had been prepared to have her stay at home with them for at least one more, but she'd decided she was bored and wanted to go back. All things considered, she was doing extremely well, and Ball knew that was in part thanks to Allye's quick thinking in getting her therapist to see her immediately, and partly because of how amazing she was.

The longer they sat on the couch cuddled up together, the more aroused Ball got. He'd been holding back from doing anything more than kissing Everly for weeks now, since she'd been released from the hospital, but last night had almost been his undoing. She'd walked out of the bathroom without a stitch of clothing on, her hair loose around her shoulders, and shimmied over to their bed.

It had almost killed him, but he'd gathered her into his arms and told her he was exhausted. She'd been disgruntled, but hadn't pressed him. Ball had spent the entire night with a hard-on, reminding himself that she'd almost died.

Remembering how beautiful she was the night before, and how she'd felt in his arms, wasn't helping his arousal now. She smelled delicious, and it was taking everything in Ball to keep his hands from wandering.

Just as he resorted to reciting baseball stats to try to calm his dick down, Everly slipped out of his grasp. He thought she was going to get up and get something to eat or drink, and was about to insist he could get whatever she needed, when she went to her knees in front of him.

"What are you—" He inhaled deeply when her fingers undid the button on his jeans and drew down his zipper. "Everly, no."

"Ball, yes," she insisted. "You've been treating me like I'm a fragile piece of glass, and I'm sick of it. It was exactly what I needed those first few weeks, but it's been way too long. My ribs are mostly healed. I love you, Ball. I *need* you."

"Oh fuck," Ball swore, and lifted his ass to shove his jeans down far enough that she could get his cock out.

She smiled and practically purred when she saw how thick and hard he was.

"All this for me?" she asked, but didn't wait for him to answer. She didn't tease, simply grabbed hold of the base of his cock and dropped her mouth over him.

Groaning, Ball brought his hands up behind his head, latching his fingers together so he didn't grab her and force her down on him. Her mouth felt amazing, hot, wet, and when she sucked him, he couldn't stop his hips from pressing upward.

She gagged a little, and Ball swore. Her throat had been bruised all to hell by Tuttle, and here he was just weeks later, trying to shove himself down her throat.

Nope. Wasn't happening. He loved her too much to hurt her.

~

Everly cried out in surprise when Ball grabbed her around the waist and pulled her off his dick. She'd had enough of him being worried about hurting her. She appreciated that he didn't want to rush her. But fuck that. She needed him. Needed him to fuck her hard. Prove in the most carnal and basic way possible that she was alive and well. And the fastest way she could think to make that happen was to suck his dick.

It was obvious he wasn't going to make the first move. She'd never been comfortable walking around naked, but she'd done it the night before in the hope that he wouldn't be able to deny her.

But dammit, he was still trying to be noble. Fuck that.

Partly to banish the thoughts of the hell the poor woman Tylor Tuttle had kept prisoner and tortured for more than a decade had been through, and partly to assuage her own needs, she'd gone after what she wanted.

Everly loved going down on Ball. Loved the feeling of power it gave her. Loved hearing his moans and feeling his thighs tighten when he was trying to hold his orgasm back.

She'd barely gotten started, however, when he'd pulled her off him and picked her up.

"Ball!" she protested. "I was in the middle of something."

"And now you're not," he told her, walking quickly toward his bedroom.

"If you think you're going to put me to bed and walk away, you better think twice," she threatened. It was all bluster, though. If he truly was able to put her down and walk away, she wasn't sure what she'd do.

Ball didn't answer. He kicked open his door and strode toward his bed. He didn't drop her, but gently placed her on the mattress, crawling on top of her the second she was out of his arms. He straddled her and whipped his shirt off over his head. Then he shoved his hands under her own shirt, and Everly happily raised her arms to help him remove it. He unzipped her work cargos, and she lifted her ass to help him. He got them down to her thighs, and she kicked them off the rest of the way.

Everly smirked at his reaction when he saw her underwear. She'd been horny as hell that morning after sleeping naked in Ball's arms all night and had planned on seducing him when she got home from work. She'd put on a lacy, sexy thong in the hope that he'd take one look at it and not be able to stop himself from taking her.

So far her plans were working out perfectly.

Leaning forward, Ball reached for the drawer next to the bed and pulled out a condom. Everly quickly pushed the thong down and off. By the time he had the condom rolled down his cock, Everly had eagerly spread her legs and was ready for him. The rough material of Ball's jeans rubbed against her inner thighs, as he hadn't taken the time to remove them. It felt extremely naughty to be completely naked under him when he was still partly dressed. Knowing he was so turned on he couldn't bother to remove his jeans was a huge turn-on.

"Fuck me, Ball," she whispered, running her hands up and down his chest.

He took a deep breath and pressed the tip of his cock to her folds. "I should make sure you're ready for me," he said, but didn't move his hips back.

"I'm ready," Everly assured him.

He clenched his teeth, and his head tipped back as he continued to struggle for control.

Deciding enough was enough, Everly reached down, grabbed hold of his ass, and yanked him toward her.

Off-balance, Ball cried out as he fell forward and threw out his hands to catch himself. His cock pushed inside her slightly, and they both moaned at the delicious feeling.

"Damn it, Ev, I could've hurt you!" he chastised.

Everly squirmed against him, trying to get him deeper. "But you didn't. I *need* you, Ball. Fuck me."

"Are you sure?" he asked.

"I'm sure." Everly grabbed hold of his face and stared into his eyes. "Make me feel alive, Kannon."

That did it.

Without warning, Ball shoved himself the rest of the way inside her, and Everly let go of him to grab hold of his arms. Then Ball fucked her as he never had before. He wasn't worrying about whether or not she was enjoying it. He simply took what he'd been denying himself for the last several weeks.

He was out of control, and Everly loved it. She couldn't do anything but lie there and take what he was giving her. It was hot as hell to see him lose the iron control he'd been holding on to for weeks. Everly wouldn't want to be taken like this every time, but right now, it was perfect.

"Yes," she breathed, encouraging him. "Just like that. Make me yours."

"You *are* mine," Ball said fiercely. "Every fucking kick-ass inch of you."

Snaking her hand between them, Everly began flicking her clit as he fucked her. He felt amazing, his jeans rubbed against her with every thrust, and the sheen of sweat that covered Ball's chest was sexy as hell. She tried to lift her ass, but wasn't able to get the traction she needed with the way he was taking her.

Ball saw, but didn't slow down. He merely put his hand under her and lifted her up as if he knew exactly what she needed. And she supposed he did.

His thrusts didn't slow, and she watched as his eyes wandered down her body. Her tits jiggled every time he pushed inside her, and she could tell that turned him on even more. She fingered herself faster and let her pinkie brush up and down his cock every time he pulled out of her.

In seconds, she felt her orgasm tingling. Her fingers moved faster and faster on her clit, and she held on to his arm with her free hand, digging her fingernails into his skin.

"That's it, Ev. Mark me. Make me yours. Come all over my cock."

And she did. His name fell from her lips in a groan. "Kannon!"

She heard Ball grunt and felt his hands dig into her ass as he pushed inside her as far as he could go, the material of his jeans scratching against her, yet increasing the carnality of the moment.

"Shit," he mumbled, seconds after he'd come. "I'm fucking dizzy as hell, and I think you sucked me dry, but I want to do that again. And again. And again."

Everly chuckled, and he moaned when her inner muscles squeezed his dick still inside her.

Ball gently let go of her butt and reached one hand into his pocket.

Without a word, he picked up her left hand and shoved a ring on her finger.

Then he gently lay down on top of her, wrapped her in his arms, and rolled until she was on top.

Everly lifted her head and stared down at the beautiful diamond on her finger. "Um . . . Ball?"

"Hmmmm?" he said absently.

"Is this what I think it is?"

"Yup."

Everly frowned. "You're not even gonna ask?"

"Nope."

"Ball!" she protested.

"What?" he asked, his eyes still closed.

Huffing out a breath, but secretly as excited as she could be, Everly put her head down on his shoulder and stared at the engagement ring.

After a few minutes, Ball said, "I'm not asking because I'm not giving you a chance to say no. You're mine, Everly. And you should know, I already talked to Elise, and she's all in. Oh, and I called Me-Maw and Pop, and they gave their blessing too. They also told me they want to move here to be closer to you and Elise."

Tears filled Everly's eyes. Ball knew how much she'd been worried about her grandparents. They'd been sad to hear about Ella, but not too surprised. She'd wanted to ask them to move to Colorado, but had been too chicken to suggest they uproot their lives.

"I love you, Ball."

"Good. Because we're getting married in a week."

She rose up quickly at that. "What?"

"Married. One week. I have an appointment at the courthouse on Saturday. Me-Maw and Pop are driving in on Thursday. The girls said they'd go with you sometime in the next couple of days to find a dress. Elise already ordered a dress that I personally think is too damn short, but I was outvoted. I'll wear a tux or just a suit. Or jeans. Whatever you want."

Everly was shocked. Was he serious? "You're serious, aren't you?"

"Everly, I love you. Nothing else in my life matters. When I realized what happened and that you'd purposely put yourself in danger, I should've been pissed. You know better than that. You could've found a way to get in touch with me even though that asshole said he was watching you. But you didn't. You marched your happy ass into danger.

"But when I really sat and thought about it, and put myself in your shoes, I knew I would've done the same thing. If it was you who'd been taken, I would've done the same damn thing you did. We're a good team. The best. I'm forty years old, and I'm sick that we've missed so much time together, but I plan on making the most of the next fifty years we've got coming."

"Are you allowed to wear your Coast Guard uniform, now that you're retired?" she asked. "I'd love to see you in it when we get married."

Ball smiled, and the lines that had been furrowing his forehead disappeared.

Everly couldn't believe he actually thought she'd protest marrying him.

"Yeah, Ev. I can do that."

"And your friends can all be there? And the girls? And can I invite some of my friends from the station?"

He chuckled. "Of course. I hope the courthouse has a big fucking room."

Laying her head back down on his chest, Everly couldn't help but admire the ring again. The middle diamond wasn't too big, and all the way around the band were smaller diamonds. She could wear this ring at work and not have to worry about snagging it on anything.

"Ball?"

"Yeah?"

"I'm pretty sure you're supposed to remove the condom before getting hard again."

He chuckled. "I don't want to leave you."

"How about you get up, take off your pants, deal with the condom, then come back to bed?"

"That I can do. I was too fast, you got me too turned on. Give me two seconds, and I'll come back and make it up to you."

Everly didn't bother to answer as he gently pulled out of her body, scooted out from under her, and tore his jeans and boxers down his legs. He headed for the bathroom and was back in less than a minute.

Without a word, he was kneeling between her legs, pushing her thighs apart, and lowering his head.

Everly had the thought that sometimes the worst things in life turned out to be the best. She'd hated Ball when she'd first met him, but slowly he'd shown her that under his bluster, he was a damn good man. And in return, she'd taught him that when you were with the right woman, everything just worked.

Then she couldn't think about anything at all, other than how good Ball was making her feel. She had a suspicion he'd do whatever it took in the near—and far—future, to always make her feel good.

Epilogue

The Mountain Mercenaries walked silently through the back alleys in a run-down neighborhood in Lima, Peru. The team had two members of the First Special Forces Brigade from the Peruvian military with them to help translate and give their mission legitimacy. Although they sometimes went into foreign countries undercover to carry out their missions, because this job involved Peruvian citizens and not Americans, they were working in tandem with the government.

Meat looked around and thought to himself that it wasn't a place he'd want anyone he cared about hanging out in. It definitely wasn't the kind of place the government was advertising in their tourist brochures.

The smell of piss and vomit was strong, but Meat ignored it, intent on the mission. There were shanties lined up side by side in a five-square-mile area, with only enough space for a small car to drive down the dirt roads between the houses. They were built with whatever materials the people could find . . . cardboard, tin, even tires. Most were small, only one room, and the river meandering through the squalor was the only source of water for most families.

Meat and his fellow mercenaries had seen poverty up close and personal more times than they could count, but this was horrifying and depressing on a whole new level.

When their target came into sight, a slightly larger shanty that had an actual padlock on the door—unlike most of the other houses around it—Gray and Ro went to the left, Arrow and Ball went to the right, and Black and Meat crept around to the alley on the other side of the house. They had the entire shanty covered in case any of the pedophiles attempted to escape.

The plan was to surround the crappy hovel and take the kidnappers by surprise.

Rex had been working with the Peruvian government to try to get a handle on the number of children going missing, especially from the poorer areas of the city. He'd agreed to undergo a joint mission with the military to rescue four to eight boys between the ages of five and twelve, who had been taken from their families and were on the verge of being sold.

The fact that they didn't know exactly how many boys they were rescuing should've been a huge red flag, but after discussing it, no one wanted to back out.

The tip they'd received said they had *already* been sold, actually, and their new owners would be picking them up sometime in the next couple of days. The mission was not only to rescue the children and return them to their families, but to take down the scum responsible for kidnapping them in the first place.

Meat sighed. He wanted to rescue the boys, but he knew that there were hundreds, or thousands, of children just like them who would disappear in the next year.

There were times when their job overwhelmed Meat. For every child or woman they rescued, there were countless others who didn't get saved. He was at least happy to be on the action side of a mission. He'd been spending more and more time behind the computer screen, tracking down the vile men and women who had no problem peddling human flesh. There were times he had the feeling his teammates had forgotten that he used to be a Delta Force soldier. They'd gotten so used to him being the go-to computer guy that when things got physical, he was often the last one asked to assist.

But tonight—or rather, this morning—they needed all the physical help they could get. There were a ton of unknowns about the raid. They weren't sure how many people were inside the target house. They knew nothing about the people living in the shanties around it . . . were they involved in the smuggling ring too? Were there guns involved? Were the boys even still there?

It was a clusterfuck, and Rex was livid that, after getting the initial intel, everything had suddenly changed, and no one apparently knew anything. The team was already in South America by that time and had decided, against Rex's better judgment, to go ahead with the joint mission.

Black and Meat's job was to guard the back of the shack. Make sure none of the bad guys escaped, and contain the raid to the one house.

Not knowing how the neighbors would react to the raid, the Mercenaries had crept into the area in the dead of night. It was three thirty in the morning, and they'd seen only the rare person up and about.

As was the plan, Gray and Ro made entry into the house by using a large rock to smash the hell out of the padlock with one swipe, and they burst into the room, Arrow and Ball at their backs. Chaos instantly reigned. Boys screamed. Men yelled. Shots rang out.

"Watch your six!" Arrow yelled through the radio headset they all wore.

"Get that kid!" Gray ordered as one of the children pushed open the back door and ran.

"I'll get him!" Black said, leaving his post to chase after the child. The last thing any of them wanted was one of the kids running off to hide and being recaptured later.

"Left room, clear!" Ball stated.

"Shit, there are two women back here," Arrow added.

"How old?" Ro barked.

"Teens. They look scared shitless," Arrow said.

"Secure everyone," Gray told the team. "Until we know who's friend and who's foe, everyone stays right here."

Meat listened to the chaos through his radio and kept his eyes on the back door. Black had taken off after the boy who'd run, and he'd expected him to be back within seconds.

When that didn't happen, Meat swore under his breath. He didn't want to leave his post, but dammit, he also couldn't leave Black on his own. Not in this neighborhood. Making a split-second decision, Meat keyed the mike on his radio and said, "Black took off after one of the kids who bolted. He's not back yet. I'm headed after him." Then he ran in the direction his teammate had disappeared. It sounded like the team had things under control in the house—as under control as they could be—and he'd hopefully only be gone for a second.

He ran the length of the alley and, when he got to the end, looked around.

He saw a small child, no more than probably six years old, pointing down another alley.

Meat didn't even have time to wonder what in the hell a little girl was doing up and awake at this time of the morning. He was too grateful for the assistance to do more than nod at her.

He ran toward where the girl had pointed and started down the neighboring alley.

He saw Black immediately—fighting three men.

Meat rushed into the fight and took out the KA-BAR knife he always carried. Without remorse, he calmly slit the throat of the man who was doing his best to get ahold of Black's pistol.

The man fell to the dirt with a thud, and Meat immediately turned to one of the others.

But before he could do more than punch the man in the kidney, they were suddenly surrounded by at least a dozen more.

"Fuck," Black said.

Meat opened his mouth to inform the rest of the team where he and Black were, and the shit storm they'd found themselves in, when the men pounced. They didn't have any conventional weapons, but the baseball bats, sticks, and rocks they *did* have were enough to do plenty of damage.

The men ripped the Mercenaries' headsets off and trampled them under their feet. They kicked, punched, and beat Meat and Black until they lay motionless in the dirt. They stripped them of their weapons and shoes, even taking their tactical pants and shirts.

The entire attack had taken place in less than three minutes.

Meat groaned in pain and looked over at his friend. Black's face was almost indistinguishable. Both eyes were swollen shut, his body was covered in bruises that were already forming, and he was bleeding from several cuts from his own knife.

Meat knew he wasn't any better off. He could barely see and knew he had at least one broken rib, maybe more. His ankle was throbbing, and he recalled one of his attackers stomping on it in the melee.

As his consciousness wavered, Meat stared at the broken radio lying ten feet away. In the distance, he could hear shouts and crying coming from the next housing row over, but it might as well have been miles.

He tried to get to his hands and knees—he'd crawl over hot coals to get his buddy help if it came to that—but immediately fell practically on his face when pain shot through his shoulder. It was most definitely dislocated.

Feeling frustrated, Meat couldn't help but think about Harlow. She would be completely heartbroken if anything happened to Black. They were madly in love, and Meat knew Black was planning the perfect proposal for when they got back home. Harlow and Black were made for each other, and loved each other with all they were, just as the rest of the Mercenaries loved their women.

He was the only one who was still single. If someone was going to die on a mission, it should be him. He had no one waiting for him. No one who loved him.

Determined to get help for Black, Meat painstakingly got up onto his knees once more. It hurt like hell, but he slowly began to shuffle forward, the rocks and dirt digging into his bare knees with every inch of ground he covered.

An inch felt like a mile, but he was barely feeling the pain anymore. His only goal was to get to the end of the alley, turn the corner, and get back to the shack where the raid was happening.

Meat made it another twenty feet or so, but the pain in his ribs and shoulder, not to mention all his other cuts and bruises, got the better of him. He fell onto his back and couldn't manage to move any farther.

He hadn't thought he'd made a noise, but he must have, because one second he was alone, and the next he was surrounded by three figures dressed all in black.

Two grabbed hold of his arms, and another hovered behind them, looking back the way the men who'd beaten the crap out of him and Black had disappeared.

Meat tried to fight off the people dragging him, but it was no use. He was completely helpless in their grasp, his body out for the count. Blackness began creeping in the sides of his eyes, and he knew he was going to pass out.

He did his best to stay conscious, but the insidious blackness was unrelenting. The last thing Meat saw as he was dragged down the narrow lane, around the corner, and into one of the shabby houses nearby was Black, lying motionless and seemingly broken in the dirt in the middle of the alley.

He'd failed his friend. And Harlow. And the Mountain Mercenaries.

Rex was gonna be pissed.

~

Chaos still ensued in the target house, with the team checking in and clearing the shanty. For a small, run-down dwelling like the one they were in, there were a surprising number of places for both men and children to hide.

It was a good ten minutes more before Gray realized he hadn't heard a status report from Black or Meat since one of the children had run out the back door.

"Black? Meat? Report in," he said through his headset.

Silence met his request.

Gray gestured with his head for Ro to check out the alley at the back of the house.

"They aren't here," Ro said seconds later. "The last thing I knew, Meat was going after Black, who was chasing after one of the kids who ran."

"Fuck. Okay, Ball, go with Ro and check it out," Gray ordered. "We've got things secured here."

Ball nodded and slipped out the back door.

It was another agonizing five minutes before Gray and the others heard anything.

"We found Black," Ro said.

"And?"

"He's in bad shape. Looks like he got jumped. They stripped him clean too," Ro reported.

"Is he conscious?"

"Barely. I can't get anything out of him yet."

"And Meat?" Arrow asked.

"Missing," Ball reported.

"What do you mean, missing?" Gray barked.

"He's not here. He *was*, because the assholes who jumped them left both headsets. But there's no sign of Meat at all."

"Fuck!" Gray swore. "Get Black back here! The last thing we need is whoever jumped them to come back and take you two out as well."

"Negative," Ball said. "Ro will bring Black to the house, but I'm going to look for Meat."

"No you fucking are *not*," Gray said in a low, deadly voice. "If they were able to take out Black and disappear with Meat, you stand no chance alone. Think about Everly and Elise. They need you. Get your ass back here now. We'll wait until it's light out and call in reinforcements. It's not as if anyone in this barrio has a car they can fucking drive him out in. We'll put up a perimeter and search every single fucking house one by one until we find him."

"Copy that," Ball said after a moment.

Gray took a frustrated breath. This mission was obviously going to take longer than they'd planned, and that sucked, because Allye was very close to her due date. She'd been concerned that he wouldn't be back in time, and he'd promised he would be.

It was a promise he might have to break, because there was no way he was leaving a teammate behind. He'd spend whatever time was necessary to find Meat, even if that meant missing the birth of his first child.

They should've listened to Rex when he'd told them to abort the mission. But they'd all been too worried about the kids. Too focused on the chance to save them.

Things had gone bad so quickly it almost made Gray's head spin.

They had half a dozen freaked-out kids, the same number of suspects, a severely wounded Black, and a fucking missing Meat to deal with.

A thought hit him. Meat was their computer expert. He'd begun teaching Black some of what he did . . . but now Black was out of commission as well. Rex would certainly do what he could, but he was thousands of miles away back in Colorado, or wherever the hell he actually lived.

Gray ran a hand through his hair in agitation. "Where are you, Meat? Where the fuck are you?"

About the Author

Photo © 2015 A&C Photography

Susan Stoker is a *New York Times*, *USA Today*, and *Wall Street Journal* bestselling author. Her series include Badge of Honor: Texas Heroes, SEAL of Protection, Ace Security, Delta Force Heroes, and the Amazon Charts bestselling Mountain Mercenaries. Married to a retired Army non-commissioned officer, Stoker has lived all over the country—from Missouri and California to Colorado and Texas—and currently lives under the big skies of Tennessee. A true believer in happily ever after, Stoker enjoys writing novels in which romance turns to love. To learn more about the author and her work, visit her website, www.stokeraces.com.

Connect with Susan Online

Susan's Facebook Profile and Page

www.facebook.com/authorsstoker

www.facebook.com/authorsusanstoker

Follow Susan on Twitter

www.twitter.com/Susan_Stoker

Find Susan's Books on Goodreads

www.goodreads.com/SusanStoker

Email

Susan@StokerAces.com

Website

www.StokerAces.com